# EVERYONE
## ON THIS
# TRAIN
## IS A
# SUSPECT

### A NOVEL

## BENJAMIN STEVENSON

**MARINER BOOKS**
*New York  Boston*

EVERYONE ON THIS TRAIN IS A SUSPECT. Copyright © 2023 by Benjamin Stevenson. All rights reserved. Printed in the United States of America. No part of this book may be used or reproduced in any manner whatsoever without written permission except in the case of brief quotations embodied in critical articles and reviews. For information, address HarperCollins Publishers, 195 Broadway, New York, NY 10007.

HarperCollins books may be purchased for educational, business, or sales promotional use. For information, please email the Special Markets Department at SPsales@harpercollins.com.

Originally published in Australia in 2023 by Michael Joseph, an imprint of Penguin Random House Australia.

FIRST U.S. EDITION

Designed by Jackie Alvarado

Library of Congress Cataloging-in-Publication Data has been applied for.

ISBN 978-0-06-327907-0 (hardcover)
ISBN 978-0-06-335785-3 (international edition)

23 24 25 26 27  LBC  5 4 3 2 1

*For Jerry Kalajian*
*Life Changer*

There must be but one detective—that is, but one protagonist of deduction—one deus ex machina. To bring the minds of three or four, or sometimes a gang of detectives to bear on a problem, is not only to disperse the interest and break the direct thread of logic, but to take an unfair advantage of the reader. If there is more than one detective the reader doesn't know who his co-deductor is. It's like making the reader run a race with a relay team.

*Rule 9, S.S. Van Dine's "Twenty Rules for*
*Writing Detective Stories," 1928*

A sequel is an admission that you've been reduced to imitating yourself.

*Don Marquis*

# THE LAYOUT OF THE GHAN

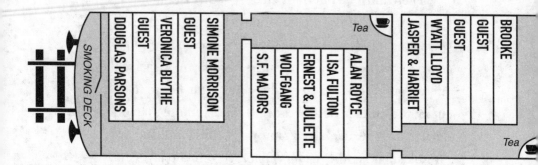

SMOKING DECK

DOUGLAS PARSONS
GUEST
VERONICA BLYTHE
GUEST
SIMONE MORRISON

S.F. MAJORS
WOLFGANG
ERNEST & JULIETTE
LISA FULTON
ALAN ROYCE

JASPER & HARRIET
WYATT LLOYD
GUEST
GUEST
BROOKE

Tea

Tea

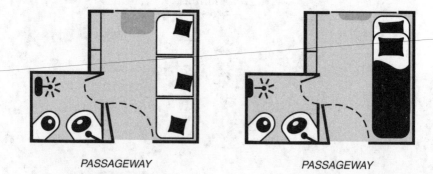

PASSAGEWAY

PASSAGEWAY

**Cabin by day**

**Cabin by night**

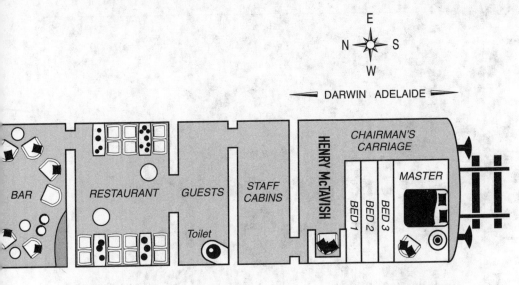

# AUSTRALIAN MYSTERY WRITERS' FESTIVAL, 50TH ANNIVERSARY PROGRAM

The AMWF extends a very special welcome to our guest of honor: Henry McTavish, globally bestselling author of the Detective Morbund series. "Unputdownable and unbeatable: McTavish is peerless." *New York Times*

**Ernest Cunningham:** Ernest Cunningham's memoir *Everyone in My Family Has Killed Someone* took us deep into the story of one of Australia's most notorious serial killers, the Black Tongue. He is currently working on a novel.

**Lisa Fulton:** Lisa Fulton's bestselling debut novel *The Balance of Justice* shook the foundations of crime fiction on release twenty-one years ago with its white-hot rage and brutal truth, and was long-listed for the Justice in Fiction Award, Women's Prize, 2003. She is currently working on her long-awaited second novel.

**S. F. Majors:** S. F. Majors's gripping thrillers have captivated the world with their psychological complexity and hair-raising twists and turns. Her books include the *New York Times* bestselling *Twists and Turns*, which has been optioned for film by Netflix. Her young adult thriller *My Lab Partner Is a Serial Killer* is being adapted into a Broadway musical. She grew up rereading the only three books in her tiny town's school library, and now lives in the Blue Mountains with her partner and two dogs.

**Alan Royce:** Alan Royce is the author of the Dr. Jane Black series, comprising eleven novels and three novellas. A former forensic pathologist before being catapulted to crime-writing stardom, he brings his expertise in morgues and autopsies to the page. "Gritty, real and uncompromising. One to watch." *Time*, 2011

**Wolfgang:** Winner, Commonwealth Book Prize 2012; short-listed, Bookseller's Favorites Award 2012; short-listed, Goodreads Readers' Choice, Literary Fiction, 2012; short-listed, Best of Amazon 2012; short-listed, Justice in Fiction Award, Women's Prize (special exemption granted), 2003; long-listed, Miles Franklin Award 2015; long-listed, Independent Library Choice Awards 2015; Archibald Packing Room Prize subject 2018; Honorary Mention: International Poetry Prize, Oceanic Region, 2020. His next project is an interactive art project titled *The Death of Literature*.

# PROLOGUE

From: ECunninghamWrites221@gmail.com
To: <REDACTED>@penguinrandomhouse.com.au
Subject: Prologue

Hi <REDACTED>,

It's a hard no on the prologue, I'm afraid. I know it's the done thing in crime novels, to hook the reader in and all that, but it just feels a bit cheap here.

I know *how* to do it, of course, the scene you want me to write. An omniscient eye would survey the cabin's destruction, lingering on signs of a struggle: the strewn sheets, the upturned mattress, the bloodied handprint on the bathroom door. Add in fleeting glimpses of clues—three words hastily scrawled in blue ink on a manuscript, at odds with the crimson, dripping tip of the murder weapon—just enough to tantalize but nondescript enough not to spoil.

The final image would be of the body. Faceless, of course. You've got to keep the victim from the reader at the start. Maybe a sprinkle of some little detail, a personal item like a piece of clothing (the blue scarf, or something, I'm not sure) that the reader can watch for in the buildup.

That's it: the book, the blood, the body. Carrots dangled. End of prologue.

It's not like I don't trust your editorial judgment. It just seems overly pointless to me to replay a scene from later in the book merely for the purpose of suspense. It's like saying, "*Hey, we know this book takes a while to get going, but it'll get there.*" Then the poor reader is just playing catch-up until we get to the murder.

Well, that scene is the second murder anyway, but you get my point.

I'm just wary of giving away too much. So, no prologue. Sound okay?

Best,
Ernest

P.S. After what's happened, I think it's fairly obvious I'll need a new literary agent. I'll be in touch about that separately.

P.P.S. Yes, we do have to include the festival program. I think there are important clues in it.

P.P.P.S. Grammar question—I've thought it funny that *Murder on the Orient Express* is titled as such, given that the murders take place *in* the train and not *on* it. *Death on the Nile* has it a bit more correct, I think, given the lack of drownings. Then again, of course you say you're *on* a train or a plane. I'm laboring the point, but I guess my question is whether we use *on* or *in* for our title? Given, of course, most of the murders take place *in* the train, except of course what happens on the roof, which would be *on*. Except for the old fella's partner and those who died alongside him, but that's a flashback. Am I making sense?

# MEMOIR

# CHAPTER 1

So I'm writing again. Which is good news, I suppose, for those wanting a second book, but more unfortunate for the people who had to die so I could write it.

I'm starting this from my cabin on the train, as I want to get a few things down before I forget or exaggerate them. We're parked, not at a station but just sitting on the tracks about an hour from Adelaide. The long red desert of the last four days has been replaced first by the golden wheat belt and then by the lush green paddocks of dairy farms, the previously flat horizon now a rolling grass ocean peppered with the slow, steady turn of dozens of wind turbines. We should have been in Adelaide by now, but we've had to stop so the authorities can clean up the bodies. I say clean up, but I think the delay is mainly that they're having trouble finding them. Or at least all the pieces.

So here I am with a head start on my writing.

My publisher tells me sequels are tricky. There are certain rules to follow, like doling out backstory for both those who've read me before and those who've never heard of me. I'm told you don't want to bore the returnees, but you don't want to confuse the newbies by leaving too much out. I'm not sure which one you are, so let's start with this:

My name's Ernest Cunningham, and I've done this before. Written a book, that is. But, also, solved a series of murders.

At the time, it came quite naturally. The writing, not the deaths, of which the causes were the opposite of *natural*, of course. Of the survivors, I thought myself the most qualified to tell the story, as I had something that could generously be called a "career" in writing already. I used to write books about how to write books: the rules for writing mystery books, to be precise. And they were more pamphlets than books, if you insist on honesty. Self-published, a buck apiece online. It's not every writer's dream, but it was a living. Then when everything happened last year up in the snow and the media came knocking, I thought I might as well apply some of what I knew and have a crack at writing it all down. I had help, of course, in the guiding principles of Golden Age murder mysteries set out by writers like Agatha Christie, Arthur Conan Doyle and, in particular, a bloke named Ronald Knox, who wrote out the "Ten Commandments of Detective Fiction." Knox isn't the only one with a set of rules: various writers over the years have had a crack at breaking down a murder mystery into a schematic. Even Henry McTavish had a set.

If you think you don't already know the rules to writing a murder mystery, trust me, you do. It's all intuitive. Let me give you an example. I'm writing this in first person. That means, in order to have sat down and physically written about it, I survive the events of the book. First person equals survival. Apologies in advance for the lack of suspense when I almost bite the dust in chapter 28.

The rules are simple: nothing supernatural; no surprise identical twins; the killer must be introduced early on (in fact, I've already done that and we're not even through the first chapter yet, though I expect you may have skipped the prelims) and be a major enough character to impact the plot. That last one's important. Gone are the days when the butler dunnit: in order to play fair, the killer must have a name, often used. To prove the point, I'll tell you that I use the killer's name, in all its forms, exactly 106 times from here. And, most important, the essence of every rule boils down to this: *absolutely* no concealing obvious truths from the reader.

That's why I'm talking to you like this. I am, you may have realized, a bit chattier than your usual detective in these books. That's because I'm not going to hide anything from you. This is a fair-play mystery, after all.

And so I promise to be that rarity in modern crime novels: a reliable narrator. You can count on me for the truth at every turn. No hoodwinking. I also promise to say the dreaded sentence "It was all a dream" only once, and even then I believe it's permissible in context.

Alas, no writers cared to jot down any rules specifically for sequels (Conan Doyle famously delighted in killing off Sherlock Holmes, begrudgingly bringing him back just for the money), so I'm going it alone here. The only help I have is my publisher, whose advice seems to come via the marketing department.

Her first piece of advice was to avoid repetition. That makes good sense—nobody wants to read the same old plots rehashed again and again. But her second piece of advice was to not deliver a book completely unlike the first, as readers will expect more of the same. Just to reiterate: I don't have any control over the events of the book. I'm just writing down what happened, so those are two difficult rules to follow. I will point out that one inadvertent mimicry is the curious coincidence that both cases are solved by a piece of punctuation. Last year it was a full stop. This time, a comma saves the day.

And what sort of mystery book would this be if we didn't have at least one anagram, code or puzzle? So that's in here as well.

My publisher also warned me to work in enough tantalizing ref-
erences to the previous book that readers will want to buy that one
also, but not to spoil the ending. She calls that "natural marketing."
Sequels, it seems, are about doing two things at once: being new
and familiar at the same time.

I'm already breaking those rules I mentioned. Golden Age mystery novelist S.S. Van Dine recommends there only be one crime
solver. This time, there are five wannabe detectives. But I guess
that's what happens when you put six crime writers in a room. I say
six writers and five detectives, because one's the murder victim. It's
not the one wearing the blue scarf; that's the other one.

I'd say Van Dine would be rolling in his grave, though that
would break one of the general rules about the supernatural. So
he'd be lying very still but disappointed all the same.

If I may repeat myself, it's not up to me which rules I break when
I'm simply cataloging what happened. How I managed to stumble
into another labyrinthine mystery is anyone's guess, and the same
people who accused me of profiteering from a serial killer picking
off my extended family one by one in the last book (natural marketing, see?) will likely accuse me of the same here. I wish it hadn't
happened, not now, and not back then.

Besides, everyone hates sequels: they are so often accused of being a pale imitation of what's come before. Being that the last murders happened on a snowy mountain and these ones happened in a
desert, the joke's on the naysayers: a pale imitation this won't be,
because at least I've got a tan.

Time to shore up my bona fides as a reliable narrator. The rap
sheet for the crimes committed in this book amounts to murder,
attempted murder, rape, stealing, trespassing, evidence tampering,
conspiracy, blackmail, smoking on public transport, headbutting
(I guess the technical term is assault), burglary (yes, this is different
from stealing) and improper use of adverbs.

Here are some further truths. Seven writers board a train. At the end of the line, five will leave it alive. One will be in cuffs.

Body count: nine. Bit lower than last time.

And me? I don't kill anybody this time around.

Let's get started. Again.

# CHAPTER 2

There was less dread instilled in witnessing the public murder (dare I say execution) of a fellow author than there was when my literary agent spotted me on the crowded train platform, elbowed her way through the throng, and asked me, "How's the new book coming?"

Simone Morrison was the last person I expected to see at Berrimah Terminal, Darwin, given her agency was based four thousand kilometers away. She'd brought Melbourne with her, wearing a coat that was a ludicrous mix of trench and oversized puffer. Then again, she was better dressed than I was. I had on cargo shorts and a buttoned short-sleeved shirt, which had been sold to me in a fishing store as "breathable." I'd always believed that was the minimum requirement for clothing, but I'd bought it anyway. The problem was that, while our journey had been duly advertised as a "sunrise start," I'd incorrectly assumed that the baking heat of the Northern Territory's tropical climate would apply at all hours, including dawn.

It hadn't.

And though there was light now, we were on the west side of the train, a slinking steel snake that blocked off all the horizon, and so half-mast wasn't going to do it for warmth; the sun had to really put some effort in. The only warm part of me was my right hand—which had been skinned during last year's murders and was only partially rehealed, thanks to an ample donation from my left butt-cheek—where I wore a single, padded glove to protect the sensitive skin underneath. In all, I was dressed more suitably for *Jurassic Park* than a train journey, and I found myself both willing the sun to hurry up and quite jealous of the cozy blue woolen scarf Simone had around her neck.

I say Simone's office is based in Melbourne, though I've never seen it: as far as I can tell, most of her business is conducted from a booth at an Italian restaurant in the city. She helped the chef there publish a cookbook once, which was successful enough to snag him a TV gig, and she's been rewarded with both a permanent reservation and an alcohol addiction. Every time I slipped into the red vinyl seat across from her, Simone would hold up a finger as she finished an email on her laptop (manicured nails clacking furiously enough that I pitied the person on the other end), take a sip of her tar-dark spiked coffee (bright pink lipstick stain on the ceramic, though, in an unnerving clue to the dishwashing standards of the place, she always wears red), and then say, completely ignoring the fact that she'd often summoned me, "Please tell me you've got good news." She's a fan of shoulder pads, teeth whitening, heavy sighs and hoop earrings—not in that order.

That said, I can't fault her ability. We first met after I'd signed the publisher contract for *Everyone in My Family Has Killed Someone*, when she invited me to lunch and asked me to bring along the contract. I then sat in silence while she leafed through the agreement underlining things and muttering various incarnations of "Unbelievable" before remembering I was there too, flipping to the back and saying, "That's your signature? No one, like, forged it or anything? You read and agreed"—she shook the pages, arched her eyebrows—"to this?"

I nodded.

"I'm surprised you can write books, because you certainly can't read. I charge fifteen percent."

I couldn't tell if it was an offer or an insult. She turned her focus to her laptop, so I considered myself dismissed and squeaked out of the plastic seat, never expecting to hear from her again. A week later a document outlining interest from a German publisher and even some people wanting to make a TV show landed in my inbox. There was also an offer for another mystery book. Fiction, this time.

She hadn't asked, and I hadn't expressed any interest in writing a novel, nor did I have any idea what I'd write about. And the catch was I'd have to write it quickly. But I'll admit I was blinded by the advance listed—it was far better than what I'd received previously—so I'd accepted. Besides, I'd reasoned at the time, it might be a nice change from writing about real people killing each other.

Obviously, that didn't pan out.

I knew Simone took her job seriously, perhaps *too* seriously, but I've always figured that if the publishers are half as scared of her as I am, I should be grateful she's on my side. And, sure, I'd been dodging her calls and texts for an update on the novel for a couple of months. But following me to Darwin seemed excessive. In any case, asking a writer how their book's coming along is like spotting lipstick on their collar. There's really no point asking: no one ever answers truthfully.

"Pretty good," I said.

"That bad, huh?" Simone replied.

Juliette, my girlfriend, standing beside me, squeezed my arm in sympathy.

"Fiction is . . . harder than I thought it would be."

"You took their money. *We* took their money." Simone fossicked around in her handbag, pulled out an electronic cigarette, and puffed. "I don't refund commission, you know."

I didn't, in fact, know that. "You've come all this way to hassle me then?"

"Not everything's about you, Ern." She exhaled a plume of blueberry scent. "Opportunity knocks, I answer."

"And what better place than in the middle of the desert to circle some carcasses," Juliette chipped in.

Simone barked a laugh, seeming charmed rather than offended. She liked to be challenged, I just lacked the confidence to do it. But Juliette had always given her the combative banter she enjoyed. Simone leaned forward and gave Juliette one of those hugs where you keep the person at arm's length, as if holding a urinating child, and an air kiss on both cheeks. "Always liked you, dear. You wound me, though, with truth. I take it you're still not convinced you need an agent?"

"Keep circling. I'm happy on my own."

"You have my number." This must have been a lie, because even *I* didn't have her number. She called me on private, not the other way around.

"I don't have a ticket for you," I cut in. "Juliette's my plus-one. How'd they even let you on the shuttle bus? I'm sorry you've come all this way—"

"I don't do shuttle buses. And I've got more clients than just you, Ern," Simone scoffed. "Wyatt sorted me out." She craned her head around the platform. "Where are the others?"

I didn't know who Wyatt was, though her tone implied that was my own shortcoming. The name didn't register as one of the other authors I'd seen in the program. Then again, I'd only flicked through it and hadn't read many of the books; they were stacked guiltily on my bedside table. If an author's biggest lie is that their writing is going well, their second biggest is that they're halfway through their peer's new book.

I did recall that there were five other writers on the program for the Australian Mystery Writers' Festival. Handpicked by the festival to cover, as the website touted, "every facet of modern crime writing," they included three popular crime writers, whose novels covered the genres of forensic procedural, psychological thriller and legal drama, as well as a literary heavyweight, who'd been shortlisted for the Commonwealth Book Prize, and the major drawcard, Scottish phenomenon and writer of the Detective Morbund series Henry McTavish, whom even I knew by name. Then there was me, doing some heavy lifting in the dual categories of debut and nonfiction, because my first book was labeled as a true-crime memoir. Juliette, former owner of the mountain resort where last year's murders took place, had also written a book on the events, but she was here as my guest. Her book had sold better than mine, and she is, I'll admit, a much better writer than I am. But she's also not related to a serial killer, and you can't buy that kind of publicity, so the invites for things like this do tend to fall my way.

If it strikes you as odd that we were milling about at a train station, when literary festivals usually take place in libraries, school auditoriums or whichever room at the local community center happens to be empty enough to accommodate an *Oh shit we totally forgot we had an author talk today*, you'd be right. But this year, in celebration of its fiftieth anniversary, the festival was to take place on the Ghan: the famous train route that bisects the immense desert of Australia almost exactly down the middle. Originally a freight route, the name comes from a shortening of "Afghan Express": a tribute to the camel-riding explorers of Australia's past, who traversed the red desert long before steel tracks and steam engines. To drill the point home, the sides of several carriages had been emblazoned with a red silhouette of a man in a turban atop a camel.

While the name and logo might have attested to an adventurous spirit, the days of sweat and grit were long gone. The train had been overhauled with comfort, luxury and arthritis in mind—it was now a world-renowned tourist destination, an opulent hotel on rails.

Over the course of four days and three nights, we were to travel from Darwin to Adelaide, with off-train excursions in the pristine wilderness of Nitmiluk National Park, the underground township of Coober Pedy, and the red center of Australia, Alice Springs. It was both a unique and an extravagant setting for a literary festival, and half the reason I'd agreed to come was that I'd never be able to afford the trip on my own: tickets didn't just run into the thousands of dollars, they sprinted.

If that was half the reason, another quarter was the hope that four days immersed in literary conversations might spark something in me. That the muse might leap out from behind the bar just as I was clinking glasses with Henry McTavish himself, who never did public events anymore, and my new novel would crack wide open. I'd gush the idea at Henry, because we'd be on a first-name basis by then, of course, and he'd raise his glass and say, "Aye, I wish I'd thought of that one, laddie."

Writing out my preposterous hopes for the journey here gives me the same shameful chill as seeing old social media photos—*Did I really post that?*—not least because of the horrifically cliché Scottish brogue I'd superimposed onto McTavish before I'd even met him. I think it's obvious that McTavish and I would not wind up on a first-name basis. Though my inspiration would still come from a drink with him, in a way, so maybe I'm clairvoyant after all.

Also, I'm aware that my motivation only adds up to three quarters—half financial, a quarter creative—as my sharp-eyed editor has duly mentioned. She's similarly pointed out that my number of writers doesn't match those on the train—I said seven will board—but that's, like, a whole thing. Juliette's a writer too, remember. I promise I can add. I've always found fractions a little more difficult, but trust me, we'll get to the other quarter.

Simone was still surveying the crowd for her other client. Around a hundred people were milling about on the platform, but

I couldn't tell which were the writers, or, given the festival was only using a few of the carriages, even the difference between the festival punters and the regular tourists. The staff, who were all wearing red-and-white striped shirts and camel-emblazoned polar-fleece vests, had started shepherding different groups of people to different areas of the platform. A young woman, shy enough of twenty to not look it in the eye, was panting and running her palms down her front as if they were steam irons, in the midst of apologizing to a man I assumed was her supervisor by the way he looked at his watch. I couldn't hear the apology, but groveling has a universal sign language.

A hostess with a clipboard approached us.

"Cunningham," I said, watching her pen trawl the list of names.

Simone gave hers over my shoulder, but then added, "It might be under Gemini's rooms, though."

"Cabin O-three," Clipboard said to me. "Easy to remember: it's oxygen!"

"Ozone," I offered instead, given that oxygen was actually $O_2$.

"Correct, you are in the O zone!" Clipboard chirped.

Behind me, Juliette disguised a laugh as a sneeze. Clipboard either didn't notice or didn't care; she pointed her pen at Simone and said, "P-one. But enter through O. I'll warn you though, it's a bit of a leg," before scurrying off to the next group.

"I'll see you later." Simone waved us away, her head still on a swivel.

"I think the warning about the distance was for the older clientele," I suggested as Juliette and I strode over to the nearest carriage. We were among the youngest there by a couple of decades. "We can handle walking the length of a train."

I was quickly humbled. The carriage in front of us was marked A. To our right, the iconic red engine cars, two huge locomotives. To our left, the train bent away so I couldn't even see the end.

I put it down, incorrectly, to curvature over distance: I was about to learn that the train ran to nearly a kilometer. So our walk was one of slowly creeping dejection, as we passed seven more carriages—including luggage, crew, restaurant and bars—and weren't even a vowel ahead.

Around G, a throaty growl thrummed in the air, and for a second the fear that the train was leaving kicked us into a jog. Then I saw a green Jaguar cut across the car park and over the curb, parking directly alongside the train, gouging thick rivets in the grass. Given the indulgence, I expected Henry McTavish to step out, but instead a spindly-limbed man emerged. He had hair that was impossibly both wild and balding, fairy floss in a hurricane, and a long, thin frame that made his movements angular and jerky, like he belonged in one of those old-fashioned clay stop-motion films. I decided he looked like the type of character who owns a gas station and tells the nubile young holiday-goers that there's a short-cut through the desert, imminent cannibals and various other nasty murdering sorts be damned, and said as much to Juliette.

"That's Wolfgang, actually. And I think he's going more for eccentric genius than lecherous imp," she said.

That did twig some recognition. Wolfgang—singular, like Madonna, Prince or even Elmo—was the prestige writer of the group, the one who'd been short-listed for the Commonwealth Book Prize. Pedigree aside, I'd been surprised he was appearing at the festival as his books didn't generally sit in the crime genre. I supposed his rhyming verse novel retelling of Truman Capote's *In Cold Blood* was his qualification.

"Clearly his books do all right," Juliette added, raising an eyebrow as the Jaguar grumbled back off to the road. "Better than ours, anyway."

I agreed; my royalties were more around the hatchback level. Secondhand.

We ducked and weaved around photographers as we got to L— people were taking selfies up against the red camel, or panoramic vistas of the length of the train—and marveled at how so many of the travelers were equipped with almost comically large telescopic lenses, near unbalanced by the weight of them, looking like untruthful Pinocchios as they raised those whoppers to eye level. In terms of magnification, the Hubble telescope hasn't got squat on a gray nomad's luggage compartment.

By carriage N we had broken a sweat. Sunrise had finally cracked like an egg yolk over the top of the train, and our shadows stretched long across the platform. A whoosh of air buffeted us from behind, and a golf cart overtook us, Simone hanging out the side, blue scarf flapping in the wind, looking like a frat boy smashing letter boxes from his mate's car. The cart came to a stop in front of us at the door to O and she hopped out, clearly catching my bemusement but shrugging it off by saying, "What? That's what they're there for. You've got to get used to the first-class travel perks, Ern."

Another clipboard-wielding staffer had produced a miniature staircase and was helping people up it and into the carriage, as the platform was level with the tracks. Beside the doors on each carriage was a series of rungs, a ladder that led to the roof. I'd love to tell you I get through the book without ascending these, but we both know Chekhov's gun applies to both mantelpieces and ladders.

We joined the queue. Wolfgang was ahead of us, given his shortcut, and I wondered if that was who Simone had been waiting for.

She must have sensed I was thinking about her, as she turned. "Just get it over with, whatever you're about to ask."

"I wasn't . . . How do you . . ." I hesitated. I had been thinking of asking her something since she'd surprised me on the platform, but I was nowhere near committing to doing it.

"You've taken three sharp breaths in, as if you're about to speak, and then fizzled out. You sound like a teenager trying to ask someone out on a date. So stop whistling in my ear like a kettle and just get on with it."

"Well." I cleared my throat, slightly annoyed because I'm supposed to do the Sherlockian deductions in these books—they are my books after all. "I wanted to ask you a favor."

"You know you pay me, right? Favors are for friends."

"It's work," I said. "But I'm stung you don't think we're friends."

"BFFs. Just don't ask me to help you move house. Out with it."

"He's hoping you can introduce him to Henry McTavish." Juliette, as ever, came to my rescue with her directness. "You used to work for him, right?"

"You've done your research." Simone seemed both impressed at Juliette's knowledge and a little annoyed to have her mystique pulled back to something as simplistic as a CV. "I was his editor, way back. Somehow landed on his first book doing a year over in the UK with Gemini as some kind of publisher's exchange program. He pinched me over to work for him directly. Real shit-kicker of a gig." She chuckled, then turned back to me. "Fan of the Scot, are you?"

She sounded, or perhaps I was imagining it, slightly disappointed. I'm still learning about the book world and my place in it, but even I knew then that McTavish was the sourest-tasting word in publishing—*popular*. It's the paradox of authorhood: apparently if you're good enough to be popular, you're too popular to be any good.

"A little," I lied. McTavish was my favorite living writer. His fictional detective, Detective Morbund, is as close to a modern-day Holmes or Poirot as they come. He's the type of character who solves the case in chapter 2 and hangs onto it until the end, only dragging it out to unspool everyone's lies. He'd have solved this murder already, even though it hasn't happened yet.

"You don't need me for that. You're on a panel together," Simone said. "You'll meet."

"I was hoping you might have the inside track. For a blurb."

The word *blurb* dropped out of my lips like a grenade. A blurb is an endorsement that a publisher can use for marketing, or even put on a cover. The more famous the person on your cover is, the better for marketing (and, let's be honest, the ego). I'm grateful to an excellent mystery writer named Jane Harper for going on the cover of my first book, and I was hoping McTavish might come through for the second. Even though, granted, I hadn't written it yet.

Simone snorted. "Henry doesn't blurb."

"I just thought—"

"Blurb. No. Go." She put a hand on my shoulder and, surprisingly, softened. "Focus on something more productive. You don't need to hunt blurbs for a book you haven't written yet. You've got four days of sitting around—use them. Get some words down."

"Soooo." Juliette wrinkled her nose comically. "If we're still doing favors, is now a bad time to ask you to help move that couch?"

I was grateful to Juliette for knowing exactly what the situation called for, and the laugh headed off the inevitable awkwardness. My hand subconsciously went to my pocket and found comfort in a small felt box I had in there.

There you go: the missing quarter. My motivations for this luxurious, creative and hopefully romantic getaway are all added up now.

More people joined the queue behind us. The fledgling sun passed behind a cloud, and the sweat we'd worked up from the walk settled icily on our necks. Juliette shivered. Simone noticed, uncurled her scarf and held it out. "Here you are, love."

Juliette took it and started wrapping it around her neck, mouthing a quick thanks just as Simone was called to the front of the queue.

At the top of the stairs, she turned back as if she'd just had a thought. "Try five thousand words by the end of the trip. That's just a thousand and spare change a day."

"It's more than just the words. It's the whole . . . fiction thing," I complained weakly. "I don't just make these things up. People, sort of, have to die."

Juliette, behind me, said, "I'll keep him to schedule."

"Blue suits you," Simone said, appraising Juliette's wearing of her scarf, then to me, "I guess I'll just cross my fingers and hope for a murder, shall I?"

Then she disappeared into the belly of the train.

# CHAPTER 3

I should introduce you to Juliette Henderson.

We didn't have the most romantic of starts, dead bodies aside. Our meet cute was me, a woefully underprepared city driver trying to get to a ski resort, and her, pulling over to help in the slush and mud. It turns out that she owned that very resort, and, even though I wound up having a hand in destroying it, we managed to get on quite well through the media frenzy that followed. Most people who read my first book are surprised we're dating. "I was so sure she was the killer!" they say. I think she's quite proud of that.

Juliette's a head taller than I am, with legs that belong on skis, knees that have paid the price for it (at only forty-one, she clicks like the Wheel of Fortune), and the freckled, often sunburned cheeks of a life enjoyed outdoors. She wound up selling the resort's land for a whopping sum of money and used her newfound time to write her own book about the events there. She's comfortable enough to never have to work again, but she insists she's not retired, she's just waiting for her next adventure. That's what she says when I ask her if she misses the mountain, anyway.

It's hard to say whether surviving a book tour or surviving a serial killer is the more arduous task, but given we'd gotten through both together over the last fifteen months, we'd fallen quite hard for one another. From the moment she first helped me affix tire chains to my slippery wheels, she's kept me on track. It's a pretty good result, seeing as we didn't exchange names until after the first murder.

And yes, I am proud of those lines, even if they are a bit cheesy. I'd written them down in advance, not for any book, but so I could memorize them to use alongside that little felt box in my pocket.

Inside carriage O, we funneled single file down a corridor that was tighter than I'd expected. Two-way traffic wasn't an option, and I'd learn that, should anyone be coming the other way, it was best to duck into the little kitchenette (which stocked not only tea, coffee and a kettle, but also an axe in a fire emergency glass case, and a handle that said *To Stop Train Pull Handle Down*) and wait for them to cross. The corridor had fake wooden paneling atop an emerald-green carpet. The cabin doors, five in our carriage, were to one side and there were wide, hip-to-ceiling-height windows to the other. I'd learn that the rooms alternated sides between carriages, which I'm mentioning here because it's kind of important. The cabins in the "O Zone," in which most of the authors were staying, were on the west side of the train.

The cabin itself was tight but comfortable. A large plush seat, lime colored and about the size of a three-person couch, filled one half of the room. This would be converted into a bed at the appropriate hour, and I could see the handles on the wall behind the seat where I assumed the top bunk came out. The bunks were singles and squeezed close enough together that sitting up quickly or a little friskiness would be rewarded with a bumped head. Not a lot of space for romance.

"No locks on any of the doors," Juliette said, wriggling the handle, perhaps thinking the same as I was. "Must be a safety feature."

With the benefit of hindsight, I can tell you that there aren't locks on many doors in the whole of the Ghan, except for the toilets (there was one public toilet in our section), the Chairman's Carriage and, assumedly, the driver's compartment. If you're hoping for a locked-room mystery, this isn't it. Everyone's room was open for anyone to come and go as they pleased.

Our cabin also had a small closet, inside which was a mini-safe and a vanity mirror, as well as a small nook at floor level for our bags (we'd only been permitted hand luggage in the cabins). Even with minimal baggage, navigating the remaining floor space did require a bit of a tango with two adults. The bathroom reminded me of an airplane's toilet, everything measured perfectly enough that the toilet seat lid lifted within one millimeter of the sink, and the door brushed both as it opened. Unlike a plane, however, there was no need for a screen or a television in the main cabin: a large window, showcasing the country we were crossing, would be our entertainment.

On the seat was a pamphlet, which I picked up. It was the program for the festival, all the guests listed on one side and the schedule of activities on the other. I was aghast to realize that for festival guests the regular off-train excursions—the crystal waters of Katherine Gorge, the red-dirt hiking of Alice Springs—had been replaced by "conversations" on board. Though it looked like we still got to explore the subterranean opal-mining city of Coober Pedy, which was a relief.

I scanned the names and tried to absorb them. I'd already encountered Wolfgang, whose bio was of too high a literary pedigree to include the phrase "he lives in the Blue Mountains with his partner and two dogs" and contained a list of awards so dense they'd had to shrink the font just to squeeze his entry in. I knew Henry McTavish's work. The other three were Lisa Fulton, who wrote legal thrillers; Alan Royce, who wrote forensics-based crime; and S. F. Majors, who wrote psychological thrillers and lived in the Blue Mountains with her partner and two dogs.

"You can have the view," Juliette said. She fumbled underneath the window until she found a latch and flicked up a small table that had been folded to the wall. She gestured to it with a magician's flourish: "Ta-da! Those thousand words don't stand a chance."

Even her good spirits couldn't lift my funk, but I appreciated her attempt enough to put on the performance of taking out my laptop and notebook and setting them up by the window. Juliette took a seat by the door and started flipping through an advance copy of S. F. Majors's new psychological thriller, which she'd been asked to blurb. It seemed a deliberate attempt to block me from conversation, and so I took the hint and opened my notebook.

To tell you the truth, the notes I did have were scant. While I'd studied all the rules of successful mystery fiction, I had no shape of plot or character on which to apply them. Last time I'd just written down what happened. Now I had to come up with it all from, God forbid, my own brain. The only thing I'd written in my notebook was a list of structural notes: what needed to happen in each section of the book, and at which stage of the word count these events should happen.

My list was:

*10,000 words: Introduce characters, victims and suspects*

*20,000 words: Explore motives (note: 90% of clues to solve the crime already present)*

*30,000 words: MURDER*

*40,000 words: Suspects identified, investigated, interviews*

*50,000 words: Red herrings + character development (romance?)*

*60,000 words: A second murder*

*70,000 words: Action scene? (must include: ALL IS LOST moment)*

*80,000 words: Mystery solved*

I'd broken it down like that in the hope that it might not seem so intimidating in smaller pieces. The last time Simone had checked in on my progress, I'd actually been confident enough to email it off to her, and she'd emailed back *Great idea, back to basics*, which seemed at the time more like an endorsement and less like the put-down that it probably was. But now, my list only reminded me of the volume of words ahead. Eighty thousand of the pesky things. I'd need to catch a hundred trains.

I took a deep breath, turned to a new page and wrote: *Setting: Train*.

Then beneath it, I wrote: *Been done before*. Obviously.

If you're wondering, we're a smidge over six thousand words thus far, which leaves me three and a half to ensure you've met every-one you need to: victims, killers and suspects. But instead I'm wasting time, writing about how I'm staring at a blank page, worried about wasting time. Nothing for it but to get started. No distractions.

My phone rang.

Just quickly: if you're expecting this sequel to be replete with returning characters, you've got the wrong book. I get it, it's nice and tidy when all the favorites come back for the sequel, but this is real life. How implausible would it be if all of my surviving ex-tended family simply found themselves at the center of another murder mystery? It's unlucky enough—or lucky if you ask Simone's checkbook—that it's happened to *me* twice, let alone the rest of them. I'm on good terms with my ex-wife, Erin, but we're more casual acquaintances these days than a crime-solving duo. My mother, Audrey, my stepfather, Marcelo, and my stepsister, Sofia, would hardly be enthused by the prospect of sitting on a train for a week. They're at a wedding in Spain actually. To be honest, if they wouldn't mind doing me a favor and stumbling on a murder there, I could use the trip and the tax deduction for another book.

My point is: real life doesn't have cameos.

I picked up the phone. It was my uncle Andy.

You need to know a few things about Andy. The first is that he's a horticulturist, which means his job is to grow grass on football fields. Perhaps in contrast to the slowness of his job, he's keen to make fast friendships and tends to reflect back the personality of whoever he's talking to rather than being himself, in the hope it will make him more appealing. Unfortunately this often only succeeds in making him the loudest voice with the least conviction. He is, suitably to his profession, a man often trodden on.

He's also a man who believes that youth is a fish that can be reeled back in. We'd recently thought he might have come to terms with his vintage (midfifties)—he'd at last shaved off his terrible goatee—but that hope was quickly dashed when he emerged with his hair bleached platinum blond. We'd all bitten our lips, except Sofia, never short of a barb, who'd asked what had frightened him so much.

I answered the video call to a nearly medical insight into Andy's nostrils. I rolled my eyes at Juliette while he fumbled with the camera. The picture spun blurrily, the scuffling sounds masking a hushed argument happening just off-mic, the snipes no doubt coming from my aunt Katherine.

Katherine is my late father's little sister. A wild youth had been transformed by a tragic accident into an uptight adulthood. She's a stickler for rules: her star sign may as well be School Principal. She roots for the umpires and is the type of person who says, with a completely straight face, "How could you forget? It's in the calendar."

Katherine is at her happiest when she's got something to fix, so Andy, who has the unfortunate affliction of doing most things incorrectly, really is the perfect match for her.

Another thing you need to know about Andy is that he wasn't too happy with how he was portrayed in the first book. He's adamant that I made him look like a bumbling airhead and he had more of a role in piecing together the mystery than I gave him credit for. He accused me of emasculating him, a word he repeated so often I was fairly sure both that it was new to him and that Katherine had taught him what it meant. He'd especially taken aim at a passage in which I'd referred to him as *a terrifically boring man*. I'd pointed out that technically I'd called him terrific, but even he wasn't falling for that one. So I'll try to do a bit better this time.

"Ernest! How are you, buddy?" Andy said, handsomely.

"We've just boarded the Ghan." I spun the camera so he could see the cabin. "Just waiting to set off."

Andy whistled. "You're a lucky sod, mate. I'd love to go one day. I don't know if you know this"—he lowered his voice, like it was a secret—"but I'm considered a bit of an amateur ferroequinol-ogist myself."

It's rare that Andy's vocabulary bamboozles me, but that was a word I had to look up later. It's a decidedly languid way of say-ing one has an interest in "iron horses," aka trains. I shouldn't have been surprised that Andy, to whom the length of grass is a passion, was also a fan of trains.

"What NR class is it hauling? I assume about one point five tons?"

"I've got to be honest, Andy, I haven't understood a single thing you've said. I think you might have confessed to being a feral ento-mologist."

"Fer-ro—" He started to sound out the word, but then there was some chatter in the background, some measure of *get to the point,* and he cleared his throat.

"Hi, Katherine!" I yelled, so she'd hear me off screen.

"I'm calling in a professional capacity," Andy said. This con-cerned me immediately; Andy and I have no professional associ-ation whatsoever. "I've got this client, and I'm hoping you might provide a consult."

"I don't know much about football fields."

"No, it's a different kind of client. It's a mystery. You're good at those."

*Client. Mystery.* Those words were more baffling than *ferroequinologist.* What he was trying to tell me slowly dawned.

"Andy," I said. "Please tell me you haven't . . ."

"I quit! I was sick of all the—"

*Grass,* I mouthed at Juliette, who snorted.

"—bureaucracy. The point is, I've got other options now, seeing as I solved all those murders up at the snow."

"Andy, *I* solved those murders."

"Well, we solved them together. Despite what you said in your book. Right?" He grimaced in an appeal for my agreement.

I remained stoic.

"And people were interested in what was next for me, you know. If I might be able to help them."

"Please don't tell me you started up a—"

"My own agency! It's called Andy Solves It!" He beamed. "I've always wanted to be a detective."

"It doesn't work like that."

"Well, private investigator."

"Don't you need a license or something?"

"Do I?"

I didn't know. I'd never looked into it. Juliette, who'd been eavesdropping, held out her phone. She'd found the web page for Andy Solves It!, the words splayed in a gigantic bubble font like it was a toy store. Beneath them was a photo of Andy wearing a fedora, an unlit cigar between his lips. I scrolled, scanning over the description, which read, *World renowned for solving the Cunningham family murders, let Andy help you with your problems today! We solve the unsolvable!*

"So I've got this client, and I'm a bit stuck. And Katherine said—"

"Andy." I shook my head. "This is a bad idea."

"I knew you'd say that." Turning away from the screen, he said, "I knew he'd say that!" He tsked, then faced me again. "I don't even know why she thinks I need your help. I've already solved a kidnapping."

"Really?" I did a terrible job masking my surprise.

"Well, it was a dog. But I tracked it down. Jilted lover."

"It's always the jilted lover," Juliette and I said in unison.

"Who wrote this biography on your site?" I scrolled past it again. "It's terrible."

"Robots, man. They can do anything."

"I'm not trying to tear you down, but have you really thought this through?" I asked.

Andy bristled. "I suppose you're the only one allowed to make money out of all those deaths? I was there too, you know. But I'm supposed to go to therapy and deal with my trauma quietly, and you're allowed to write these big books, and cash checks and be on TV and go on trains—"

His final complaint felt small compared to the others, and I wasn't so much "cashing checks" as counting coins, but I had to admit he was right. I had processed my grief and trauma publicly, and even though the real reason I wrote it all down was to remember it, and *them*, in a way that ink and paper only can, I had indeed made a small amount of money from it. If Andy wanted to cash in on some infamy, deluded or not, I'd be a hypocrite to disagree.

"Okay," I acquiesced. "This client . . ."

"I knew you wouldn't let me down!" The video jolted like an earthquake had hit it, and I realized Andy was doing a fist pump. "So there's this old lady, right, and she's like a florist or whatever and someone broke into her shop. I need to know who did it."

"Okay."

"Great." Andy grinned expectantly. "Soooooo . . ."

"That was a digestive *okay*, not an I-know-who-did-it *okay*."

"Okay," Andy said.

I want to note here, as I write this out, that Andy is making it very difficult to paint him in a better light than in the first book.

"Look, Andy, I can't just tell you who committed a crime without anything to go on. First of all, you need a list of suspects."

Andy looked down, off-camera, and I could tell he was writing something. "That's a good idea," he mumbled.

"You don't have any suspects?"

"I mean, there are a lot of potential—"

"The population of metropolitan Sydney is not a list of potential suspects, Andrew."

"It's interstate," Andy said proudly. "I've always wanted to go to Tasmania. Plus, I get expenses!"

"You are ripping off this woman," I said. I heard him suck his teeth, decided I'd rubbed it in enough, and hastily added, "What about clues?"

I heard the scratch as he wrote something down again. I imagined a big yellow legal pad with the words *Crime Solving: To Do* scrawled across the top and, underneath, the words *Suspects* and *Evidence*. I hoped the old lady hadn't paid a deposit.

"I mean, I interviewed her," Andy said at last. "She was a bit shaken up and all, but her husband was much more helpful." He paused. "Hang on. Maybe it was her brother."

"There's a big difference between husband and brother, Andy. You need to be specific. Words are important."

Any mystery writer will tell you that word choice is crucial. A story changes drastically if you replace the word *husband* with the word *brother*, and while it might have made the scene of his domestic burglary more salacious, he was better off getting it right. Given we're on the topic of word choice: Andy's client was a botanist, not a florist. While it might be picky of me to point this out, there's a big difference between an incestuous florist and an elderly botanist, and I did promise you accuracy.

"Let's start with something easier," I said. "What's her name?"

"Uh . ." Andy clicked his teeth as he searched for a note somewhere. "Poppy," he said eventually, which is, in fact, not her name. Details.

"Okay, so Poppy—"

"Now, was her name Poppy or did she sell poppies?"

"Andy—"

"Or maybe it's—"

"Maybe her name's Poppy and she sells poppies."

"Yes, that's what I was saying . . ." Having a conversation with Andy is sometimes like watching a hurdler barge through all the hurdles without jumping and drag the wooden planks along: no matter the obstacle, he trudges on. "But the weird thing is, you should see the security on this place. Security cameras, keypads—man, it's a fortress. For a florist!" Reminder: botanist. "Weird, right?"

"You think the security is there for something else? That the burglar was after whatever that was?"

"That's my working theory." He looked pretty proud of himself, or, at least, the inside of his nostrils did. I had to agree, it wasn't a bad piece of reasoning, or evidence gathering. He'd successfully jumped over one hurdle. "That . . . or it's like a flower fetish. Like a sex thing."

I take it back: hurdles still clanked around his ankles.

"I've solved it then," I said bluntly.

He lit up. "Really?"

"No, Andy. Suspects and evidence. Ask some questions. Call me back when you know, for a start, the victim's actual name. Then I'll try and help."

As I hung up, the seat beneath me jolted and a long slow groan came up through the floor as the wheels ground to life for a few inches. A voice crackled through an intercom, which I realized was embedded in the roof. Juliette looked up from her book.

"Ladies and gentlemen, welcome aboard the Ghan. We'll be departing Berrimah in fifteen minutes. Please join us in the lounge for a welcome, the chance to meet your hosts, and for tea and coffee at your leisure. And may we extend a very special welcome to the Australian Mystery Writers' Festival, joining us on board for their fiftieth anniversary. Let's keep the murders to a minimum, please."

"Good title," Juliette said, pulling on a sweater and picking up Simone's blue scarf. "*Keep the Murders to a Minimum*."

"Speaking of minimums—I wrote a few words. Break?" I said, knowing I hadn't earned one.

Juliette had the good sense not to ask just how honest I was being with my definition of *few*. She nodded and I stood up, but she blocked me from the door. She put both hands on my shoulders, leaned forward and kissed me on the cheek.

"I know you're stressed. First of all, I think you need to stop worrying about McTavish. Don't worry about some stupid blurb. Think about that *after* you've written the book. Speaking of—trust me, it'll come."

I was surprised to find my face warming, neck flushed. Staring at a blank page can make you feel alone; I wasn't prepared for how affecting it was simply to have someone tell me I wasn't. I nodded.

She shook me gently. "And if it doesn't, that's okay too. You can spend these four days staring out the window if you like. Or you can spend them writing. But we're spending them together. So keep the *moping* to a minimum, huh?"

I nodded, managing to croak out, "Thanks for the pep talk."

"Purely selfish." She smiled. "If you're going to be a melancholy sod the whole trip, it's going to be a long four days. Because once this hunk of metal starts moving, we're trapped on it."

# CHAPTER 4

We joined a throng of people moving slowly through the single-file corridor, which felt more like a queue for a post office than the start of a holiday. In the next carriage along, the bloke in front of us patted his pockets and looked forlornly back at his cabin door, only meters away, before accepting that the current was against him. I recognized it as the same look Juliette gives me every time we reverse out of the driveway at home. That's not sexist, by the way; I refuse to be the male protagonist who makes snide remarks about his girlfriend's forgetfulness. I mention it because it's a plot point.

After two more accommodation carriages, the corridor opened up to the bar. It was the most spacious carriage so far: hip-height maroon and brown booths ringed the walls, alongside select pairs of swivel chairs and, further toward the end, bar stools, all bolted in place to suit the train's motion. The bar itself looked like one you'd find in a speakeasy, a wood-paneled front, racks of spirits behind and hanging glasses above. Juliette, anticipating the popularity of the seats, snagged us two chairs by the east-facing window, a slash of sunlight and a tiny table no bigger than a paperback between us. Everything was three-quarter size in keeping with the train's space-saving design—the seat edge sat beneath my thighs instead of my knees, which wasn't to say it was uncomfortable, but it did make me feel like I was visiting a hobbit.

As the carriage continued to fill, I was glad of our seats. The air was thick with voices: the lulling murmur of general conversation mixed with the slightly higher-pitched tone of overenthusiastic introductions: *So nice to meet you!* Over it all, a coffee machine behind the bar whined with a rickety tiredness that sounded like it had not properly anticipated servicing a carriage full of writers for half a week. On the liquor shelf, I spied a three-quarters-empty bottle of vodka that was similarly underprepared.

Juliette draped the blue scarf over the back of her chair and headed to the bar to snag us coffees. There was quite a line, and the girl serving—the one who'd been self-ironing with her palms on the platform—seemed quite overwhelmed.

I looked around at the rest of the clientele. I figured our O carriage was the middle of three between the bar and the back of the train (as P was further to the back and we'd walked through N), which would fit about thirty people, though I also noticed people entering the carriage from the bar end, which implied there were cabins toward the engines and maybe doubled the attendance. Subtracting the six festival writers and their guests didn't leave much of an audience. That it was the festival's fiftieth anniversary was probably an excuse for the excess, as this was clearly not a traditional event that relied on ticket sales. Perhaps that was also how the festival had gotten away with setting up in such an expensive location: attendees had been promised an intimacy not usually catered for at events. Meals, drinks and socializing with the writers: the chance for everyone to let their hair down together. This would wind up being true—if you counted both being murdered and murdering as letting one's hair down—so at least everyone would get their money's worth.

I tried to weigh up the attendees, to better gauge how the rest of my long weekend was likely to play out, or, more specifically, which wannabe—embittered by years of rejection from publishers, clutching a coffee-stained handwritten manuscript and ready to spring it on you at any time—was best avoided. The carriage had a celebratory air to it, the pre-disembarkment holiday excitement that accompanies the phrase *It's five o'clock somewhere* and a glass of champagne that you don't really want but got anyway because it feels like an adequate signpost that you're up for a good time. It was still before breakfast, but that didn't matter to most. Holidays are, after all, mostly extravagant charades with which to justify an addiction. A group of three silver-haired women who'd staked out a booth clinked glasses amid cheering and laughter that seemed to prove my theory.

According to my structural cheat sheet, in order to play fair I'm running out of words left to introduce victim(s), killer(s) and suspects, and I fear I'm coming up short on at least two categories. So I'll take the opportunity to whip around the carriage now.

Given I didn't recognize all the writers yet, the only linking characteristic I could find was people's choice of beverage: caffeine or champagne. So I'll start there.

Champagne:
- A man, older but not elder, seated in a two-seater across from me—gold-rimmed glasses and beard flecked with equal parts orange and gray—had one glass of bubbles in hand, another full flute in front of the vacant seat across from him.
- S. F. Majors, whom I recognized from her photograph in Juliette's advance copy, was dressed in a light gray pantsuit, with black hair pulled tightly back into a ponytail—looking better dressed for court than a holiday, and far too serious for the undrunk bubbles in her hand.

- A woman with a brunette bob and a blouse adorned with native flowers was playing on her phone, squeezed onto the end seat in the booth of the ribald senior ladies and doing her best to ignore them. From the effort she was making to keep to herself, I pegged her as a writer: Lisa Fulton, by process of elimination.

Coffee:

- An eager-eyed, spindly-limbed man, somewhere in his forties, whose shoulders had an IT worker's computer hunch that threatened to swallow his head like a tortoiseshell, was surveying the room, pointing out each writer to a woman. The woman had her curly hair in a messy bun, two tendrils hanging beside her cheeks like a picture frame, and I assumed she was his similarly aged wife by her obliging yet uncaring nod, as if he were explaining to her the backstories of *Star Wars* figurines. He was an easy addition to the fan category.
- A woman who looked far too young to enjoy or afford such a trip stirred a spoon idly through her cappuccino while reading a paperback copy of Stephen King's *Misery*. I assumed at first she must have been a university student but gave her the benefit of the doubt of having a youthful face and landed on thinking she was probably a graduate publicist, because she'd chosen a work-safe nonalcoholic option and was wearing a T-shirt that said *A nod's as guid as a wink tae a blind horse*, which associated her directly with McTavish's Detective Morbund novels.
- A short, stocky man wearing colorful suspenders, definitely a writer based on the quirky outfit alone, but also because he was scribbling in a notebook, was most likely Alan Royce.

And fitting into neither category was Wolfgang, standing on his own in a little alcove by the bar, holding a glass of blood-red wine that he kept sniffing unhappily.

I spied Juliette delicately carrying two rattling coffees back to our table. Of the remaining expected attendees, Simone hadn't made the effort to attend—meet-and-greets not really being her style—which made Juliette's bringing her scarf pointless. Neither could I see Henry McTavish. I was confident in my naming of both Alan Royce and Lisa Fulton as the ones keeping to themselves in groups of one or two and who, like me, had a look on their face that was half sizing up the rest of the room and half trying to decide if there was still time to leave the train.

I fear I'm going to break my own rule here. Mystery books like these are only fair if all the cards are on the table from the start, so to speak, and I haven't managed to properly introduce everyone by my self-imposed limitation of the first ten thousand words, which is here. Someone important has just missed out.

I felt a hand on my shoulder.

"Your book did well," said a man in his sixties, not towering but tall enough to be looming over me in my hobbit seat, the same man who had patted his pockets on leaving his cabin. He was well dressed in a dinner jacket and leather shoes, an open collar and a loosened navy silk tie. His accent was imported—English—and he spoke with a belief that volume was equal to meaning. Which, for a man who seemed to believe everything he had to say was important, means loud.

I've found that people sometimes talk about how your book's doing if they don't want to give you a direct compliment. It sounds like a compliment, but it's just an observation. There's a difference between *You look nice today* and *So I hear you're a model*, for example. I didn't like the way he'd said it—almost leering, mocking.

"I'm very pleased it's found an audience," I said, choosing humility instead of matching his aggression. "I'm sorry"—I held out my hand—"I don't think we've met?"

"You're Simone's boy, aren't you?"

"Ernest," I said, choosing not to be Simone's property.

"Yeah. Ernest." It was as if he was agreeing that my name was, in fact, what it was. He glanced around the carriage, muttering. His sentences had a way of cascading over one another, the oven between thought and speech undercooking everything: he spoke in first drafts. "Good numbers. Well published. She's not here?"

I realized he was looking at her blue scarf, draped across the empty seat. He'd recognized it. "Oh. No, we're giving that back to her."

"Okay. Well, while I'm here . . ." He paused, leaned down and lowered his voice. "Look, I'd like to take the opportunity to apologize about our little . . . indiscretion."

"I don't think we've met." I waved it off, confused. "No need for apologies."

"I mean, it's not *polite*. But it's not really something we can police, you agree? And I figure we're all adults. Right? And your book's—well, it's not for everybody. On the plus side, I've always been telling him to interact more online. So I guess this is a start."

I still wasn't sure what the apology was for, but this was certainly on the low end of apologies I'd accepted.

He sneezed, wiped his nose with the back of his hand. "Allergies," he said apologetically. It was a much better apology than the one he was trying to give.

"I'm really sorry, but"—I pointed to my chest—"I'm Ernest Cunningham, and my list of beefs is rather small. So unless you're the guy who backed into my car two weeks ago, for which following me here would seem excessive for an apology, I think we're probably square." I noticed Juliette had been caught in conversation with Majors, and wished she'd hurry up and rescue me.

"Course. I should introduce myself." He straightened his tie, sniffed again. His eyes were slightly bloodshot. If I'm honest, he looked like he was coming down off something, and not just a high horse. Finally he took my hand and shook it. "Wyatt Lloyd. I own Gemini Publishing. I publish—"

Suddenly there was a commotion from the bar. "It's all-inclusive, isn't it?" a man shouted in a vaguely Scottish accent. "If I want the bottle, just give me the bottle."

I could only see the tweed-shouldered, heavyset back of the speaker, but the tone of the command, of someone quite used to asking people if they knew who he was, gave me an idea: here was the festival's biggest draw, Henry McTavish.

"—I publish *that*," Wyatt said, turning to the ruckus and raising his eyebrows. "You don't have any antihistamines on you, do you?" He fossicked a small white packet from his pocket. "Jasper gave me these, but they're rubbish."

I looked at the branding. "Well, that's because those are for seasickness, not hay fever."

"Damn." He sneezed again, then cocked his head back to the argument at the bar. "I better go sort it out. Glad we could smooth this over. And if you see Simone"—his head was on a swivel—"tell her I'm looking for her."

Still having no idea what we'd smoothed over, I settled on smiling sagely, while feeling, admittedly, quite wrinkled. I felt more out of place than ever, because if I really belonged here, I should have known—as Simone had clearly expected—who Wyatt was. I did know Gemini Publishing was a big deal, based in the UK but with an Australian outfit. They'd pretty much built their business publishing McTavish. Their other authors—Royce, for one—had been dragged into prominence by association. And I now know that Wyatt, who'd discovered McTavish, had risen to co-own the company off the back of it. He had taken the time to come over and talk to me, and I'd responded by cracking jokes? By shrugging him off? I replayed the conversation in my head, feeling (irrationally, because I had my own publisher already) like

I'd blown it somehow. I was clearly still figuring out how to play the social politics of being an author.

Wyatt strode off toward the hubbub, where McTavish had just slapped away the hand that a man in a red-camel-emblazoned vest had calmingly placed on his shoulder. I was left with a carriage full of writers and a now completed roll call. Suspects: check. Victims: check. Killer(s?): check.

# CHAPTER 5

Juliette slid into her seat and sucked at her flat white with the relief and thirst of a traveler who'd just crossed the desert. "God," she said. "I just had to lie to S. F. Majors. Said I'd almost finished her book." She looked behind her to make sure nobody was close enough to hear. "*And* that I was enjoying it."

"Aren't you?"

"I've got no idea. I've read like three pages. The writing's fine, I guess. But I have a sinking feeling it's got one of those twists where the first-person narrator has been dead the whole time."

I looked at her, amused. That went against one of the most obvious rules of fair-play mysteries. "No ghosts."

"I know, right? No *bloody* ghosts. Psychological thrillers these days don't have to follow any rules. I shouldn't have said anything at all, but I was trying to fill the dead air. Now I'm going to have to give her a bloody blurb." She necked half her coffee in a gulp and closed her eyes for a second. "This place is chaos—McTavish wants an IV of whiskey and that poor girl up the front looks like it's her first time using a coffee machine. And she is not happy that he is treating her like his personal butler. Sorry I took so long. How was it down here?"

"I met Wyatt Lloyd." I nodded over at him, in case Juliette didn't know who he was, but she seemed to understand without needing to look. "McTavish's publisher."

"Yeah, I wondered about that when Simone mentioned him before. Four days at a festival seems a bit beneath the pay grade of a bigwig: authors come to him, he doesn't come to authors." She shrugged. "Maybe he's got business with McTavish. What did you talk about?"

"It was so strange, actually." I grinned. "He *apologized*."

"Oh." Juliette paused, like someone who didn't get a joke that's just been told, her cheeks a little tighter than they should have been. Then she read my face and relaxed. "You're taking it well, then. Very noble of you. That's a relief."

"Taking what well?"

Juliette's cup stopped halfway to her mouth. "Didn't you just say he apologized?"

"Yeah, that's what's so funny about it. It's absurd." I felt like a comedian trying desperately to save a crowd, the only choice being to double down on the joke and make something funny by sheer force of will. This *was* funny, right? "He must have thought I was someone else. I have no idea what he was apologizing for."

Juliette scratched her forehead and sucked air through her teeth. "You haven't seen it, have you?"

"Seen what?"

"I'm sorry, Ern, I just didn't think you were in the right headspace—"

"Right headspace for *what*?"

A loud clap of hands interrupted us. The staff member who had been defusing McTavish now commanded the attention of the cabin. A stockman's Akubra hat was snug on his head, hair hanging underneath like vines. His shirtsleeves were rolled up to reveal sinewy muscled forearms, the type that could hold down either a sheep for shearing or a disgruntled alcoholic Scotsman. He waited for the room to settle—the table of rebellious seniors took the longest—and then spread his arms widely.

"Guests," he began, and I recognized his voice from the intercom, "on behalf of me and my team, I'd like to welcome you to the start of our historic journey aboard the Ghan. I invite you to reflect on the traditional owners of the many lands we will travel through on our journey, including my people, the Arrernte people, whose lands you may know as Alice Springs, and the Larrakia people, on whose land we begin our expedition today." He paused to a round of applause. "My name's Aaron and I am your journey director. I hope we'll get to know each other well over the next four days. I'm here if you need anything, as is Cynthia"—he pointed behind the bar—"who will keep you both caffeinated and intoxicated. So out of the two of us, she's the one to keep on your side."

This was met with the half chuckle that meets the basic expectation of a pause and a smile in a formal speech.

"And now for the exciting part. Our end of the train has the special privilege of hosting the Australian Mystery Writers' Festival's fiftieth anniversary"—a clap—"for a trip filled with scintillating insights into the minds of some of the country's best writers." Clap. "We will be departing momentarily, and the first session, a meet-and-greet panel with all the guest authors, will be held at midday." He paused again, but the clapping had run out of stamina, and this was welcomed only by the plodding slap of a couple of hands. "But before we start the fun stuff, we will be serving breakfast." This rejuvenated the applause, with perhaps the most enthusiastic response yet.

"This Writers' Festival has the run of eight carriages, including this bar, the Queen Adelaide Restaurant and the Chairman's Carriage, which we have specially borrowed for this trip from our friends at the Indian Pacific. The Ghan today has two locomotives hauling thirty-five carriages, at a length of seven hundred and eighty meters and with a total weight of one thousand four hundred and fifteen tons."

I expected people to be disappointed by the replacement of breakfast with statistics, so was surprised to hear a murmur through the crowd, one of both interest and opinion, as if several people were scratching their chins and agreeing *Yes, I was thinking that was an appropriate weight for the journey*, which taught me a lesson about hobbyists I should have already known: everyone's an expert.

Aaron continued to list off figures, and I quickly realized, from the bent backs and leaned-forward concentration of the guests, that Andy's fellow ferroequinologists found this dull tirade of data frothingly exciting. "Across our two-thousand-nine-hundred-and-seventy-nine-kilometer journey, we expect to use seventy-five kilograms of barramundi, sixty-two kilograms of cheese, over a thousand bottles of wine"—this got a small cheer from the rambunctious retirees—"and approximately forty thousand liters of fuel." This was again met with a murmur of definitely educated opinions on the fuel required for the trip, this time with a line of dissent (easy to identify—it's a semitone lower in a murmur): *I would suggest that they could do it in thirty-nine if they optimized the engines.*

"I hope they've got a coupon," Juliette whispered, leaning forward.

I snorted, which turned Aaron's attention, and therefore that of the rest of the room, on us.

"Did we have a question?" He meant it genuinely, but it was impossible to not feel spotlighted.

Juliette's cheeks flamed. "Oh, sorry. Just a joke." When Aaron continued smiling gently at us, Juliette added, "I just thought you might need a coupon . . . for the fuel . . . Four cents a liter on forty thousand liters . . . it's a solid discount."

Nothing kills a joke's momentum like overexplanation. Juliette did get a couple of laughs, but I caught one passenger looking aghast at us, as if horrified we dared joke about something so crucial as fuel quantities.

Juliette was saved from any further humiliation by a jolt of the carriage, just violent enough that those standing rocked and gripped the chair backs nearest to them. This was accompanied by the metallic groan of one thousand four hundred tons waking up. The scenery started to roll horizontally past the windows.

"That's my cue to wrap it up, I suppose. Just one caution—you're likely to see a bit of smoke occasionally. It might be in the distance, but it might be closer than you'd like. Don't panic. These bushfires are natural, though, to be fair, deliberately lit." This drew a little gasp, which he'd clearly hoped for, and he grinned. "Believe it or not, our little arsonist is a *bird*. A kite bird, to be precise. They hunt down bushfires and pick up flaming sticks, which they fly over and drop in dry patches of grass. Once the area is aflame, they catch the fleeing rodents. So if you see fire, unless it's on board, nothing to worry about!" Aaron gestured toward the restaurant carriage. "Breakfast is served, at your convenience."

The hungriest were up quickly, but I was happy to sit for a minute. Now that we'd set off, the spell of the journey had taken hold of me slightly. Watching the chicken-wire fences of Berrimah terminal trundle past, replaced by pristine blue sky and vibrant monsoon-season-flourishing greenery, underpinned by the click-clack of the wheels rolling over the tracks beneath us and piping-hot coffee in hand, I had to admit to feeling the magic. I felt, well, posh.

In fact, I was so charmed, it took me at least another fifteen minutes to remember to ask Juliette what exactly she was hiding from me about Wyatt Lloyd.

# CHAPTER 6

"One star?!"

I almost flung the phone across the table, as if it were a hot coal superheated by the incriminating internet browser I had just opened. On-screen was the Goodreads page for my book, *Everyone in My Family Has Killed Someone*, where a new review had been posted. The review had a little red star. Just one.

"One bloody star?! Where the hell is he?"

"Ern," Juliette said gently, "I think you might be overreacting."

I looked around. A few heads had turned from their breakfast at my outburst. The restaurant carriage was fitted out with a dozen or so four-seater booths with flip-down seats. Pristine white tablecloths and polished silver cutlery glinted in the shafts of sunlight shining through the panel windows, and jade-green strip lights lined the roof. I spied Henry McTavish dining in the far corner with Wyatt and—and this incensed me further—Simone. They were all leaning forward, shoulder blades hunched like vultures' wings. That's a posture exclusively reserved for scheming.

I made to stand, but Juliette put a hand on my arm and gave a pointed cough. I followed her gaze and was surprised to see my left hand had curled around a knife. It was more of a reflex, grasping something nearby as I went to stand, but it surprised me enough that I dropped it with a clatter.

"A bit of the old Cunningham family blood still in me," I said with as much lightness as I could muster. I put the phone down, and Juliette flipped it screen-to-tablecloth so the red star wasn't staring me in the face. She needn't have bothered; it was seared into the back of my eyelids.

Today's date. A single red star. One word underneath: *Ghastly*. Author of the review: Henry McTavish.

Wyatt's apology ran through my memory: *I mean, it's not po-lite. But it's not really something we can police, you agree?*

"Maybe his finger slipped," Juliette suggested.

"*Ghastly* is a seven-letter word."

"I meant the star rating."

"So he's capable enough to log in, type in the name of my book, pull up the page, enter the review field, and type his review, and *then* he fumbles on hitting the five-star button?" I stared back at McTavish's table. What the hell were they talking about? How could my agent buddy up to them after *this*?

"Ern?" This time Juliette snapped her fingers in front of my nose.

Cynthia heard the snap and interpreted it as a summons, which made us feel both classist and apologetic as we ordered our pancakes and scrambled eggs.

"Sorry," I said, after we were alone again. "I'm just . . . processing. Has it been up long?"

She shook her head. "I don't think so. I only saw it in our cabin, just before we left for breakfast. I didn't want to freak you out. I wasn't, like, deliberately hiding it." Her lips tightened in an appeal for understanding. I remembered her telling me to forget about petitioning McTavish.

"I'm sorry," I said. "I shouldn't have snapped at you."

"It's fair enough. Although"—she looked at the table setting—"in retrospect, I probably should have told you when there weren't knives to hand. Just remember, the only people who read reviews are the authors themselves, and other writers."

"That's what I'm worried about," I said, then admitted, "I was hoping I'd fit in a little better." It sounded childish, but I'd been worried about it since the invite. All the other invitees had published multiple books or had multiple accolades; they were *writers.* I'd simply been at a place where a bunch of people had killed another bunch of people and been the one to write it all down. I'd already felt like an imposter; now I knew for sure that at least one of my contemporaries considered me one. I figured it wouldn't be long before the others joined the chorus.

"You haven't even met everyone yet—"

"I don't . . . I don't know if I deserve to be here."

There was more to it than that, of course, but that was the best way of saying both of my concerns in the same sentence. It was about as much as I was ready to admit to, in any case.

"Hey! Your book's just as good as any of theirs. Besides, we'll be out of mobile reception in a few hours. No one is even going to see—"

"Copped a pasting from the old Scot, I see." The man in rainbow suspenders whom I'd suspected of being Alan Royce stuck out a hand and proved me right. "Alan Royce. Mind?"

He didn't wait for an answer or a shake, wriggling his way into the seat across from Juliette with a grunt. His blocky frame did not sit comfortably in the little table booth. His bulbous ears had more hair than his head, protruding antennae of such length that I decided he could hardly be unaware of them and likely they served some function similar to a cat's whiskers, considering his peripheral vision was reduced by his tiny teddy-bear eyes. When he got himself settled, he looked around, or perhaps his ear hair thrummed, and he snapped his fingers at Cynthia. Embarrassment flooded through me: now she'd definitely think we were a table of *snappers*.

While he ordered, I noticed he'd placed the little notebook he'd been carrying around open on the table. It was a cluttered mess of notes, but I caught that he'd written in all caps: *KEEP THE MURDERS TO A MINIMUM* and next to it the word *TITLE?* Underneath that was a list of names, including both mine and Juliette's, and dot-point descriptions. Next to my name he'd written: *cherub-esque face: wide-eyed, often confused, unacademic.* Next to Juliette he'd written: *out of his league.* This is probably why I've focused so much of my own description on his ear hair. Authors are a petty bunch. He also had a list of notes about the train, which you've already read in my own descriptions. There are only so many ways to describe the carriage: *emerald-green carpet; in case of emergency, pull here; axe; barramundi = 75 kgs.* He'd even nicked Juliette's joke, having written: *fuel coupon.*

He caught me reading and flipped the notebook over. Authors are a protective bunch, too.

"You write forensic thrillers, don't you?" Juliette attempted to change the topic away from my review.

"My protagonist is a forensic pathologist, if that's what you mean. Dr. Jane Black: eleven books, three novellas."

"I used to love *CSI*," I said.

Alan rolled his eyes. "I prefer to think that I write novels about society, depravity and humanity, and the crime itself is just the engine for a more . . ."—he paused in obvious affectation—"enlightened conversation around some real-world issues. I find all that *CSI* stuff quite"—his lips curled into a cruel smile as he deliberately chose his next word—"*ghastly.*"

This was all a bit rich coming from someone who, I've since researched, has a novella in which Dr. Jane Black travels back in time and conducts a forensic investigation on the murder of a dinosaur. But witty comebacks are capably served by both hindsight and Google, and given I had neither at the time, I could only respond with an unacademic glare.

"You know, what you *want* is a one," Alan rolled on, oblivious to my bristling. "Or a five, obviously. Because you can use both for publicity. A two, blah, that's just bad news. But a one: that's a history-making calamity. People will be inclined to check it out just to see how bad it is."

"This may surprise you, Alan, but you're not making me feel any better."

"You know Wyatt Lloyd rejected my first manuscript four times before he agreed to publish it?" That did, actually, help my spirits a little. "It's all part of the game."

"You got McTavish-ed?" A female voice joined in, speaking as its owner slid in beside Alan. She'd been looking at me when she spoke, which meant she'd also seen the review. "Ernest, right?"

I nodded.

"I'm Lisa." (Not to brag, but nailed it.) "You're the other writers, I assume? I'd rather not sit with the guests."

"Nice to meet you. Juliette." Hands were extended and taken.

"Pleasure."

"Alan . . ." Royce waited just a little too long in hope of recognition. "Royce."

"Oh, the gory autopsy guy. My mum reads your books."

This is another of those publishing compliments: *I wouldn't subject myself, but someone I know reads you.*

"I prefer to think I write novels about socie—"

"McTavish-ed?" I moaned. "Oh God, it's so bad it's a verb. Has *anyone* not seen it?"

"Don't worry," Lisa said, "the only people who read reviews are—"

"—everyone on this train."

"You're not the only one to get a review, man," Alan said, as if it were a competition. "He gave us all one, you know."

"Really?" The hope in my voice was pathetic, that my misery might be shared.

"Well, he didn't give us all *one*, he gave us all a review. Everyone on the program. Gave me a four." He held up a correcting finger. "But it reads like a five."

"Maybe his finger slipped," Juliette said quietly.

"What did he say?" I couldn't resist asking.

"Just one word, same as you: *Splendid*."

"Maybe Ernest has had enough of the review talk," Lisa interjected. Her eyes gave me an apology.

"Oh, come on. As if you don't want to talk about yours?"

She looked at the table. "I really don't."

"Five stars!" Alan held up five stubby digits in Juliette's face. "'Tremendous,' wasn't it?"

"Something like that."

"That's weird." Juliette had picked up my phone and clicked through a few pages. She offered it back to me for a look. "His profile is completely inactive. He's literally never reviewed anyone until this morning, and then he reviewed the five of you. All at once."

I saw on McTavish's profile that he had indeed only made five reviews ever, and they were all from this morning. Lisa Fulton's only published book, *The Balance of Justice*, a legal drama from twenty-one years ago about a car thief who'd been sexually assaulted by the judge presiding over her case, had five stars, accompanied by the word *Tremendous*. Alan Royce's *Cold Skin: Dr. Jane Black #11* had four stars and the word *Splendid*. So far so accurate. S. F. Majors's upcoming book, *Dark Stranger,* the psychological thriller that Juliette was currently reading, had a three-star rating and, again, a lone word: *Overblown*.

"He's ranked us," I said before I even checked Wolfgang's rating. It was, as I'd anticipated, a two.

"*Heavenly*," Juliette recited from beside me.

"Reads like a five," I said. *Heavenly* was a strangely complimentary word to use on a two-star review. Unless the context was: *I'd rather die.*

"I doubt Wolfgang's seen it," Lisa said. "Literary writers don't brood online quite so much as we do. I wouldn't tell him if I were you."

Juliette and I nodded in agreement. You didn't need the approval of strangers when you had awards laurels. Wolfgang wrote books that didn't apologize or cater to readers, as if to say: if his works are too difficult for you (and they were for me), that's your fault.

"It's not exactly a fair ranking though, is it?" Alan preened, turning to Lisa. "Five stars? Come on." He realized he was the only one laughing and folded his chortle back into his mouth. "What? You've always been his favorite."

Lisa looked like she was about to hit him, before Juliette cut in to defuse things. "It's not a competition. It's not even a critical opinion. It's just one man sitting at a keyboard, trying to mess with you—which you're all falling for, by the way. It's meaningless."

Just so you know, it's not *exactly* meaningless. I write this because that's what I thought at the time, and, even now, writing it all out again—although for different reasons—I maintain this position.

"Doesn't bother me," Alan finally agreed. "He can give me a one for all I care. The blurb's way more important than an online review."

"He's giving *you* a blurb?" I got the emphasis all wrong in my surprise, and Alan physically reeled.

"And what do you mean, exactly, by that?"

I backtracked. "I thought McTavish didn't blurb is all."

"He doesn't." Alan now had the smug look of a child with a secret. "Unless he owes you a favor."

The arrival of food cut him off from elaborating further, and we moved away from the comparison game. I ate quickly. Unlike the train itself, I didn't have forty thousand liters of social fuel, and I feared I'd used too much too early dealing with Wyatt Lloyd's chattering and Alan Royce's ego. I wanted to get back to my cabin and try to enjoy myself again, even though Lisa struck me as someone deserving of getting to know a little better.

"I really liked your book," Lisa said as we stood up to leave. "About what happened on the mountain. Very respectful. What are you working on now?"

If *respectful* strikes you as a word not often used to describe me, you'd be right. She was talking to Juliette. I felt a rush of shame. I'd been so worried about fitting in that I hadn't even given a thought to how Juliette might feel not being on the program, or how she deserved to be treated as a writer in her own light, and not just my shadow, which Lisa had just done. I said *seven* writers, remember?

"Oh," Juliette said, "I'm tossing up between a few bits—"

"Waiting on her next adventure," I said, squeezing her hand.

"Something like that." I can tell you with the benefit of hindsight that Juliette's smile was forced, though I didn't clue into it at the time.

Still, Juliette, warmed by Lisa's compliment, was cheerful on the walk back to our cabin. I was more contemplative, dragging my feet and trying to get my head around the morning. Not *just* because of McTavish, and the review, and the blurb, and Simone's camaraderie with him and Wyatt, and the general indignation that four writers at a table can't resist competing, but because Alan Royce's notepad had annoyed me.

It seemed odd to me that he had a list of everyone on the journey. Why did he write down all our names, what we looked like? Of course, some writers scribble everything down as a matter of course, but this seemed excessive, specific. Why take those kinds of notes? Was he writing a book about the trip? I'm aware of the hypocrisy that *I'm* currently writing about the trip, but at least I waited until someone died to start. I couldn't shake the feeling that it was more than simple note taking.

It was almost like he knew something was about to happen.

# BLOCKBUSTER

# CHAPTER 7

The Ghan rolled on. The Northern Territory whipped past our window.

Rocky outcrops with scraggly, crooked trees, no taller than Alan Royce, backs bent low as if shielding themselves from the bright sun, gave way to spinifex-pocked orange sand, made all the more vibrant by the unblemished blue sky above. The horizon was far, still and flat, and the expanse of the Australian desert, which we were yet to even hit the edge of, dawned on me. We may as well have been an ant making our way across a sandpit.

Three hours after we set off, we made our first stop, in Nitmiluk National Park, Katherine. I crunched down the portable steps onto gravel. There was no station here; we had simply stopped in the middle of the tracks, and the Ghan seemed somehow more impressive by how out of place it was, shiny steel among nothing but trees and sky and birdsong. I became very aware of the footprints I was leaving in the dirt, in this place where neither I nor a giant man-made metal snake really belonged.

Up near the head of the train, almost a kilometer away, waited a queue of buses. They would take the nonfestival tourists on their scheduled day trip sailing down the magnificent Katherine Gorge: high rock walls bordering pristine, crocodile-filled waters. In front of our carriages were forty or so black fold-out chairs set up in the red dirt for the festival attendees. Another six chairs faced the group, a wireless microphone on each and portable speakers either side. Behind these was an easel with a rectangular canvas mounted on it, hidden by a black felt covering.

Juliette kissed me on the cheek, which I took to be for luck, until I realized she was walking in the wrong direction and had meant farewell.

"You're not staying?"

"Aaron said he'd sneak me onto the gorge tour." She grimaced with the confession, but it was a cheeky guilt. Of course, the choice between one of Australia's natural wonders and six writers having an ego-off wasn't really a choice at all, but I didn't do a very good job of hiding my disappointment. She overamped her enthusiasm. "You'll be great! . . . Unless you want me to—"

The offer was half-hearted, her body already tilted toward the tour buses like a runner waiting for a starting pistol. Behind us, people had begun to mill about in the crowd, and the writers were choosing their seats. S. F. Majors was walking up and down, carrying a clipboard stacked with paper and notes; Henry McTavish was ambling, his back to us, clutching a cane with an ornate silver top that he ground into the dirt with each step and looked at risk of splintering; and Alan Royce lap-dogged behind while chewing his ear. Henry chose the furthest of the six seats, on the end next to an already seated Lisa Fulton, perhaps hoping to shake Royce. Royce was marooned for a second, looking around to see Wolfgang already seated dead center in the prime focal point, and then shamelessly trotted to the other end of the row, picked up the last chair, and relocated it to McTavish's empty side. I couldn't hear him from where I was, but his mouth remained flapping in conversation, as if he hadn't broken his train of thought at all to consider that McTavish didn't want to sit next to him. As soon as Royce sat down, though, Lisa stood up and moved herself to the opposite end—whether this was to rub in the wasted effort of Alan's circus or her own disinterest in sitting next to McTavish, I wasn't sure.

"Don't be ridiculous," I said to Juliette, forcing a smile onto my face. "Take lots of photos. Try not to get eaten."

Juliette flicked a final look over at the impromptu staging, at the gathering writers. "You too."


"Welcome to our first thrilling panel!"

S. F. Majors, it turned out, was on hosting duties. I knew she chaired the festival board, because she'd invited me, which I mention here because in murder mystery books like these it's generally quite a key point who invited the cannon fodder to the specific location they become trapped in. You know the scene: a character turns, holding an invitation, and says to another, *"You invited me here,"* to which the other character holds up the same invitation and says, as lightning flashes against their face, *"No, I didn't—YOU invited ME here."* Cue calamity. So you have that answered now: she's the one who brought us all together.

The reason I was invited may not be important to the plot. But it's damn well important to someone. I just don't know that yet.

Majors introduced the panel to a smattering of applause that, in the expanse of the open, sounded more pathetic than it had indoors. I caught a couple of craned necks lusting after the final departing tour bus. I'd ended up next to Lisa Fulton on the opposite end to Royce and McTavish. Wolfgang was next to me, and Majors had filled the space between him and McTavish. We'd all shuffled our chairs down a bit to compensate for Royce's seat switching.

I tuned out of the introductions and took my first proper look at McTavish. The main thing that struck me was that he didn't look how I'd expected. Of course, writers can look like anybody, and it was nothing physical—his stature slotted somewhere between the blocky Royce and the spindly Wolfgang, and his wispy hair was wild enough to be uncared for but not enough to be eccentric, which is all par for the authorial course—but writers do have a *look*. There are a couple of variations to it—S. F. Majors's sternness is that of a writer by whom everything is analyzed as an opportunity, for example, and Royce's eagerness for plaudits is ego plastered over a true lack of confidence—but it's all in the eyes: the dead giveaway. A writer's eyes are wide and curious, taking in the world and flipping it over, interrogating and interpreting it, regardless of whether it's for vanity or creativity. I saw it beneath Wolfgang's scowl, beneath Lisa's shyness, even in Royce's maligned notebook. But McTavish had none of that: his eyes were giving off the petulant clock-watching of a student waiting out a detention. It was jarring to see my favorite writer in this light. I knew his agreeing to attend this festival was quite the coup, but now I could see why he abstained from these kinds of things: it must have started to feel like serving time.

Noticeably, his left side, the one he'd propped up walking with the cane, was, for want of a better word, crumpled. His tweed jacket seemed to hang more loosely around a coat hanger of a shoulder, his trousers baggier around a bony knee, while his right side filled out the fabric much more naturally. He wasn't disfigured, but he was unbalanced: he looked like a loaf of bread you've accidentally put the rest of the groceries on top of. A drunk driver had cleaned him up one night, sped off and left him twisted and broken in a gutter. This had, of course, been bundled into his publicity: he'd been told he'd never walk again, never *write* again. And look at him now. Back from the brink.

His cane was leaning on the seat next to him, and I could see now that the ornate topping was a gleaming silver falcon. He slugged from a similarly gleaming flask, produced from the inside chest pocket of his tweed jacket, often enough that I wondered why he bothered to screw the cap back on each time.

"Let's start with you, Lisa." Majors kicked off the interviews proper. "Your debut, the striking novel *The Balance of Justice*, was released twenty-one years ago. It was a worldwide phenomenon, breathing new life into the courtroom drama, and from a fresh female voice too. It's still reprinting today! A lot of people, me included, have been clamoring for your next book. We're set to finally get it this Christmas. Excuse my bluntness, but what took you so long?"

"Well, following up *The Balance of Justice* was a tricky thing." Lisa spoke out to the crowd, and I noticed she'd put on a hint of fake radio-announcer voice. "Certain parts of that novel were maybe ahead of their time, and I think the world has finally caught up to the conversation I wanted to have about women and our rights."

"Fascinating." Majors had the air of someone reading ahead to the next question. "So it wasn't the pressure of the follow-up? That didn't contribute to the gap?"

"I get writer's block like anybody," Lisa said, but a little uncomfortably. "I wanted the right idea . . . but I can't say that really influenced it. I wanted to be in the right space to publish again—writing a book is a soul-baring thing, as you'll know. Besides, I think a good book is a good book, no matter how long it takes to write."

"Kids didn't derail you? I understand you're a single mum, not long after your debut? A book baby and a real baby in the same year. Must have been tough."

"I don't think you'd ask a single dad that." Lisa didn't even bother painting on a smile. "I'd ask the other women here, but seems I'm the token guest on the panel. Shame, when we should be sticking together."

Majors took the hint. "That's a good opportunity to move on to our next guest. Ernest Cunningham, I guess you're different from Lisa in a way: I don't think anyone's hanging out for your next book."

This insult blindsided me, and I took a second to steady myself. "Um . . . well . . . I think people actually quite liked my first. I hope they might read another."

Majors faked a droll laugh. "Of course, of course. I simply meant we're all hoping you don't *have* to write another book. Given what happened to you and, more importantly, those around you, the last time."

"Oh, sorry," I mumbled. There was a loud cough and I saw a plume of assumedly blueberry-scented smoke arise from the crowd. Beneath it, Simone tapped one hand under her chin and used the index finger on her other to trace a line across her cheek. She was telling me to look up, speak up and smile more. To an onlooker, however, it might have looked like she was slicing her finger across her neck. I forced some energy. "Absolutely, I wouldn't wish to go through that again. Especially not for the same royalties!" Even Simone smiled at that. Relieved, I relaxed into the conversation. "I am writing though. I'm working on a novel."

"Good luck," Wolfgang said, in the not-quiet-enough way where his surprise that I'd heard him had to be completely faked.

"Tell me about it," I agreed. "No one told me fiction would be this hard."

"Harder for some," Wolfgang said, and I realized his first comment had not been the self-deprecating alliance I'd taken it as.

"Excuse me?"

"Your book. Stranded on a mountain, a serial killer." He wriggled his fingers as if describing a scary movie. "All very sensational. The kind of sordid stuff that sells a lot of books, I'm sure."

"I wasn't thinking about book sales at the time," I said. "I was rather busy trying to stay alive." This got a gentle laugh from the audience.

"Excellent deflection. Media training kicking in."

"I'm sorry, are you accusing me of something?"

"Festivals welcome feisty conversation, but let's keep things civil," interjected our host.

"I mean no offense." Wolfgang wasn't even speaking to me. He was pandering to the crowd, like he was the narrator and I the hapless clown in a pantomime, righteousness puffing out of him with every word. "There's obviously demand—that's how a writer like you can sell a lot of books."

"What exactly is a *writer like me*?" I fumed.

"A connoisseur in the fine art of pulp." He leered. "I mean that as a compliment, of course. Different strokes for different folks."

Majors had crumpled the top sheet on her clipboard with her anxious hands. She made a feeble attempt to regain our attention. "Okay, I think we might—"

"No, sorry. I'm curious." I turned to Wolfgang. "What exactly makes my writing *pulp* and yours *literature*? You can't come to a crime festival and sneer at our whole genre, when all you did was copy Capote."

He shriveled a little at that.

"It's all words on a page," I continued. "I put as much of myself into my work as anyone here."

"If you don't know the difference between pulp and literature, that would be a serviceable definition of the problem." He crossed his legs and leaned back, as if to imply that his response was of such inarguable caliber he would not indulge a retort.

"It's nothing to be ashamed of. We all start somewhere," Alan Royce chipped in, predictably.

"Sounds to me like the only difference is having a last name or not, *Wolfgang*." This got me another laugh from the crowd, which incensed Wolfgang enough for him to sit up straight again.

"You write blood and guts for the sake of it, as if it's entertainment. It's distasteful. In fifty years, books like yours will be spat out of machines. And of course, your prose is amateurish. I'm not the only one here who thinks that."

He looked over at McTavish, who glanced up from his flask somewhat confusedly, and I realized that we'd been wrong about Wolfgang being too lofty to read the online reviews. Apparently no amount of acclaim can bandage the cut from a stranger on the internet. I'd done panels before, when the book had first come out, and I was familiar with the occasional barbed question, sure. But the majority of writers are generous and warm. For a literary confrontation, this had struck me as particularly aggressive. Now I knew why. Wolfgang was incensed that McTavish had ranked him down low alongside me, and so was now trying to assert himself above our commonality. It still came down to ego.

"You want the difference between pulp and literature? Between a real writer and just a writer? I'll tell you: adverbs."

"Adverbs?"

"You use too many of them," he said, derisively.

It seemed to me quite snobbish to say that real writers didn't use an entire group of legitimate words in the English language, but here is where I confess that I was too flustered to articulate this. I shut up, embarrassed and enraged in equal measures.

"Leave the lad alone," McTavish said, surprising me by both coming to my defense and revealing that he'd actually been paying attention. He used the microphone like a father of the bride: inexpertly, alternating between too far from his mouth so the words came patchily, and too close so the wincing ring of feedback echoed. "Nothing wrong with a bit of blood and guts. I'm sure it's fine."

And just like a flare of lit magnesium burning bright and short, we settled back into the usual panel rhythm, though not without a few whispers of excitement from the crowd, no longer regretting missing the gorge tour. The next set of questions went to Wolfgang, beginning with his *In Cold Blood* adaptation and then moving on to his future works. It turned out he wasn't writing anything new at the moment, but was instead focused on an "interactive art installation" titled *The Death of Literature*. He started most of his sentences with *Well, you see* and *As you know* as he discussed influences almost entirely comprising obscure philosophers. I found it grating but kept my mouth shut.

"Nothing like a little bit of literary snobbery to get us started," Lisa whispered in my ear. "Don't let it get to you."

"What's an adverb?"

It took her a second to realize I wasn't joking. I had a sinking feeling my only alliance was about to disintegrate. What had started as a grin melted off her face. Slowly.

Wolfgang's pontification finally ended, and the questioning moved on to McTavish. Backs straightened in the crowd with interest; it was obvious, given it was one of his rare international outings, he was who people were here to see. To my surprise, now that the spotlight was on him, it was like a switch was flipped. No longer was he half slumped in his chair peering into the black hole of his flask. He came alive: impressing with tales of drizzly Scottish moors, of growing up poor and how hard he'd had to fight to not only get his books published, but then to be taken seriously as a writer (perhaps this was why he stuck up for me, I thought, though I was still struggling to forget that little red star), and how, recovering in the hospital after his accident, he feared he'd never write again. He finally finished on how much he hoped people enjoyed his most recent Detective Morbund novel: *The Night Comes.*

At this, a hand shot up immediately. It was the young woman I'd seen clutching a copy of *Misery*.

"There'll be time for questions at the end," Majors said.

"It's just—" The girl jigged like she needed the bathroom. "I was hoping you'd talk more about *The Dawn Rises*, given it's the newest. Henry, it's incredible, by the way. I loved the way you—"

"Thank you, there'll be time for questions at the end," Majors said again with teacherly steel before turning to the wider crowd.

"The young lady is correct," McTavish interrupted. "Though I do consider both books one half of a two-parter. Of course, *The Dawn Rises* won't make any sense if you don't read *The Night Comes* first, which is out in a new paperback this week. There are so many release dates and formats and countries to keep track of, it's easy to get muddled. What I'm really saying is: just buy both." McTavish mugged for the crowd and was rewarded with a laugh.

"I can't imagine how complicated it is bringing a series of sixteen books together for a finale." Majors got back on topic. "How did it feel to say goodbye to such a popular character?"

"Uh, well that's a tough one." McTavish faltered. A light slur nudged on the edges of his words and the previous sparkle had disappeared. He clearly had an alcoholic's touch for delivering prerehearsed lines but little room for improv. He was scanning the crowd, and I noticed his eye line settled on Wyatt, but it wasn't for reassurance, like why I'd hunted out Simone. His eyes blazed with annoyance. Wyatt shrank a little in his chair. Owner of the company or not, it was clear who was in charge. McTavish directed his answer at him. "*Goodbye* is such a strong word. I don't want to spoil it for the people here who haven't finished it yet, but no door is ever closed."

"I feel like that's as much of a scoop as we're going to get from you," Majors responded smoothly, reading McTavish's deliberate aloofness. "One more question for the craftspeople in the audience, then. Is it true you write all your books by typewriter? I heard that you do it to protect against spoilers, by only having a single typed copy of every manuscript. That seems quite an extreme solution."

"It's not so extreme if you think about it. J. K. Rowling's manuscripts used to be handcuffed to her publisher's wrist, like the U.S. president's nuclear codes. Dan Brown's publishers required his translators to work out of a basement in Milan for a month: no internet, security guards if you wanted to use the bathroom. You can't take it lightly. You should see some of the things people have threatened to do to me to get their hands on a manuscript. And with everything online these days, I just don't trust my computer. Besides, I like the feel of the keys."

"What if your house burns down?" I couldn't resist asking. Admittedly, I was a little emboldened by the fact he'd taken my side earlier.

It was the first time I'd spoken directly to McTavish and he looked askance, as if he was trying to decide if he was offended. I wondered if he'd really been sticking up for me, or if he'd just wanted to disagree with Wolfgang. Eventually he said, "I would take that as a sign from the universe that I probably need another draft." He unscrewed his flask again and took a long swig, in a clear sign to move on.

Royce looked like a dog ready to go outside, such was his enthusiasm to finally have a question of his own.

"And last—"

"But not least!" he chipped in.

"Yes. Of course." I realized here that Majors said *of course* as a polite way of saying *shut up*. Whenever she was interrupted, in fact. I chalked her up as a woman who took great care with her words and didn't wish to be either diverted from them or spoken for. "Alan Royce, author of the Dr. Jane Black series, whose novels take place on steel tables and in morgues. Very chilling reading!"

"I prefer to think that I write novels about society, depravity and humanity, and the crime itself is just the engine for a more . . ." Royce paused in the same deliberate spot as he had over breakfast, and I realized this was a man who took himself very seriously and wanted to advertise that he did everything with great effort. He was the type of person who picked up and carried a suitcase with wheels, just so he could complain about how heavy it was. "A more enlightened conversation around some real-world issues."

"Of course."

"I think that's our job, really. To interrogate society. Which I think is what Wolfgang was saying, with regard to the French modernist move—"

"Plus you've got firsthand experience with all the gore and grisliness, right?" Majors was taking pleasure in reducing Royce to his most sensationalist identifiers. To her credit, the crowd did prefer to hear about morgues over Wolfgang's tangent on French modernism. "You used to be a forensic pathologist yourself?"

"Oh yes, that's what inspired me to write fiction." Royce exaggerated the last word, lingering on the f sound by pulling his bottom lip under his front teeth and flinging it like a trebuchet. It looked like he was aiming the word at me for some reason, which didn't make any sense, given that I was the only one there who hadn't published any.

"Wonderful," Majors said. "Let's move on to audience questions." Royce deflated a little at getting timed out, but she either didn't notice or didn't care, as she gestured toward the black-cloth-covered easel behind her. "And after that, we have a special treat for you. So. Questions?"

*Misery*-girl's hand was up first. Majors made a show of looking around at the otherwise unmoving crowd, before selecting her with an obvious lack of enthusiasm. A wireless microphone was delivered into the audience by a staff member, and the young woman stood up.

"My question's for Henry." She bounced a little on her toes as she spoke. "My name's Brooke and you might know me as the president of Morbund's Mongrels!"

Morbund's Mongrels were McTavish's die-hard fans. McTavish showed little recognition of the mention of his fan club, nor did he noticeably clock the phrase on her T-shirt (*A nod's as guid as a wink tae a blind horse*, which is a Scottish colloquialism for plain speaking and as close to a catchphrase as Morbund had, as he often delivered it during his monologuing solve). I'd suspected Brooke was his publicist when I'd first seen the T-shirt, but now that I knew she was Head Mongrel, it made sense that she was on the train specifically to fawn over Henry. The price of the trip still seemed excessive for her age (I still pegged her as early twenties, not least because I figured the passion to organize *anything*, let alone be the president of a global fan club, dissolves like sugar in water after you turn twenty-five) but I supposed she came from money. Either that or her adulation was such that it didn't matter how hard she'd had to scrape, from how many shifts of bar work or mopping fast-food floors, to meet her idol. Henry's words echoed—*the things people have threatened to do to me to get their hands on a manuscript*—and I wondered if there were any other Mongrels on the train, and if their obsession was another reason he no longer did events like these.

"I wanted to ask, without spoiling anything"—she looked around with a guilty expression—"Morbund's not, well . . . is he? I mean, in *The Dawn Rises* certain things happen and I just wanted to ask if he's *actually*—"

There was a groan from the back row familiar to anyone who has a spoiler-defensive friend (this, for me, is Andy, who once berated me for spoiling the ending of, of all things, *Titanic*). I must admit I was a little cheesed at Brooke too, because although I'd known from the marketing that *The Dawn Rises* was Morbund's supposed swan song (it was emblazoned on the cover, alongside a *New York*

*Times* pull quote—"Unputdownable and unbeatable: McTavish is peerless"—that meant McTavish would never have to beg for blurbs), I hadn't thought that McTavish would kill off his prized character. His books were, after all, in first person, and you already know that is a cardinal sin for fair-play mysteries in my eyes. How does a book get written down when the protagonist is dead?

Take me, for example. You *know* I'm not currently in the dirt, being bullied by writers under a burning sun. No: I am in a hospital room in Adelaide, finally off the train and in a plastic-sheeted bed but not yet allowed home, as the police are still gathering everyone's statements and body parts. I'm typing this out while occasionally requesting more painkillers and scratching a thin sheet of skin from my peeling neck.

"Thank you, Brooke," McTavish said, clearing his throat, the mere act of his remembering her name from fifteen seconds before almost making her spontaneously levitate. "I'll keep the secret for the rest of the audience here, but I think it's up to your own interpretation."

It was a nothing answer, and Brooke wrinkled her nose. The Ghan staff member held their hand out for the microphone. Brooke clutched it like a toddler scared of losing a toy. She seemed to have forgotten she had four more days in which to harass McTavish, and to want to capitalize on this moment: to win him over.

"Okay, well, it's just that the innkeeper, in the book—his name is Archibald Bench. *Archie* Bench." She squinted expectantly and pronounced the innkeeper's name in syllables, the way you gossip about an ex's new partner (*You'll never believe who she's dating . . . Arch-i-bald Bench*), as if she and McTavish were in on the same secret.

I itched for her to get to the point. I could feel the back of my neck reddening, and I wished I'd put on sunscreen: I remember feeling certain my neck would blister and peel later.

"Am I right?"

McTavish glanced over to Wyatt, who shot him a boggled *I don't know* grimace. I was pretty confused myself. I'd read all the Morbund books except the last and I'm normally pretty good at piecing things together, yet the name Archibald Bench meant nothing to me other than that an editor should have suggested swapping out the surname for something more realistic. Then again, just like I'd told Andy and like I've already told you, everything in a mystery is deliberate, and McTavish was up there with the best in trickery, puzzles and wordplay, and so I figured that if it was Archie Bench instead of Archie Bus-Stop or Archie Church-Pew, it must have had some significance.

"I think you've outsmarted me there, girl," McTavish said at last. It was a general enough statement but, apparently, exactly what Brooke wanted to hear, as she pretty much clicked her heels with excitement and thrust the microphone back at the staff member, well satisfied that this moment, one she must have rehearsed over and over, had gone as she'd hoped.

Just quickly: I swear I didn't conjure up that the book she was reading in the bar earlier was *Misery*, in which a psychopathic fan takes a writer hostage and forces him to write a dead character back to life (sorry, Andy, for the spoiler). That's what she *actually* was reading. Until it got covered in vomit, at least. I assume she discarded it after that, but then again, seeing as it was McTavish's vomit, I wouldn't put it past her to souvenir it.

Majors offered a chance for further questions. Brooke must have been doing biceps curls in preparation for the number of times her hand shot up, and Majors did her best to pick around her but struggled with a lethargic crowd. Most of the questions were for Henry, which I didn't mind one bit but had Royce practically wriggling out of his chair in the hope someone would target him. He almost imploded when the man with the speckled beard—I recalled the second glass of undrunk champagne in front of him—received a microphone and said, "My question's for Ernest."

I fumbled my own microphone to my lips and smiled to welcome the question.

"It's a simple one," the man said. I noticed he was on his own here, just as he had been at breakfast, on the end of a row, the seat beside him spare. "Did you kill him?"

As if on cue, a sudden surge of wind planted a stinging plume of red dust in all of our eyes. I scrambled to wipe the dust and collar my thoughts at the same time, and the best I could do was utter, "I beg your pardon?"

"Did you kill him?"

I'm sorry to rob you of the dialogue here, but my editor has censored the answer I gave, as it directly relates to the killings on the mountain last year. I can tell you that I answered simply by repeating what I wrote in the last book—the phrasing of which has been legaled enough to keep me safe. It seemed to go over well. Royce's eyes were lava, on me the whole time.

A new hand rose. "I have a question for Henry." It was the curly-haired wife from the couple I'd assumed to be fans: more Mongrels. She had a light Irish accent, the pitch riding up and down mountainsides. Her husband was sitting next to her, and he made a gentle grab at her elbow to pull her arm down, but she shook him off. "Where do you get your ideas?"

"Harriet." Her husband tried to shush her and his cheeks flared with embarrassment. As a fan, he seemed the opposite of Brooke, in that McTavish's turning their way seemed to panic him.

"I'm allowed to ask a question, Jasper," Harriet said firmly.

McTavish headed off a lover's tiff by leaning forward and spreading his arms. "What a fabulous question!" he said, before launching into a well-practiced answer.

If you're wondering, writers fall into two categories: plotters, who outline their work before writing it; and pantsers, who sit down at their desk each day with no idea where the work will take them, thus flying by the seat of their pants. I suppose I am a bit of both, being that when I live the events of my books I have not much idea what is going to happen, but by the time I sit down to write, the killer has had the decency to plot most of it out for me (though I would stop short of calling the murderers I've encountered *co-writers*). McTavish revealed himself to be a pantser, stating that he started with an image, a feeling or even a color, and let that inspire where Morbund would wind up in each adventure.

It was a pedestrian answer to a pedestrian question, and I apologize that you're having to suffer through this entire panel discussion as if you were there in both length and banal conversation, but I figure you deserve the proper feel of a literary convention. And, besides, there are too many clues in this chapter to skip over even the seemingly innocuous dialogue. Like what's about to happen.

Archie Bench, it turns out, is rather important too.

"My favorite of yours is *Off the Rails*," Majors said (this is, for those who don't have an encyclopedic knowledge of McTavish's work, his third Morbund novel).

Brooke nodded along. I dimly remembered the book, in which a couple staged a car accident with a commuter train to cover up the murder of their son. There was a particularly sordid scene involving the setup to the collision, in which the parents substituted two freshly dug-up corpses as their own in the front seats, designed to be pulverized beyond identification, but other than that I remembered little of the overarching plot.

"I recall a news story that was somewhat similar actually," Majors added. "So, on top of colors and mood boards, you must find inspiration from"—she stole Royce's trick of faking effort into word choice—"elsewhere."

"Nae." McTavish shook his head. His accent came out more

heavily now, as his tongue tired and slipped around his consonants. "I don't really take stock of much news. Of course the world around me sinks in every now and then, and I have to keep up with policing and technology, but if I paid too much attention to the news I'd never have an original idea for a book. You know what they say: truth is stranger than fiction."

"There *was* a similar story though. In my hometown actually," Majors said. "When I was a kid."

Someone cleared their throat loudly in the audience. I looked over and saw Wyatt coughing into his hand. His focus was locked on to Majors, the expression on his face clear: *Watch it*. I saw Jasper roll his eyes at Harriet, as if the tension was her fault for asking a question.

"Was there?" McTavish asked, interested.

"You don't remember? Lisa, you'd know the story. It was thirty-two years ago. Nineteen ninety-one."

Lisa shrunk into her shoulder blades. "I don't think I want to—"

"That's a long time ago, lass," McTavish cut in. "Where'd you grow up?"

"Out here," Majors said. "We'll cross right past it, actually. The train line, that is. About a hundred kays out of Alice Springs."

"Aye. And the odds of me stumbling on an article from regional Australia, when I'm over in Scotland—well, it's slim I'd say. I'm sorry if the book touched a nerve. If you knew someone who died or was hurt in a similar way as I imagined in my book, I imagine it would be painful to read about. But every one of us here"—he picked up his cane and scanned it across us all—"has killed an infinite number of people in an infinite number of ways. It's inevitable that, somewhere, real life mimics it."

"You don't think—" Majors pressed.

McTavish laughed. "Thank God we're just *inventing* it! If one of the six of us was to die right now, you'd have five suspects who all know how to get away with murder."

Majors blanched. Her eyes flickered over to Lisa but found no hold. Lisa was busy tracing circles in the dirt with her toes.

"If each of your books is a color," I said, trying to rescue the conversation, "what color is *The Dawn Rises*?"

"Red." He delivered this with relish. "*Blood* red."

This got a round of applause from Brooke, as it was clearly a reference to Detective Morbund's fate. Even Wyatt smirked. *How's that for media training*, I thought, looking over at Wolfgang. Maybe it was just being out of practice; I shouldn't have doubted McTavish was anything but a pro.

Majors cut back in. "And, Henry, *Off the Rails*?"

If words could hammer nails, McTavish could have driven in a railway spike with his sharp reply. "Green."

Majors made a great show of checking her watch and stood, creating a rustle of movement in the crowd, less of excitement and more in anticipation of a bathroom break. Bladders are the opposite of writers' egos—finite—and many had been tested by our discussion. The morning champagnes hadn't helped either. Thinking back, the alcohol had probably fueled the argumentative streak in us writers as well: normally literary talks aren't so combative.

"It's been a lively hour. To round out our morning's program, we have a very special treat for you all." Majors walked over to the easel on display. "We've had special permission from Penguin Random House to unveil to you, today, exclusively"—she gripped the corner of the black cloth draped over the easel—"the cover of Lisa Fulton's new novel, *The Fall of Justice*, over two decades in the making." She whipped the cloth off like a magician, revealing a large cardboard printout.

The cover showed a regal building, assumedly a courthouse, lit by the blood-red of a setting sun, the silhouette of a city behind it. Lisa's name was in bright gold letters, lanky and stretched, bigger than the title itself. But most noticeable of all, in stark white type against the blacksmith's forge of a sky, were four words.

Everyone reacted differently to these four words. Lisa's hand went to her mouth. I could see her jaw quivering, eyes wet. She would have had approval over the cover design, but she clearly hadn't seen the *final* version and was duly overwhelmed. Royce's hands curled into fists and clawed up his knees. His mouth was set in such a thin line he'd probably cracked a tooth. Wolfgang hadn't even bothered to turn around. Majors had her eyes set on Lisa, an expression in them I couldn't figure out. It wasn't quite jealousy but lacked the warmth of *Happy for you*.

McTavish was the easiest of all to read: he had a well-fed belly-slapping smugness to him.

Of course he did. Of the four words, two of them were his.

*"A firecracker." Henry McTavish*

An endorsement from the man who *never* blurbed. And from where it sat on the cover, unmissable in size and brightness, it would definitely sell books. Lisa's cheeks bunched like she was about to cry, and clearly afraid of doing so in front of everyone, she stood up and hurried back toward the train.

People in the crowd followed her cue and started to stand and break off. Wyatt stood up and came over to McTavish, wrapping one hand around McTavish's good shoulder. I couldn't hear what they were saying, but I saw McTavish laugh in response to something Wyatt said. I headed quickly for the train, as I'd seen Simone start to rise. I did want to talk to her, but I didn't have the energy just then to be properly mad at her and wanted to do it right.

I hurried back into the bar, where I ordered a Stella, served in a tall bulbous glass with the foam sliced off the top with a knife, and sat by the window, taking a miniature booth all to myself, waiting for the plume of dust to signal the returning buses. I was looking forward to complaining to Juliette—all-inclusive drink in hand, plush seat beneath me, as our first-class train continued on its world-famous journey—about how hard done by I was.

My position turned out to be fortuitous, because otherwise I might not have seen Alan Royce, dawdling behind the other guests, guiltily looking around until he was sure he was alone. I swear he looked right at me, but the glare of the sun on the window must have made me invisible.

Which meant he didn't know I saw him glance around one last time, and then punch a fist straight through Lisa Fulton's cover.

# CHAPTER 8

The first beer didn't touch the sides, but the buzz of alcohol helped my hands stop shaking. Writers are, universally, far more polite than what I'd just experienced. But there was something about this festival in particular that had us all at each other's throats. Was it the isolation, the locked-off feeling of the train—no live-streaming, no journalists—implying we were on our own and therefore our actions might not follow us back to the real world in some kind of bizarre *Lord of the Flies* satire? Or was it simpler: S. F. Majors had clearly selected a combustible cocktail of writers. They all had their links, their grievances and their arguments, which, adding ego and cooking under the desert sun, baked into nothing less than a resentful quiche. Except for me. This was my first time meeting every one of these writers. So why was I here?

I told myself I was overthinking it and got up to get a refill, but when I came back the husband-and-wife team, Jasper and Harriet, had commandeered my table by the window. I looked around. The bar was filling up. The boisterous flock of older women had a spare seat at their table but I didn't think I could handle them. McTavish had a stool at the bar, elbows keeping him upright, where he could mainline fluids, and though there were spare stools beside him, I didn't think that was a much better option. No one else I knew was in the carriage, as many had retreated to their rooms. I must have hovered long enough that Jasper noticed.

"Sorry, mate. Did we pinch your spot?" He slid over, and I sat down. "Jasper Murdoch, good to meet you."

His blackberry-dark hair contrasted with the Gatsby-lantern green of his eyes. He was wearing a T-shirt belted into a pair of jeans. I shook his hand, which bore the hardened fingertip calluses of a tradesman, and turned to his wife. "And Harriet, right?" This caught her off guard; she brushed a tendril of hair behind an ear. "I heard you talking during the panel. I'm not a stalker or anything. Ernest."

"The adverb guy," Harriet said. It was a warm insult, an alliance in thinking Wolfgang had been a bit harsh.

"That was all quite lively, wasn't it?" Jasper said.

"That's one word for it." I sipped my beer, looking out the window at a staff member picking up the collapsed easel from the dirt, scratching their head at the lack of wind to knock it over. "I don't think I realized what I was getting myself into." I laughed. "But you're the guests. Money's worth for you, at least?"

"Don't take it personally," Jasper said. Harriet nodded.

"Like all good advice, that's easy to say and tough to follow."

"Think about it this way—to Royce and Wolfgang, fresh meat like you is a scary thought, because there're only so many spaces on a shelf. And you're standing there, ready to jump in their graves. So to speak." Jasper shrugged. "That's how they see it, I reckon."

It was too astute a summary to not be lived experience. I hazarded a guess. "Which publisher do you work for? Gemini?"

"He's a writer, actually," Harriet said.

"Part of the festival?" I asked.

Jasper physically waved my question away. "I have business with Wyatt Lloyd. This seemed as good a place as any to chase him down and do it. Not often you get the chance to go all the way up and down Australia." In the air, he traced a finger in a line up and a line down. I remembered the Ghan went both ways. "Especially for the Irish." He whispered it almost conspiratorially, nodding at Harriet.

She playfully punched his arm and said to me, "Don't listen to him. My parents are Irish, but I was born in Melbourne." That explained why her accent was so light.

"So you caught the train up from Adelaide just to catch it down?"

"We rented a car. Drive up, train down," Jasper said.

"Long drive." I thought of the seasickness tablets that he'd mistakenly handed Wyatt. They seemed unnecessary for a desert road trip; he must have been the queasy carsick type.

"If you've never done it, I recommend it. Beautiful country. Nothing better than open roads, dingy motels and clear air to finish some projects."

"Okay then, writer to writer. Am I being fragile, or was everyone picking on me?"

"I think you crave their validation too much. Who cares!" He shrugged. "It's the stories themselves, not the covers and the shelf space or the festival invites, that outlive us." This struck me as poignant, but it sounded just a little rehearsed. It seemed to me in particular that he'd convinced himself a festival invite wasn't important, partially in defense of never having had one. His mention of shelf space, and specifically how little it mattered, twigged a better understanding.

"You self-publish?" I guessed. An online success trying to make the jump into print made sense: it was a reason to tail Wyatt on the trip. There's always at least one guest at every writers' festival clutching a manuscript, waiting to shove it into an unsuspecting publisher's hands. "Ebooks? I used to do that."

"Ah—"

"He's very good," Harriet bragged. "Sold just as many books as McTavish."

"Thanks, Harry, that's enough." He clearly disliked her speaking on his behalf, like a child bemoaning a proud mother. He turned back to me. "I do okay."

It wasn't quite humility. He was suddenly a little more shy, protective, and I wondered if it was a glimmer of the same kind of imposter syndrome I felt. Of course, Harriet may have been inflating his ego, but the truth was simple: even if Jasper had great sales for his self-published work, he'd still had to come chasing a publisher on this train.

I turned to Harriet to change the topic. "And you're a fan of McTavish, I assume?" She had, after all, been the one to ask him a question.

Harriet smiled. "I'm a big fan of his books."

"What about you?" Jasper cut in. He seemed to me a gentle guy, but one with the uncomfortable habit of interrupting his wife when she was talking, as he had during the panel, which was a little too possessive for my tastes.

"Yeah. I'm not, like, a Mongrel or anything. But a fan. Well," I half-laughed, "I'm deciding if I still am, to be honest."

"If it's any consolation," Jasper said, "I heard that lady—she's your agent, right?—arguing with Wyatt about taking those reviews down."

"You've seen it too?"

"Word gets around. Everyone gets a bad review sometimes. Don't let it bother you. Hey"—he held up his empty glass—"we might freshen up before dinner, right, Harry?"

Harriet nodded. "It was nice meeting you, Ernest."

They stood up to go, and like I was at a speed-dating table, the man who'd asked me the question at the panel—gold-rimmed glasses and graying, red-flecked beard—sat right down. He had a leathered face and black-diamond moguls for furrows on his brow, and he wore an Akubra that was too clean to have been purchased anywhere other than the Berrimah gift shop. He was holding two beers, and just as I wondered if his mystery companion was joining him, he slid one over to me. This was too many drinks for my constitution—I still had a third of my second beer to go—but I hooked the glass with my finger out of politeness and nodded my thanks.

"Douglas Parsons." He extended a hand and we shook. I didn't feel the need to give my name, considering he'd read my book and had addressed me at the panel, but then I felt self-conscious that I was being arrogant in assuming he knew who I was, and so spluttered out *Ernest* after far too long a pause.

"Yeah. I was in the audience before." He spoke in a light Texan accent.

"Oh." Now that I'd indebted myself to the charade of pretending I didn't know who he was, I had no choice but to continue with it. "The sun was in my eyes a bit. Thanks for sitting through it."

"I asked you a question during the Q and A. I'm sorry if I was a bit . . . well . . . direct."

"Don't worry about it. Are you enjoying the trip?"

"It's fine enough. It's strange actually being here. I've thought about this trip for a long time." His voice faded and his eyes looked past mine, like he was hypnotized by the rolling countryside, then he refocused with a sip of his beer. "Free booze. Can't complain."

"Are you here with someone?" I asked.

He shook his head a little. "Just me."

It felt overly nosy asking about his second glass of champagne that morning. So I let the conversation fizzle and we sat in silence for a moment.

"My question, though. It's just—" he started.

I'd had a feeling this was coming, and I cut him off like I was stealing his parking space. "You'll understand I can't talk about it. Legally."

"I know. I know. It's just, well, it's funny that you're here. Is all."

I frowned. "Is it?"

"Because I was just reading your book on the flight over. One of those coincidences that aren't really allowed in mystery novels, right?"

"Right. Well, you had to fly to Australia for this and I assume they sell my book at the airport. It's not the wildest coincidence."

He pushed his glasses up his nose. "For me it is."

"That's a long way to come. Favorite author? McTavish?" I assumed, given he rarely toured, that McTavish never traveled stateside. It seemed quite extreme to fly to Australia just to see one person, but, then again, it was coupled with an internationally renowned holiday. Maybe McTavish was simply the cherry and not the cake.

"It's a rare opportunity."

I half stood, knees bent but not quite risen, which was the most apologetic body language I could come up with to escape the conversation. The condensation from my undrunk beer pooled accusingly under the glass.

"I know you can't talk about it."

I was stuck, thighs burning, in my hovering stance. "I really can't."

"Hypothetically."

"Not even hyp—"

"That person took a lot from you. Loved ones. Friends. They caused you pain. *If* you did—"

"I didn't."

"Hypothetically."

"Fine." I decided to indulge him.

"What would it have felt like? Revenge on this person."

"There was no revenge. It was just survival." This was true, but I paused for a second. Perhaps the two beers helped me forget the cautions of my legal team, perhaps I was just so sick of the posturing surrounding me, or perhaps it was Douglas's beard, shaking like a bird had just taken flight from a treetop, hiding a quivering lip. Whatever it was, I added some truth: "It would have made me feel sad."

"Sad?"

"Powerless instead of powerful. Which is what you might assume you'd feel before something like that happens. Hands around someone's neck is control, right? No. Revenge has no power or control in it. Think of all the things that would lead you to that moment, all the things that had to go right, all the things that had to go wrong. I imagine it would feel like being a victim all over again." I spotted the buses lumbering up the side of the track and stood up fully. "Hypothetically."

As I left the bar, I glanced back and saw Douglas staring thoughtfully into his glass. Then he clinked it against my full one, in a solitary cheers.

I had an uneasy rumbling in my stomach as I made my way back to my room. It wasn't so much the nature of the questions—we live in a world where people listen to the grisliest crime podcasts you can imagine while cooking dinner—it was the tone. It almost felt like he'd been asking for, well, permission. I hoped my answer had been suitably glum so that it couldn't be taken as an endorsement.

Admittedly, that's quite an analysis to give someone I'd only shared a third of a beer with. And I normally would have accused myself of overthinking it if, of course, he hadn't just lied to me.

He'd definitely had two glasses of champagne at Berrimah Terminal.

So why had he said he was traveling alone?

And who was he traveling with?

# CHAPTER 9

Juliette had the decency to lie about how good a time she'd had exploring the gorge. It was particularly artificial when she attempted to describe the forty-thousand-year-old rock paintings as *so-so*, but I appreciated the effort all the same.

By the time the last bus had disembarked and we'd both showered (the Ghan started moving in the middle of my shower, with a jolt that almost made me slip and break my neck) and dressed for dinner in the Queen Adelaide carriage, night had crept up and the flickering film reel outside our window had turned a deep navy blue, the shrubbery now only shadows as it passed. Neither of us was sure how formal dinner was expected to be: Juliette wore an orange-and-brown checked dress that she said felt "desert-y" and I'd brought a dinner jacket. We needn't have worried, as there was a mix of suits and shorts in the restaurant. My theory is that the less wealthy you are, the better you tend to dress for expensive events—meals, the theater—as your effort in dressing matches your effort in expenditure. A week's wage: better pop on a tie. One billable six-minute increment: I'll wear boardies to the opera, no worries.

We both had crocodile dumplings for appetizers, which tasted like chicken, and kangaroo fillet for mains, which tasted like beef, and shared a table with a retired book-loving couple from rural Queensland who had taken the trip to celebrate their fiftieth wedding anniversary. They'd been saving up for quite some time, which they didn't tell me, but she was wearing a vibrant floral dress, and he, believe it or not, a tuxedo. I won't describe what they looked like, because they're not important to the murders. There are plenty of guests on board who are simply that—guests—and I worry if I give them too much descriptive detail it may start you thinking that they are more relevant to the plot than they are. Just like there are many more staff than I've named, but I've got a tally to consider here. Imagine your grandparents: our dinner companions looked like them.

Dining was in three sessions; we were the second. Lisa Fulton was also there, eating with Jasper and Harriet Murdoch. Douglas, the Texan, sat across from S. F. Majors and Alan Royce, though it seemed a designated seating as Douglas and Majors were urgently whispering to each other, not including Royce. Wyatt and Wolfgang were at a different table, with Wolfgang doing the talking and Wyatt listening intently, a pointer finger on each temple. I didn't want to make too much of it, but it looked like he was receiving very bad news indeed. McTavish and Simone were absent, though a waiter with a silver cloche returned from the engine-side rooms a couple of times, which meant someone was getting room service.

Your grandparents decided to retire, and Juliette and I stayed for a nightcap of red wine, for which we were joined by two women who worked as museum curators, one in London and one in Tasmania, and who had skipped dinner but come for dessert. The navy blue outside had disappeared, and while I had anticipated some kind of beautiful twilight desert-scape, it was instead, with no cities near or lights on the outside of the train, completely black.

"So you haven't even mentioned the panel . . ." Juliette waded in.

"Not much to say." I shrugged. "Wolfgang *adamantly* thinks I'm a bad writer. The only person who seems to be on my side is bloody one-star McTavish."

"Hey." She grabbed my uninjured hand and stroked it with her thumb. "Everyone's just on edge. Traveling yesterday, early start today. Plus the heat and the grog—that'd make anyone a bit snappy."

I sighed. "You're right. It wasn't just me anyway. Majors and McTavish had a tiff. Oh, and get this, you should have seen Royce's face when they revealed that McTavish had blurbed Lisa's new book: it could have boiled a kettle."

"McTavish blurbed Lisa?" She frowned thoughtfully. "That's awfully generous. It could really broaden her audience."

"They set it up as a surprise: she was shocked. On the verge of tears."

"I can imagine. Well," Juliette said, swirling her wine in an evil pantomime, "also no harm in sticking one up to Royce. See? Everyone's at each other's throats."

We turned at the sound of a bang and the clatter of cutlery. Wyatt had smacked the table, causing the spoons to bounce. He was half out of his seat. "You can't do that," he was hissing over the table at Wolfgang, who was cradling his red wine, a smug and stained smile on his lips. "It'll ruin—" Wyatt realized everyone was watching and course-corrected. "Sorry," he yelled overenthusiastically, the way a kidnapper talks at a random police stop, body in the trunk. "Sorry! Got caught up in the excitement." He pointed at Wolfgang. "New book. Sounds amazing." He lowered himself back into his chair, still flapping his hand apologetically at the rest of the carriage.

"I didn't think Gemini published Wolfgang." Juliette frowned.

I pulled my hand from Juliette's and rubbed my eyes. "I just can't help feeling I don't . . ." The words I'd found difficult to say before ran up against my teeth and rattled them, begging to get out. This time I let them. "I don't deserve to be here."

"You *do*. No one here's any better than you are. You're a good writer. You deserve to be here just as much as—"

"No. Jules. It's not just *here*. I'm saying it feels like I don't deserve any of this. Anywhere."

She blinked in confusion and leaned forward. I had no choice but to keep talking, but I couldn't look at her, so instead I stared out into the ink dark.

"Everyone who died . . . They didn't do anything wrong. And I didn't do anything special. So why am I here and they aren't? I don't deserve it over them. To sit on this train, to cash the royalty checks . . . I don't deserve even—even this ridiculously expensive wine. It shouldn't be me. Why is it me?"

"Oh, Ern." Juliette didn't say anything more, just sat in understanding, for which I was grateful, as I'd run out of words.

Writing it out now, I know why I felt so personally attacked by the other writers. We all have imposter syndrome sometimes, it's not unique to novelists. No one is immune from trying to prove something to themselves. But here at the festival were five people who were trying to prove their worth creatively. And though it may seem like I was motivated by the same vanity, I was trying to prove something else: that when fate had decided that some in my family should die while I should live it hadn't gotten it wrong.

My therapist gave me a name for it: survivor's guilt. You don't really see it that much in Golden Age mystery novels. The protagonists finish one book and then live in stasis before it all just starts again on page one of the next. There's no cumulative impact of the sheer volume of death and violence they see; every crime doesn't embed in their psyche, eat away at them at night. For all my wishes to be like those famous fictional detectives, I am haunted in a way they aren't, asleep between when their authors pick up a pen. Miss Marple doesn't have nightmares, is what I'm trying to say.

Having finally told Juliette, I felt a little better. The gentle rocking of the train helped lull me further, and our silence was comfortable. Most people had filtered out of the carriage, though Wyatt and Wolfgang were still there. Wyatt had what looked like a checkbook on the table and was tapping a pen on it. I couldn't hear what they were talking about, but judging by Wyatt's other hand curling the tablecloth and the pen not moving to create many zeroes, Wolfgang was not to be bought.

At last Juliette yawned. "I think I might pack it in. I want to get up early and catch the sunrise—Aaron says it's once-in-a-lifetime stuff." She nodded down the carriage. "Shall we?"

"I wish." I grimaced. "I was hoping to bump into Simone in the bar. It'll be quick."

"Shit!" Juliette started patting herself down, despite the fact that what she was looking for would hardly fit in her pockets. "Her scarf! I left it behind at breakfast, completely forgot to give it back to her. Oh, damn. I'll check if they have a lost and found in the morning, or maybe someone picked it up. Would you mind not mentioning it when you see her? Say I'm still using it. Not that I've lost it."

I did mention Juliette's forgetfulness would be a plot point. Here it is: a blue scarf changing hands. This grim pass-the-parcel ends in a corpse.

"So you *are* scared of her," I gloated. She shot me a look that said, *If you're not going to help . . . ,* so I backpedaled. "At least it's not going to go far. I won't mention it. And I'll try to be quick."

"Not too late." She kissed me. "And for what it's worth, *I'm* glad you're here. Right here. With me."

*

The froth from an espresso martini sailed off Simone's top lip and onto my cheek as she spoke. "It's not that big a deal, Ernie. Let it go."

"It is to me."

"What do you want me to do? If you had a problem with it, you shouldn't have accepted Wyatt's apology."

"I didn't know what it was for!"

"Then why'd you accept it?"

I huffed. "I was being polite."

"And the polite thing to do now is to drop this whole thing before you embarrass yourself."

I exhaled heavily through my nose, counted three breaths in and out. Simone was like cobblestones: I very rarely put my foot down firmly around her. But it had been a hard day and espresso martinis aren't known for their defusing properties. If we served them at political summits, there'd be a world war every three months.

I straightened my posture and cleared my throat. "All right. I'm your client. I hired you. And I am asking you to act on my behalf on an issue that I believe will have a negative effect on my career. Okay?"

Simone took a second to weigh up the seriousness in my expression, then snorted. "If I'd known you had a backbone, Ernest, our friendship might have blossomed earlier." She put a flat hand on my chest and gave it a condescending pat. "I'm not going to talk to Wyatt about it, no way, but I am proud of you."

"But you did talk to him—a guest heard you arguing. So what you're saying is not that you wouldn't do it, but that it's too hard and you're giving up?"

"Okay, fine. I raised it with him, like your pal heard. Trust me on this, though, Ern: no author wants to hear every conversation their team has about them. I tell you what you need to know."

I deflated. "Do you even care about my career?"

"What's that supposed to mean?"

"Well, you seemed awfully chummy with McTavish and Wyatt this morning. After the review went up."

Simone finished her drink and looked around the bar. Given the dawn start and the blackness outside, it was easy to think it was later than it was. Harriet and Jasper were having a drink in a booth opposite us. The president of the Mongrels, Brooke, was reading in the far corner. The only part of McTavish that had changed in the last hour was, repeatedly, the angle of his elbow. The three older women, two of whom had shared dessert with Juliette and me, were acting like it was a bachelorette party, sloshing drinks. Each had a copy of the same book out on the table, as if it were a book club, although the title wasn't by any of the festival guests: *The Eleven Orgasms of Deborah Winstock* by Erica Mathison.

I knew that book. It had been a viral phenomenon. Too much sex to be mainstream, not enough to be considered outright pornographic, tittered about in enough salons and high teas to have sold well into the millions. If the established writers hated *me*, they'd surely despise Erica Mathison. The book had taken off on TikTok, which was both a social media app and the sound people like Royce must hear when new writers find new audiences in new mediums. The one I hadn't met, hair twisted up in a silver beehive, was showing off her signed copy (*To V!*) with gold-bangles-jangling glee. It had the logo for Gemini Publishing on the spine and a sticker on the front from a Darwin bookshop—I knew the logo because I'd gone in there to shuffle my books to the front of the shelves, only to find none.

McTavish drew my attention with a thump of his cane. He slid off the seat and propped himself into a standing position. "Right! Off ter bed with this one." He thumbed at his own chest as he called across the bar to Cynthia. A guest took the opportunity to dart up and cut him off, a copy of *The Night Comes* folded open, pen at the ready. I thought Brooke might follow suit, but Jasper was next to join the mini-queue. He didn't have a book on him, so when it was his turn he stuck out a hand too early and then had to walk several steps with it out like a ship's rudder until it landed awkwardly in front of McTavish's belt.

"Jasper," Jasper said.

McTavish gave him a murmured hello, but Jasper's hand remained unshook.

Jasper coughed lightly. "Jasper Murdoch."

"Yeah. All right. Hang on," McTavish said. He fished a pen from his coat pocket and then took a cardboard beer coaster from the bar, scribbled on it and handed it to Jasper. "There you go."

Jasper stood there a second, flipping the coaster over in his hand, then made his way back to his table and handed the coaster to his wife as he took a seat and a long sip of his drink. He looked like someone who's just crossed the schoolyard to ask out a crush and depleted all their reserves of shame and energy simultaneously.

"To Jasper Murdoch," Harriet read out from the coaster, then put it in her handbag. "Wow. That's a keeper."

McTavish ambled down the corridor toward the restaurant and his cabin further up the train, the heavy thump of his cane carrying through the thin floor with each step.

"Okay," Simone said, after McTavish was out of sight and the rhythmic clunk of his cane was fading away. She spoke firmly, with a hiss, but in more of an *I'm going to tell you something you need to hear* tone than an admonishment. "Just so you know, we're a *partnership*. You don't get to tell me what to do. We're supposed to trust each other."

"I was just—"

She held up a finger. "I'm not finished. I know you're upset. I get it. But I don't need you involving yourself with McTavish, okay? I heard there's a bit of tension between Wyatt and Henry. They've been in business directly for a long time—Wyatt snapped him up before any agent even got a sniff, and he still doesn't have one. So friction between a certain author and a certain publisher might lead to opportunities for someone like me to work with someone like our Scottish friend. No offense, but I don't come on a trip like this to watch the panels. If I get Henry on board, it increases the profile of my business. It increases *your* profile, by virtue of being a part of my business, like it does all my authors. And that's when backs get scratched, and how someone like you might wind up with a blurb."

"You're trying to sign McTavish?" I thought aloud. "And of course Wyatt would hate that, because he's probably got the Morbund books tied to a shit deal for McTavish. Or you could threaten to take him somewhere else, I suppose."

She shushed me, scanning the bar to see if anyone had heard. "Could you be a bit more discreet about it? *Jesus.*"

"So you don't want to make a scene about McTavish's reviews because, what, it will ruin your chances of signing him if it gets back around? And I'm supposed to think that's you doing *me* a favor?"

"No. I'm doing it for me. Of course I'm doing it for me. Ever heard of capitalism?" She looked at me like I was a moron. "But I'm saying it might benefit you as well. Long term."

"Jeez, does everybody just steal everyone else these days?"

"Not from me they don't. Don't get any ideas."

A thought struck me. "Who publishes Wolfgang?"

"Ah." She ran through her mental Rolodex. "Brett Davis. At HarperCollins. Why?"

"Wyatt's trying to buy him."

"Really?" She snorted. "Didn't think that was his style. Humph. Trying to add a bit of class to his list, I suppose. Balance out that crap." She nodded to the book club table behind us, whose occupants were discussing Erica Mathison's book with unbridled glee. I raised my voice to speak over them.

"Another thing: you said McTavish didn't blurb." I put a defensive hand out. "This bit isn't about me, I swear. It's just interesting."

"He doesn't," Simone said. "I was just as surprised by that as you were. Either Lisa or her publisher has got some serious dirt on him, or he did it just for the look on Royce's face."

"Worth it," I said cruelly. This was rewarded with a wry smile from Simone, which I took as a standing ovation.

The discussion of the soft-porn book had started to bleed over to our chairs.

"It's . . . honestly, it's . . . genius!" Silver Beehive said.

"There are so many layers," her friend agreed. "Just true vision."

The third kissed her fingers. "It's a revelation!"

"Excuse me." Simone leaned over the back of her chair to interrupt. "You're not talking about *that* book, are you? The Erica Mathison?"

"Perhaps." Beehive wriggled her neck, preening and offended. "Have you read it?"

"I haven't," Simone said, in a way that meant *I wouldn't.*

"Well, it's people like you who could learn a lot from this book," Beehive said, to a chorus of sniggering from her friends.

Simone gave a tight smile. "Thanks for the recommendation."

"Come on, ladies, I think we should finish our drinks on the smoking deck," Beehive said, deliberately loud enough for Simone to hear. She stood and the rest followed suit, clutching their precious books. It was less of a dramatic exit than planned, given they had to gather their bags, books and beverages, but Silver Beehive still made the pretense of striding out of the carriage.

"Gee, the word *genius* is worn to threadbare these days," Simone said when they were gone. "Veronica should know better."

"Veronica? You know that woman? Is she another publisher?"

Simone gave me one of those *I don't know why I bother* looks. "Blythe? Chief books critic for the *Herald*?"

I stared back blankly.

"She wouldn't have reviewed you. Up a level—or so I thought. I wonder who she was with just now. Not critics."

"They work in museums," I said. "I met them earlier."

"No wonder they need the raunchy stuff." Simone slapped her knees. "Right. I'm off. Early start and all."

"One more quick thing. Promise I'm done complaining."

"Don't make promises you can't keep, Ernest."

"Archibald Bench? Mean anything to you?"

She shook her head, sucking her teeth in a clueless fashion. "I mean, I assume it's some kind of puzzle. That's how you have to talk to Henry. To get his attention, to impress him, you have to use his own tricks. He loves codes and riddles and wordplay and all that Golden Age stuff. That girl seemed pretty desperate . . ." She spun a finger in the air, hunting a name.

"Brooke."

"Brooke! The superfan. She seemed pretty desperate to impress, so she'd come ready to play his own game. It'll be some kind of in-joke. A clue in the book or something. But I have no idea what it is. Now"—she stood up—"I'm off to bed. I hear the sunrise is to die for."


Like all good mistakes, which are often made quickly and in volume, I careered through my next three before I'd even recognized I'd made the first. These came in the order of: ruminating in the bar until I was the last one there; having another martini while I did so; and deciding to confront McTavish.

I hadn't quite decided on the last mistake until I'd stood up to leave the bar and gone in the complete wrong direction, finding myself in the empty restaurant carriage. That was enough of an omen that I decided my feet knew more than my head and continued into the next batch of accommodation, across the rattling gap where the carriages latched together, and through a door marked *Platinum*. The first set of cabins was on the opposite side of the train to mine, so the passenger windows would get the sunrise. The second was marked *Staff* with a small sign, and suffered the inferior western view, like my own. I could hear a loud banging sound, which I assumed came from the tracks or the restaurant's kitchen, accompanying my steps. I soon came to another set of double doors and crossed the gap into the final carriage of our section. But instead of another hallway, I found myself in front of a closed door with the sign *Chairman's Carriage*. It was the end of the line.

I wasn't surprised that McTavish had the stateliest cabin, as close to the penthouse suite as you could get on a train, I suppose.

But I *was* surprised that I wasn't the only one there.

Royce had his back to me. He was leaning into the door with his shoulder and banging a raised fist repeatedly against the wood. He looked like an unfaithful husband begging to be let back inside the family home. The smell of stale breath and beer wafted over me as I stepped between the carriages. The clatter of the tracks was louder at these joining points, where the floor was only gently overlaid and not sealed. A blur of gray stony earth was visible through the gaps, lit up every few seconds by the sparks from the wheels on the tracks.

"Henry!" Royce yelled, not noticing me. *Thump-thump-thump*. "Henry!"

The thumping was the sound I'd heard through the last car. I put my hand on Royce's shoulder, and something like an electric shock passed through him. He whipped around and scowled. His eyes were bloodshot. He had a red mark above one eye, where he'd been leaning on the door.

"Pissssss off," he said, spending S's like he'd robbed a bank of them.

He lumbered at me, and I took a step back in case he took a swing, but he just stood there, swaying. He looked dejected, pitiful. Was that how I seemed to Simone? Grasping at dignity? This pathetic vision knocked some sense into me. I vowed to be more professional tomorrow.

"I know how you feel, trust me," I said. "I came here to do the same thing. But let's not embarrass ourselves tonight. Why don't we sleep on it, shower, and see how we feel in the morning."

Royce scowled back at the door like it had insulted him. "They're in there."

"They?"

"I heard them talking. A woman's voice. He *owes* me, and he's in there with *her*." Royce turned and yelled, "I heard you talking!"

I put a hand gingerly on his shoulder. "You don't want to do anything you'll regret in the morning."

"Come out and talk to me!" He stepped back to the door but I moved in quickly, deftly hooking under his armpit and spinning him around. He blinked widely, unsure of why he was suddenly pointing in the wrong direction, but accepted his new path without complaint.

"Why *her*?" he drooled in my ear. "Why did he choose *her*?"

"It's just a blurb, mate," I said, talking to myself more than him.

Royce half-walked, and I half-dragged him, through the restaurant and the bar and into our set of cabins. My shoulder was wet by now and I assumed it was saliva, but then I realized he was crying into my neck.

He hiccupped. "It's just a few words. He doesn't even have to read the damn thing. Wyatt used to care. He said he'd help me when I needed it, and he never did. But sales . . ." He burped. "It's not like it used to be."

"Hey." I felt a surprising amount of empathy for Royce in this moment. "You told me yourself you got through four rejections for your first book. You've gotten over bigger hurdles. Chin up."

"I begged. This time, please. Don't *ask* Henry to blurb it, *make* him. Wyatt said he'd do what he could. He knew it could change my life." He arrived at a door. "This one."

We stopped in front of his room, and he spent a moment patting his coat for a key before remembering the door didn't have a lock and staggering in. My kindness for Royce stopped short of stripping him down and tucking him in, so I stood in the doorway while he faceplanted onto the bottom bunk.

"Tell me," he said into his pillow, and it was more a groan than words. "It didn't happen, did it? All that stuff up on the mountain? You faked it, right? For the publicity."

"It happened. I don't wish it on anyone." Then, because I figured he wouldn't remember it, "Not even you."

Royce made a cat-meowing sound, then laughed, hiccupped and belched all at the same time. It was impressive auditorily, but also quite pungent. "So you're just lucky then, huh? That you somehow fell into those murders."

"Yeah, mate. Lucky."

"Of course, there's another option."

"Oh yeah?"

"If you didn't make it up, I mean. Maybe you just did it all yourself." His words strung out of his teeth like chewing gum, his sentences a single monotonous drone. "That's one way to write a book."

"You're drunk."

"And you're *lying*," he teased. "It's not a bad idea. Automatic publicity. Easier than research."

"Good night, Royce."

"Henry better be careful," Royce said, just as I went to close the door. I thought he was murmuring to himself, but I looked back and saw one blood-red eye staring straight up at me. "The things I've done for that man. He shouldn't be so . . . so . . . caviar . . . with my friendship."

"Cavalier?"

"Huh?"

"Did you mean cavalier?"

"Mmmm."

"What have you done for McTavish?"

Royce blinked then, and it was as if a stupor was lifted. "Cunningham? What are you doing here?"

"I'm helping you to bed, mate. Few too many."

"Be honest. It didn't happen, did it?"

We'd come full circle: he'd completely forgotten everything he'd told me up to now, and surely he'd forget the rest by morning. It's not far-fetched that Royce would accuse me of fakery: the great literary hoax is a grand tradition. Drug addicts' harrowing stories of trauma despite never touching a single substance; Hiroshima survivors writing from the comfort of their imagination; a fifteen-year-old's diary concocted by a fifty-four-year-old woman. In one memoir a woman claimed to have escaped Nazi persecution and been raised in the snow by a family of wolves, and the whole world believed it. Her story was even made into a successful film before the accusations flowed, leaving behind a red-faced publisher. Royce wasn't the first to disparage me by any means—I've been on morning television *and* I have Twitter.

"It happened," I said again.

"Then I guess you're just the unluckiest bastard I've ever crossed. And if bad luck follows you, maybe something's going to happen here."

"Careful what you wish for."

He blew a raspberry at me. "I *do* wish it. We'll wake up tomorrow and one of us will be dead."

"Don't say that."

"You're just scared."

"Of what?"

"That I'm right. And if I'm not, I'd love to see how you'd react to a *real* murder."

"Good night, Royce."

I closed the door, and I could hear his thunderous snoring within seconds. Juliette was fast asleep, dead still, by the time I got back to our cabin. She'd taken the top bunk. One arm, pale in the moonlight, hung limp over the side. I changed as quietly as I could into my pajamas and lay down in the bottom bunk, where I shut my eyes and tried to sleep.

The train rocketed along in darkness.

# CHAPTER 10

It's a staple of mystery novels that, just before the murder happens, certain conversations are overheard in the deep of night. This is to be the case here.

I didn't sleep easily. I'd expected the gentle rocking of the train to be quite restful and meditative, and it may well have been had I not forgotten to account for the washing-machine sloshing of two martinis and two beers in me. Each pair would have been fine on its own but as a foursome they were having a keys-in-the-bowl swingers party in my stomach. I awoke to a gurgling shortly after I lay down, and not wanting to inflict carnage on our squeezed living space, this was how I found myself in the corridor, headed for the communal toilet.

There was just one public toilet in our section: it replaced the tea and coffee station past the restaurant. Now, it's my duty as a fair-play detective to disclose to you everything I see, but I'll spare you the details of what happened in the bathroom except to tell you it was far grislier than any murder that's about to take place on the train. Wiping my mouth on the walk back to my room, I checked my phone and learned two things: it had just gone midnight, and we were officially out of reception. My phone would be useless until Alice Springs. I spotted some flower petals in a trail on the carpet, pink and dainty, that hinted at someone's lavish attempt at romance. That explained Wyatt's hay fever, or, I thought to myself, perhaps it was more likely he was allergic to affection.

That was when I heard Wyatt's voice.

"I don't care what *you* want," he was saying inside his room. His voice was raised, but not loud enough to wake anyone. "It's in your contract. More Morbund. It's simple. Why change it after all this time?"

I paused but didn't catch McTavish's quiet reply, muffled through the door.

"That was just for *publicity*. Everyone's going to read it if they think it's the last one, and then everyone's going to get excited when it's not."

There were footsteps as one of them paced.

"You promised me you'd bring him back. Not that you'd write . . . *this*."

Another muffled answer. I leaned into the door to hear better. I recalled McTavish's discomfort over the question of Morbund's finale, his glare toward Wyatt. This argument must have been a follow-up to that.

"I know, I know. Archie Bench. Real fucking cute."

A pause.

"Don't threaten me."

Suddenly the train hit a curve. I smacked my head loudly against the door and, to my horror, the voices stopped. I bolted down the hall, slipping into the tea alcove just as I heard the door click open. I pretended to make a cup of tea, just in case Wyatt or McTavish came out to investigate, but my charade was hobbled by the fact that the kettle had been tossed, assumedly broken, into the nearby bin.

It didn't matter; I heard the door click shut and, after a minute, edged my way back through the corridor. Wyatt had lowered his voice or the argument had subsided naturally; either way, I couldn't hear anything this time, so I hurried back to my bed.

I still couldn't sleep. Juliette was dozing so contentedly above me, one arm still hanging over the side of the top bunk, that I couldn't even hear the small whistle of her breathing over the train. How did she do it? Ignore everything around her, be at peace, so successfully? I'd thought that praise and acclaim were what was missing from my career, what would make me a *real* writer, but hearing that argument with Wyatt had made me realize McTavish felt just as trapped as I did. Was there any light at the end of this tunnel? Or did it not matter who you were or how well you'd done: someone always owned you. Someone always asked for more, more, more.

The whole day had left a sour taste in my mouth that wasn't just from the regurgitated martinis. I had a feeling that tomorrow was only going to get worse.

I had no idea.

# CHAPTER 11

This may be a surprise, but everyone survives the night.

I know that's not how things usually go in a mystery. There's the night before, in which halves of conversations are overheard (check) and the complex motives and backstories of everyone are introduced (check), then everyone retreats, as if Broadway choreographed, to their rooms, doors clicking in unison, only for dawn to rise on a tussle in the night, a bloodstained cabin and a victim. Alas, not here. Not yet.

The sunrise was, however, as impressive as advertised: a furnace of gold that bled over the sand and turned it into shimmering lava. As we approached the center of Australia, the land had become indescribably flat. It may strike you, as it has my editor, as lackluster that I can't describe *flat*. But there's flat, sure, and then there's endless, barren levelness the likes of which an explorer, atop a camel perhaps, must have looked out across and thought was the end of the world. *That's* flat. That's the middle of Australia.

Juliette and I watched the sunrise from the corridor in our pajamas. Then we showered and dressed, navigating our confined cabin tango, and made our way to the bar for the morning's panel.

It was a congregation familiar to anyone as the first morning of a holiday—a mix of the overeager and the ravaged who'd hit it too hard the night before—and no corpses to speak of. The book club ladies (not dead) who'd been reading erotica bore the pale-faced regret of overindulgence. Brooke (not dead) was in the too-keen camp, staking out a seat right down the front, her copy of *Misery* on the floor and a large scrapbook in her hand, edges overflowing with jagged, hastily glued-in leaflets. Today's was to be a smaller panel, just S. F. Majors (not dead), who was flicking through notes, and McTavish (not yet arrived), and so two fold-out chairs had been placed at the end of the carriage, and the audience seating was whatever we could snag from the bar.

McTavish (not dead) showed soon after, in a vest and a red tie, with Wyatt (not dead). They were both in jovial spirits, seemingly having moved past their midnight argument—though McTavish did have a slight bump on the bridge of his nose, a redness that looked like the prologue to a bruise. Had it been getting physical before I interrupted them? Brooke tried to shove her journal, pen extended, at McTavish as he passed her on the way to his seat, but Wyatt squeezed between them and reminded her there'd be a signing after the panel.

Simone (not dead) gave me a shoulder squeeze as she moved by me to sit down next to Douglas (not dead), who was carrying a single coffee this morning, perhaps out of awareness I'd been counting his drinks. Wolfgang (not dead), his back to the speakers, was reading a scuffed hardback titled *The Price of Intelligence*, which looked—from its plainness and size—like a science textbook, but I figured there was an equal chance it was an incredibly self-indulgent poetry collection. Jasper and Harriet (not dead) were unsurprisingly there, having proved to be autograph-hunting Mongrels themselves. Cynthia (not dead) was working the coffee machine again, under the supervision of our host, Aaron (not dead). Royce (not dead, but he looked halfway there) stumbled in just as Majors cleared her throat, seemingly about to start the panel; the scruffiness of a hangover still blurred his edges, and he dropped into a seat like he'd been shot in the knee. The only person truly absent was Lisa Fulton (liveliness to be determined).

As unslit throats were cleared with light coughs, hangovers were massaged from unshot foreheads, glasses of water were poured from unpoisoned jugs, and the remainder of the guests assembled and caffeinated themselves, McTavish leaned forward and whispered to Brooke, "It's a mighty fine drop to drink alone."

Before he could say anything more, the shrill feedback of a microphone indicated the start of the event. For her part, Majors had worked hard to make sure that this morning's panel sought a closer examination of McTavish and his works. Despite her efforts, McTavish took those familiar swigs from his flask as he launched into the same anecdotes as yesterday. My attention drifted out the window. There hadn't been much wildlife beside the train—the land was too barren even for kangaroos—but a circling bird, clawing talons extended, floated beside us.

Far on the horizon, thick black smoke blemished the blue in several spots. A helicopter dotted the horizon with a full vessel of water suspended underneath. It made me think there was probably more concern about the bushfire-lighting kite bird than Aaron had let on. Natural ecosystem, circle-of-life stuff it might be, but all that destruction for one's own benefit didn't seem all that natural to me. Burn a whole forest for one measly breakfast. It seemed, well, *human*.

Then I heard Majors say, "Are you okay?" and everything changed.

I turned to see McTavish with a hand over his mouth, shoulders heaving. He half-burped, half-hiccupped, and a stream of vomit gushed into his hand, spraying between the gaps in his fingers and over the front row, where the seated attendees squealed and scrambled backward. McTavish doubled over, dropping his flask to the floor, and gave up covering his mouth, spewing onto the carpet and coating Brooke's copy of *Misery*.

I stood up, along with everyone else in the room, hovering, unsure how to help. Aaron was pushing his way to the front of the car, first-aid kit in hand. McTavish's face was stark white now but had a tinge of blue to it, and he'd started to shiver. He gripped his cane and levered himself up to a standing position. His breath was coming in short sharp bursts.

McTavish seemed to have regained his composure, though he still leaned unsteadily on his cane. His skin was pale and clammy, his pupils pinpricks. The flask glugged in slow heaves, soaking alcohol into the carpet. He looked at us all, wiped his mouth and said, "I don't seem to be feeling all that well."

And then he died.

I mean that literally. He was looking right at me, and it was like someone switched his brain off. There was no slow eyes rolling back into his head, no gradual closing of his eyelids. He was looking at me one second, and then his circuits fried, his eyeballs snapped to different directions (one up and to the left, one completely sideways), and everything in them was gone. He stayed upright for a second after this, by virtue of his cane, and then his body slackened and he crumpled to the floor.

Unmoving. Dead.

No one budged. It was too absurd, too unexpected and too violent for anyone to even think to scream. No one made a sound: just a single, horrified silence.

Except, of course, for the scratching of Alan Royce's pencil, scribbling in his notebook.

# CHAPTER 11.5

Here's what you're thinking:

- Lisa Fulton is your current primary suspect, by virtue of her being the only person who's been remotely nice to me so far on this trip. Her lack of incrimination is, ironically, incriminating. She was also the only person not in the room during McTavish's death.
- Alan Royce is currently lowest on your list of suspects, given that he is the kind of reprehensible cockroach who normally winds up the victim in these books, and you consider him too obvious as a murderer.
- S. F. Majors and Wolfgang are on equal footing, somewhere around the middle, as are Simone and Wyatt. They're all clearly hiding something, but it's not clear whose secrets are worth killing for. Wyatt seems to be in the middle of a lot of webs, given he has relationships with most, if not all, on board due to his position at Gemini Publishing. You're keeping an eye on all four.
- You have also considered that the killer may not be one of the

writers but could be one of the guests, in which pool you have Brooke, Jasper and Harriet Murdoch, the erotic book club ladies and Douglas. You're not convinced that any of them have reason enough to qualify as a murderer—but out of the lot of them, Douglas's "mysterious stranger" act has perhaps drawn the most attention.

- You haven't ruled out the staff: Cynthia, the bartender, and Aaron, the journey director, because Aaron and Cynthia are the only staff members I've given a name to. Of course, Aaron and Cynthia may be on your mind because you know there is also a second murder to come, and you may have considered this reason enough for Aaron and Cynthia to be named.

- Juliette has thus far avoided your scrutiny, because a returning character doesn't tend to commit the murders in the sequel unless their character changes completely, and such an inconsistency wouldn't be considered fair. Sure, you might suspect a little bit of jealousy given that we both wrote a book on the same topic and I'm the one with the invitation to the festival. But to be clear: *only an idiot* would accuse Juliette of murder.

So now we know where we sit with regard to suspicions. You also find yourself wondering about the following plot points:

- Is Henry McTavish really dead? Because people sometimes come back in these kinds of books. I'll tell you now that you can as much wink at a blind horse as you can at a dead Scottish author: he's stone-cold deceased.
- You think the plot of *Off the Rails* may be significant.
- It has occurred to you that not everyone in these books is who they say they are. You wonder if someone whose real name is Archibald Bench is on the train under a different identity.

- I also promised you I'd use the killer's name, in all its forms, 106 times. To be fair, if there are multiple identities at play, I will consider the cumulative total of both. The running tally is:
  - ~~Henry McTavish: 136~~
  - Alan Royce: 70
  - Simone Morrison: 56
  - Wyatt Lloyd: 51
  - S. F. Majors: 46
  - Lisa Fulton: 40
  - Wolfgang: 40
  - Jasper Murdoch: 27
  - Harriet Murdoch: 21
  - Brooke: 20
  - ~~Aaron: 14~~
  - Book Club/Veronica Blythe/Beehive: 14
  - Archibald Bench: 10
  - Cynthia: 9
  - Douglas Parsons: 8
  - Erica Mathison: 4
  - Juliette: EXEMPT

This may feel unusually candid for a narrator in a detective story. Maybe. I say all this because, believe it or not, mystery novels are a team sport. Some authors, the bad ones, work against the reader. But we are a team, and in order to play fair, you need to see what I see. I want you to succeed in figuring it out, just as I have.

Of course, you still don't trust me. You can't help but think I'm feeding you a batch of misdirecting red herrings to keep the truth hidden. That when I tell you someone is the most likely suspect they are the least likely, and vice versa. Of course, if you're thinking that, you're also thinking that maybe I *want* you to think that, and so I'm telling you the most likely suspect in order to make you think you are outsmarting me by thinking they are the *least* likely, when in fact, they really *are* the most likely. And so on forever. A key part of mysteries is working with not only a reader's beliefs but their disbeliefs as well. So you're thinking the very list is the red herring.

All I can tell you is what I've been telling you so far: the truth. After all, I told you Henry McTavish would be poisoned, didn't I?

Well, not in those words, I suppose. But I *did* say the inspiration for this book would come from a drink with him.

# FORENSIC

# CHAPTER 12

We were all swiftly banished to our cabins while the staff organized the cleanup. It sounds heartless to put it like that, but no matter how dramatic a dead body may be, there is *always* a moment where it just comes down to someone getting out a bucket and mop.

Besides, the Ghan was populated with twilight-years tourists: it can't have been the first dead body the staff had faced. And a hirsute man who punished his organs with lashings from a silver flask wasn't an unlikely candidate for an early demise. As such, while the guests oscillated between shivering shock and tear-streaked panic (the former being Majors, the latter being Brooke), the staff were remarkably calm. No one even mentioned stopping the train as an option. Of course, we were also in the middle of nowhere, and there was nowhere to stop. That's the thing about trains: they rattle on.

I paced our tiny cabin—it was, unfortunately, not an appropriate size for grand deductions—while Juliette sat and stared out the window. Our room had been converted back into the comfortable seating arrangement, the beds packed up and flipped into the wall by the invisible team of service staff when we went for breakfast.

Outside there was smoke on the horizon. Juliette tilted her knees to the wall every time I got to her.

"I think you should sit down," she said after my hundredth lap, patting the seat next to her. "You're going to walk a hole through the floor."

"It doesn't make sense," I said, turning back for another five-step lap.

"It makes perfect sense. An overweight alcoholic had a heart attack." She acted out dusting her hands. "Case closed, Detective."

"An overweight alcoholic *who everyone on this train hated*."

"Just because you hated him doesn't mean everyone else did," Juliette cautioned.

"Everyone had cause to." I counted them off on my fingers. "Royce felt betrayed he didn't get the endorsement. Wyatt wants him to keep writing the Morbund books—I heard them arguing. Simone wants to sign him up."

"Listen to yourself! None of this is worth killing for. A few petty jealousies and disagreements." Juliette mimicked my counting, exaggeratedly flicking each finger. "Lisa has the endorsement. Simone, I'd wager, wants him *alive* to sign him, just like Wyatt would want him *alive* to write more books."

"They might feel spurned if he said no."

"I'm not an expert, but killing your cash cow seems like a bad negotiation tactic. And then everyone else is a fan of his."

"Exactly."

"Exactly?" She tucked her legs to the wall.

I spun. "Maybe Brooke's obsessed with him."

"Ooooh." She wriggled her fingers spookily at me. "Motive."

"You weren't at the panel yesterday. It was supercharged. S. F. Majors has some kind of grudge against him too. Their conversation was fiery. *And*"—I got excited, remembering—"there was a woman in his room last night."

Juliette folded her arms, but I could tell there was a new spark of curiosity. "Last night?"

"I heard—"

"You were snooping even before he'd been killed?"

"No. I went to confront him about the review."

Legs to the wall. "Really? Ernest—"

"I changed my mind. When I got to his cabin, Royce was already there, banging on the door. But McTavish wouldn't come out. Royce said he heard a woman in there with him."

Juliette seemed unconvinced but sat a little forward. "And is this when you heard Wyatt tell him he wanted more Morbund books?"

"That was later," I said sheepishly. "In the hall."

"And you weren't snooping."

"I got up to . . . be sick. I'd had too much to drink."

"So you were drunk, then."

I stumbled into her knees; she hadn't tilted them this time. I steeled my reply. "I know what I heard."

"All I'm saying is, if this was in a mystery, you wouldn't trust the intoxicated witness."

"I wasn't drunk."

"I'm not trying to argue with you, Ern. I'm trying to help. All this is, it's simply confirmation bias. You want it to not add up."

"Why would I want that?"

"Because you're thinking there's a book in it."

"I'm thinking there's a *crime*."

"Is there a difference, to you?"

I stopped pacing and collapsed into the seat next to her. I put a hand on her knee and watched the desert flick past for a moment. "Okay," I said at last. "My curiosity is a little selfish. But think about how these things play out." I thought about my list, my schematic for how a murder mystery is supposed to go: *60,000 words:*

A *second murder*. "There's never just one murder in these things. There's always at least two."

Juliette put a hand on top of mine. "This is real life, not a book. It doesn't have to follow any of your rules. Most importantly, it doesn't have to play fair."

"But what if I'm right? What if this person's just getting started? What if," I appealed, "I can stop them . . . this time?"

That was the key to it all, those two words. *This time*. So many people had died on the mountain. If I'd been smarter, if I'd acted faster, maybe it could have been different. There were too many links and too many secrets bubbling under our little group to write off McTavish's death as a coincidence. Didn't I at least have a responsibility to see what I could find out?

And maybe, not that I believe in this kind of stuff, but maybe even if I didn't *deserve* to be here, I was meant to be.

"If I do nothing," I said, "everything that happens from here is my fault."

"It's not your job," Juliette said softly. "And it's not—not now and not then—your fault."

"I know that," I said, in a way that made it clear that I didn't.

Juliette chewed her lip, knowing I was both waiting for and not really asking for her permission. "If you need this—just for you, not for any other reason—then ask some questions. Sure. But just enough to feel comfortable that this is exactly what it looks like. Don't try and prove that McTavish was murdered. Try and prove to yourself that he *wasn't*."

It feels smug writing this out in retrospect, because, well . . . *obviously* I have the hindsight and the stab wound to say how wrong she was. But Juliette's advice was, at the time, really quite good. I found my agitation calming.

"Okay. So it'll come down to *how* he died. If it was murder"—I caught her eye—"which I'm not saying it was! But I need to either find or rule out the method."

"Sounds like a starting point."

"It must be poison. In his flask?"

"That's how I'd do it." Juliette shrugged.

The intercom crackled and Aaron's voice came on, telling us that we'd be reaching Alice Springs in two hours, and the staff would appreciate it enormously if we could all stay in our rooms until then.

Alice Springs was a rural community, home to about thirty thousand people. Enough for a police station and a morgue. They would take McTavish's body off the train there. I was on the clock.

I stood up. "I need to see the body."

"What? Why?"

"To see if he's been poisoned."

"And how are you going to tell? You're not a doctor. You're not even a detective."

"Last time—"

"There was an *actual* doctor with us. This is not the same. You'd need an autopsy, for starters, toxicology tests. Wait for Alice Springs. You need the experts."

Something McTavish said bounced up inside my brain. *If one of the six of us was to die right now, you'd have five suspects who all know how to get away with murder.*

Maybe we had experts on the train after all. Five crime writers, each specializing in a different field. Five people who had spent decades researching every way to solve a crime. Or commit one.

I hadn't even spoken but Juliette started vehemently shaking her head. "No. Ern. That doesn't count."

"Hear me out."

"You need an *autopsy*. And someone who knows the actual law, otherwise you risk compromising evidence."

"We've got both of those."

"No, you don't. These people are *writers*."

"Royce used to be a forensic pathologist. Lisa was in law. They're experts." I was talking mostly to myself now, ticking off everyone's qualifications in a rapid mutter. "Forensic thrillers. Legal thrillers. Majors knows criminal psychology—interviews, profiles, that sort of thing. That'll help. And Wolfgang—well, I suppose literary fiction is a bit useless."

This is, for the most part, true. Wolfgang's contributions, except for a stunning bit of literary deduction involving a comma late in the piece, are lackluster.

"And where do you put yourself in this crack crime-fighting team?"

"Well," I said, a little proudly, "I know the rules."

At this, Juliette threw up her hands. "If this makes it into the book, I refuse to be a nagging girlfriend. So it feels pointless to remind you, again, that this is real life and no one has to follow any murder-mystery rules. But if you *insist* on making me a side character, I won't be a part of this don't-go-in-there pantomime any longer." She turned away from me and looked out the window.

Silence is a tap left running: it fills and fills until it overflows and becomes insurmountable.

Honestly, we'd never really fought before. Clothes on the floor and who takes the trash out are small-fry compared to the serial killer we'd fought, and so it had never occurred to us that we possessed any household dramatics worth raised voices. But the cabin was flooded and the felt box in my pocket heavier than ever. This wasn't in my plan.

If one advantage of writing this out again is to gloat when I am correct, a disadvantage is having to relive when I am wrong. I should have said a lot more in that moment. I should have realized that Juliette wasn't asking me to not care about McTavish's death, she was asking me to care about her. That she wasn't asking me not to go, she was asking me to stay. Those words may seem the same on paper, but they mean very different things.

Those of you hoping I said the right thing next haven't paid enough attention: my mistakes are voluminous and swift. I'm a double-down kind of guy. So I stood, which was a bad start, as no one likes arguing from a height difference. And then I said the worst possible combination of words (dare I say, not only in this conversation, but in general social terms) I could have chosen:

"I need to talk to Alan Royce."

# CHAPTER 13

Royce was in the corridor, fist raised, when I opened my door. He wore a frog-faced look of surprise. It took me a second to realize that he hadn't been magically summoned by my words: he had been just about to knock on my door.

I pushed him back into the hallway and stepped out before Juliette could see him.

"Good timing," I said, leading without asking. I knew where his room was from putting him to bed last night. "Shall we talk in your cabin?"

Royce took a beat, clearly unfamiliar with being delightedly received, before trotting along behind me. He'd taken the forced quarantine as an opportunity to have a shower, but the hangover was still a coat hanger around his shoulders, over his slumped head, as if the vapors of his excess were marionette strings holding him up and dragging him along.

I hadn't chosen Royce's cabin merely to get him away from Juliette. I also wanted to snoop. I hardly thought he'd have vials of poison open on the windowsill (preferably with unsubtle skull-and-crossbones labels), but it was worth a shot.

I gave him the courtesy of opening his own door: the illusion of an invitation. I hadn't seen the room properly in the dark, but I was shocked by the state of it now. It looked like he'd been there a month, not a mere twenty-four hours: clothes spilled across the carpet and junk-food wrappers, sheaves of random papers and empty bottles ranging from water to beer filled the gaps. His carpet should have been on the side of a milk carton: it was that missing. I sidestepped into the room like I was avoiding mousetraps. My ankle nudged something damp, and I shivered as I kicked aside a balled-up towel.

Perhaps because he'd slept in, the bunks hadn't been flipped, so Royce and I frowned and grunted and managed to figure out how to roll the top bunk into the wall so we could at least sit down on the bottom bed. Royce positioned himself by the little table at the window, took out his notebook and tapped a capped pen on the page. The page was filled with scribbles in blue ink. I could see my name underlined halfway down.

"So," he said. "You got that murder you wanted, then."

I didn't mention that it was Royce who had wished for the murder, not me. Instead, I said, "You think it's murder?"

"Why else are we here?" He uncapped the pen. It was elegant, thumb-thick and with ornate silver details on the body and the cap. The tip had been designed to look like an antique dip pen, though with a modern ink feed so a well wasn't needed, and sharp enough that it must have felt tortured by serving Royce's dull words. "Shall we start with last night?"

"Yes, please." He was surprisingly open to being interrogated. I gave myself a mental pat on the back for the refinement of my detective skills. "What do you remember?"

"I remember you." He jabbed the pen at me. "You were all steamed up, wanting to talk to Henry. Quite aggressive, I thought."

"I think you have the two of us confused. You were the one bashing down his door."

"So you didn't want to talk to Henry?"

"Of course I did. That's not the point. You said last night you heard voices. Through the door?"

Royce nodded. "They shut up when I started knocking. But Henry was talking to someone. A woman. Lisa Fulton."

"You're sure it was Lisa?"

He shrugged. "It sounded like her."

"It sounded like her, or it *was* her?"

"I keep forgetting you're new to this"—Royce raised an eyebrow—"but there's more than one way to get a blurb. Follow?"

What had Royce said over breakfast the day before? *Unless he owes you a favor.* I understood the implication. Lisa and Henry.

Sex is always a good motive in these books, of course, but it felt a little easy here. A relationship between Lisa and McTavish certainly mounted a case against Royce's jealousy. But if that was true, the victim was wrong. Royce was far more likely to lash out at Lisa than Henry. I could see it in the way his lip curled around the words *more than one way.* There's nothing like good old-fashioned sexism, and it fit Royce well enough to be tailored.

Of course, Royce had been drunk and he had a reason to dislike Lisa. How certain was I that he'd heard correctly? Plenty of women were at the festival: Cynthia, Harriet, Majors, Simone, Brooke, Juliette and Veronica Blythe's book club to name the most notable. And, depending on his drunkenness, the person with McTavish might not even have been a woman. Can you tell gender from a whisper? It's hard to identify a voice speaking behind a door.

On the other hand, while it takes two to tango and only one remained alive, it seemed that Lisa already had what she wanted out of their possible exchange. The cover was revealed, the book endorsed. She'd hurried from the panel with grateful tears in her eyes. The late-night rendezvous could have been, well, a reward. Salacious, sure. But motive it wasn't.

Still, Lisa and McTavish having a clandestine meeting the night before he was murdered seemed a pretty good starting point.

"You said you wanted to talk to Henry," Royce interrupted my thoughts, "and then you changed your mind. Why?"

"I saw you there," I said honestly. "I realized I was being rash, and I thought better of it." I stopped short of explaining that seeing him as a cringe-worthy vision of my future had knocked some sense into me.

"You were angry?"

"Of course I was angry. About that bloody review."

He wrote that down.

I took the pause as a chance to ask the next question. "This morning, you saw everything that happened. Poison?"

"Was it?"

"You're the forensic pathologist."

"Where . . . put it?" He mumbled this sentence so I only half caught it and reconstructed from the words I did hear. *Where would you put it?*

"In the hip flask," I said. "Right?"

Royce wrote it down. "Suppose so."

"Suppose?"

"If that's what you're telling me."

If I may, here: you're lucky Royce isn't writing this book because I believe he'd be the unreliable sort.

"I'm not telling you anything. I'm seeking your . . ."—I had to root-canal the word out of my teeth—"*expertise.*"

Royce picked up his notepad and flipped it back a page like a traffic cop giving a fine. He blew out his cheeks in thought, and I reckon if I'd lit a match the cabin would have exploded with the pure gasoline he hissed into the air. I peered over at his page of scribbles. Among the other notes I saw he had all those Goodreads reviews written out, one per line, in ascending order, starting with my one-star review and then following with the others:

*Wolfgang:* ★★ *Heavenly*

*S. F. Majors:* ★★★ *Overblown*

*Me:* ★★★★ *Splendid*

Instead of Lisa's name, he'd violently written *Trollop*. Then, clearly with shaking hands, her five stars and the review: *Tremendous.*

On my quick glimpse, I noted both the oddity of S. F. Majors's rather harsh wording against her rather mild stars, and the inverse for Wolfgang. It was almost like they were deliberately the wrong way around.

Royce saw me spying on his notes and tilted the notebook away. He cleared his throat, glanced at the door. "Maybe we should talk in the bar?" His words wobbled, a little nervous.

"I'm okay here. You all right?"

"Why me?"

"Because—are you serious?—how many times do I have to tell you? I want your help. You used to work in forensics. You're as close to a doctor as I've got."

Royce puffed a little at that. "You want me to solve it?"

I shrugged, which was the most I could summon.

He cleared his throat. "Okay. I think I've got it all. There's just one thing I don't understand."

I was, if I'm honest with you, a bit affronted that he had the crime worked out not only so early on, but also so far ahead of me. I know it seems heartless. Solving crimes is supposed to be about bringing a murderer to justice, not about who got there first, but still . . . out of everyone, did it have to be Royce?

Of course, there's a whole lot of this book to go, and so you already know that means that either Royce is wrong, or he'll be killed before he can tell me. I will refrain from stating my preference on this particular matter. I will tell you that I won't figure everything out myself until chapter 31, when Andy, it pains me to write, provides an assist.

I stood. "You've solved it?"

Royce's head swiveled, looking past me to the door. "Almost," he squeaked.

I took an excited step toward him. "Tell me, then. What's missing?"

Royce squeezed against the window, away from me, then said, "Where you got the heroin."

"Heroin?"

"I mean, we can call it poison if you like. Heroin is technically poison, even if it's not as commonly used as cyanide or arsenic or whatever else is popular in novels these days. But effective all the same. That was an overdose we saw. Heroin is a nervous system suppressant, so it slows down things like circulation, breathing. I researched it for Dr. Jane Black, Book Nine. The cause of death, I'd say, was an anoxic brain injury. Means no oxygen gets to the brain. Cells die, and it switches off."

I remembered McTavish's blue-tinged face, his sharp breaths. His eyes disconnecting from his brain, like a switch flipped. On. Off. Dead. It made sense. "Heroin," I muttered to myself. Then realized, "Wait, you just said where did I—"

I paused. Took in the scene. I was standing up. Royce was squeezed hard against the wall, glancing at the door. My name in his notebook, underlined. "Hang on. What do *you* think's going on here?"

"You've just confessed," Royce said.

"Confessed?"

"Well, I'm interviewing you."

"*I'm* interviewing *you*," I huffed.

"Why do you get to interview me, and I don't get to interview you?"

"Because I'm the narrator!"

"Not in my book."

Thinking back on our conversation, I realized Royce had indeed been asking many of the questions. I'd been following the rules for mystery novels, such as excluding Juliette, predicated on myself being the detective. In Royce's book, in his head, he was the detective and I was a suspect. Hell, apparently, I was the killer.

"You can't seriously think I'd—" I couldn't finish the sentence.

Royce flicked through his notebook pages. Read his notes aloud. "You went to Henry's cabin last night in a"—he drew his finger down the page until he found it—"*rash* mood. You were angry with him over that review. One star, *ghastl*—"

"I know the review, mate."

Royce's finger moved along his page. He sounded like a child reading in front of class. "You changed your mind about confronting him because a witness was there. That would be myself. You decided to use poison. You put it in his hip flask."

"I thought you said where *would* the murderer put it. I was asking if you thought it was poison, not telling you it was." I flung up my hands.

Royce flinched.

"Disregarding the fact that your theory has holes all over it— I don't carry around bloody heroin, and if I did I wouldn't just waltz in and confess to the first person who asked me any questions about it—I don't have any motive. A bad review isn't motive. I don't care how mad I was, it's not worth killing over."

"It isn't," Royce said, and flipped back two pages. I couldn't see the writing, but it was clearly a note he'd taken before our conversation. "But a hundred thousand dollars might be."

"What?"

"You have an undelivered book to write," Royce went on. "If you don't deliver, you'll have to hand the money back, and you're suffering for inspiration because no one's bitten the dust around you for a while."

I faltered. One hundred thousand dollars was annoyingly correct. "Who told you—"

He cut me off. "You told your literary agent"—he flicked back even further, right to the inside cover—"that *people, sort of, have to die* in order for you to write a book. I was standing right behind you in the line to get on board. And I always knew there was something unsavory about your first book. Something that didn't quite add up. So I knew you were planning something. I've been watching you this whole time, taking notes, making sure that I'd see what you were trying to do before you did it."

My mouth flapped like a fish's. Royce hadn't been writing general notes: he'd been keeping track of me. The world's worst amateur detective had invented an entire murder mystery out of one overheard sentence as I stepped on the train.

But Royce wasn't done. "And now you're here, telling me exactly what you did, because you're going to kill me and pin me as the villain and then write another book about it." He stood up, uncapped the pen and held it out like a sword. "Not today! Not with this writer."

I took what I thought was a placating step toward him, but he jabbed the pen in the general air in front of me. "Keep away from me. I took a self-defense class while researching Dr. Jane Black, Book Six."

"That's the most ridiculous thing I've ever heard," I said.

"It taught me some valuable techniques."

"Not the self-defense class, that you think I'm a murderer." I reached forward and plucked the pen, quite easily as it happens, out of his grasp.

I am not one for reflexes but Royce's required an archaeologist to find. He clutched the air where the pen used to be, then gave a little yelp and plopped back onto the bed, arms raised in front of his head in an X.

"I didn't kill anybody," I said. "And I'm not about to start with you."

He lowered his hands slightly, peering at me from above his forearms. "You just wanted my . . . opinion?" Royce, who is a man so comfortable giving his opinion when it is *not* asked for that he assumedly found being asked for it quite the rarity, still seemed confused.

"I suspected there might be something in the flask. You're the only one with forensic experience, so I thought if we put our heads together we might figure it out. And voilà: heroin. It wasn't the conversation I thought we'd have, but we got there."

Royce had settled back enough into his skin to choose petulance. "Can I have my pen back? It's special."

I held it up, noticing it had *Gemini Publishing* on the side. McTavish and Royce's publisher, and Wyatt Lloyd's company. "It's nice." I pressed my thumb into the tip. Watched it dimple the skin. "Sharp. A gift?"

"For my first book. A welcome-to-the-party kind of thing." He held his hand out, begging for it back.

Fair enough, I thought, publishers liked giving welcome gifts. I'd gotten a mug and a bottle of champagne, which ironically reflected a writer's hobbies somewhat more than a pen did.

"I'm not ruling you out as a suspect, you know," Royce huffed. "Or . . . or . . . maybe someone's trying to help *you* write. Provide you inspiration from afar."

I'd already opened the door to leave.

"Where are you going?"

"I'm going to see if they'll let me look at the body." I tossed the pen at him. "You coming?"

# CHAPTER 14

"Absolutely no way"—Aaron's arms clamped shut so fast over his chest they could have been a bear trap—"am I letting you lot poke a corpse."

He blockaded the walkway from the bar through to the restaurant. The sound of Cynthia scrubbing the spot where McTavish had vomited, a bucket of soapy water beside her, carried through the now empty carriage. The body had been cleared away, the wet stain the only evidence that someone had died there an hour ago. Without the hubbub of the guests, I could hear the glasses behind the bar tinkle and chime as the train rocked.

"We can help," I pleaded. "We have experience."

Aaron looked us up and down like he was choosing us for five-a-side. "The poor bloke's past helping. We're an hour from Alice. If I can ask you to sit tight in your rooms for just a little longer, we'll have this all cleared up."

"We're not offering to help Henry," Royce said. "We're offering to help *you*."

"I appreciate it, Mr. Royce, but we have it very much under control. As unfortunate as the circumstances are, we are well trained in such eventualities." Aaron extended an arm behind us, toward our cabins. Behind him, Cynthia still scratched at the floor, yellow gloves to her elbows. The carriage smelled like bleach. "Now, if I could ask you to return to your cabins."

"You have murders on this train often, then?" I asked.

"I'm sorry?"

"We think Henry McTavish was murdered," I said, grimacing at including Royce in that *we*, but needs must. "And while you might be practiced in the odd old bird dropping off in their sleep, when it comes to murder, trust me, you're going to need our help."

Aaron clicked his tongue. I could see him replaying McTavish's death in his mind. He huffed air through his nose as he settled on a decision. "I appreciate your concerns, but Mr. McTavish lived a life of excess, it appears. It caught up to him. That's all there is here."

"You're wrong," Royce spat.

Aaron's eyes went hard. "I've been very accommodating with you both—"

"He means, *what if* you're wrong? If there's been a murder on the train, that means there's a *murderer*," I added, with a smile I hoped was more magnanimous than deviant. "You can cart off the body in Alice, sure, but by the time you figure out we're right, we'll be halfway to Adelaide, and you and all your guests will be trapped with a killer." I lingered on the word *guests*. The magic password here was so obvious I only had to hint at it: corporate liability.

Aaron frowned and checked his watch. I could see him calculating the value in our opinions versus the time it would take to get to Alice Springs, where the real police would be better placed to help him, killer or not. "When you say . . . experience . . ." He twirled a finger in the air, speaking warily, still unsure, but the opening was there. "You're not police."

"We have skills," I said.

"You're writers."

"Royce used to be a forensic pathologist."

Aaron was unimpressed. "And what did you *used* to be?"

I ignored the dig and tried one more Hail Mary, spreading my arms wide. "Look, I get it. It seems ridiculous. But I've been here before. I've looked a serial killer in the eye. I've had people die in front of me. People I could have—should have—helped. So when I tell you I know what we might be up against, I'm not doing it for bragging rights, I'm not doing it for kicks." I paused, and then decided to just tell him the truth. "I'm doing it because I'm scared."

Royce gave me a judgmental look: *Wuss.* I heard Cynthia rip her dishwashing gloves off behind me with a wet *thuck* and toss them in her bucket.

I lowered my voice. I knew I was cooking up a pantomime here, but I needed to be as over-the-top as possible to get past Aaron's disinterest. "This killer doesn't strike at night or in shadows. They struck in broad daylight, in front of all the other passengers. You think a killer like that stops at just one? You think they're following the train timetable? No. McTavish was just the start. And if you think an hour's not so long, that you can wait it out, well, I hope for your sake we're wrong." I grabbed Royce's shoulder. "Come on, Alan. We're going back to our cabins and barricading the doors. Aaron, I advise you to do the same. Otherwise some people on this train are going to *'used to be'* a lot of things. And I don't mean retirement."

Royce, who hadn't figured out my plan, was like a boulder to turn around, but eventually fell into grumbling step. "Ernest, we have to see the body," he mumbled under his breath.

I hissed at him to shut up.

We kept walking.

Aaron's hand on my shoulder came right on cue.

"Five minutes, okay? And just so you can tell me if any of the guests are in danger. You better not be screwing around. So help me God, there's coppers in Alice who owe me a favor and they will throw the bloody book at you."

Henry McTavish's death had been violent, but without gore or evisceration, and so his body was unmarked. He looked physically similar to when he was alive—a little paler, perhaps—and there was a trickle of vomit on his chin, though that could be passed off as sleeping drool. But, in death, his body lacked something more indefinable, like an elastic band without the snap. A lettuce without the crunch. Prose without voice.

I raised a fist to my mouth and covered a dry retch. This was the eighth dead body I'd been unfortunate enough to come across in my life. I don't know the magic number to desensitize a person, but I do know I wasn't quite there. As I write this, thankfully as an outpatient and in a hotel room now, I'm up to ten and it still makes me queasy.

We were in cabin L1, in the staff carriage between the restaurant and the Chairman's Carriage. Aaron had explained that these were actually all staff cabins, but that L1 doubled as a spare room for medical needs. I read between the lines: most people, if they died on the train, were simply tucked up into bed until the next station. If a body had to be moved, because the deceased was, say, sharing with someone, it was placed in L1. Despite his private carriage, I assumed McTavish had been relegated here as the Ghan wouldn't want rumor of the finest class of room being haunted. Aaron told me that on full trains, which this was not, the staff members drew straws for who slept in L1. Clean sheets mean nothing on a mattress's memories.

Royce, aware that we were on a countdown to both Alice Springs and Aaron's feeble allowance being overtaken by sanity, immediately got on his knees and started fossicking around the corpse.

I peered over from behind him, and Aaron hovered anxiously in the doorway.

Royce prised McTavish's mouth open, using a handkerchief in the absence of gloves, pulled out his tongue like it was a toy and probed his inner cheeks. Aaron swallowed audibly.

"This kind of stuff happen much on your shift?" I asked him, as a distraction.

"Oh, um. I mean there's the occasional—" His eyes flickered to McTavish, then back to me. He forgot the rest of his sentence and simply said, "Natural causes."

I've always found that phrase fascinating. Human beings, by nature, are so easily overtaken by emotion, our base urges. We feel certain things so keenly—love, sure, but also hatred—that we are practically designed to implode. Murder, it seems to me, is about as natural a cause as it gets.

"You've never had problems with the guests?" I pressed. "Fights and that?"

"We're a luxury experience, not a backpackers' cruise." He looked over at Royce, who was currently pulling down the fleshy sacks under McTavish's eyes and peering into the corners. "Although we've never had writers before."

"You must have contingencies? Detainment?"

"I guess we could lock someone in the freezer if we had to, but I've never really thought about it. The Royal Flying Doctor Service would come in if it was something life-threatening, but for a big chunk of this journey we're pretty remote, so we've all got a certain get-on-with-it attitude. We're trained in crisis response, medical and such, in case something goes wildly off course, but it's not like it's hardwired. We do the best we can."

"Does this count as *off course*?"

Aaron shrugged. "I've seen worse."

My boggled eyes meant I didn't need to ask him to continue.

"About thirty years ago a school bus parked across the tracks. Before we were a hotel, back when we were doing freight. *That's* haywire." He blew air out through his teeth. Shook his head in memory. "Four kids and a teacher died, plus the bus driver of course."

I know you'll have twigged to the phrase *about thirty years ago* because the past, in mystery novels, never sleeps. A second case always becomes important to the overall solution, which, I'll tell you now, is going to be the situation here. Of course, there are a few timelines and second cases to choose from.

I thought about the school bus. Rural communities tend to have only one school to cover very large areas, and the bus would not have been the traditional coach, it would have been a bulbous white minivan that relayed around the rural farmlands. The trip may have taken a couple of hours, crisscrossing the rail several times. "The conductor didn't see it on the tracks?"

"This thing weighs—"

"Fourteen hundred tons," Royce called from the floor, proving himself a ferroequinologist. He currently had McTavish's left shoe and sock off and was fiddling with his toes. Whether we'd passed from autopsy into fetish, I wasn't quite sure. McTavish had died from a poisoned hip flask, not a rusty nail.

"Exactly." Aaron turned back to me. "We can't stop on a dime. You should see our three-point turns. I was an apprentice engineer back then. First job, eighteen. It's hard to forget. It wasn't our fault."

I had a sudden image of tiny palms pressed against windows. A thousand tons of steel barreling down. "How could the bus miss this huge train coming at them?"

"Bus driver was a bit hard to ask, flat as he was. Hard to check things like the engine or transmission weren't busted too—they were all blown apart. Is this going to take much longer?"

Royce hustled McTavish into a seated position, muttered *hold this* like he was a mechanic with a screwdriver between his teeth, and shoved McTavish in my direction. I had a second's hesitation at adding my fingerprints to a crime scene, but the corpse was drooping toward me and I figured, with Royce's hands all over his tongue and toes, we were past such decisions. I stepped in and held on to his shoulders, keeping him tilted forward, while Royce fumbled off his coat, tapping me to lift one hand here, another there.

Without his coat, McTavish showed more signs of death. The veins in his neck were bold rivulets of blue. Royce set about rolling up McTavish's sleeves, and I noticed that the skin on McTavish's left arm was rippled and glossy, the type of mottled flesh caused by burns long healed. This continued up to the side of his neck and assumedly also down his leg. The hit-and-run he'd barely survived, remembered by his skin.

Royce looked inside the creases of both elbows. Then he stood up. "I need to see his room. And the flask."

Aaron checked his watch again. He'd indulged us with a look at the body under the guise of passenger security, but now we had fewer than forty-five minutes before the real police would board the train, and his caution was kicking in again.

Royce stepped into the bathroom and called out over the sound of the faucet as he washed his hands, "I suspect it's a drug overdose. I'm sorry we alarmed you, but it pays to be prudent. I just need to check his room and see if any environmental factors, drug paraphernalia and the like, can contribute to my conclusions."

This mix of truth, in the cause of death, and lies, in our reason for looking at McTavish's room, was a particularly brilliant piece of manipulation, sold all the more heavily by the casualness with which Royce had expressed it while drying his hands, swapping our intimidation tactics for exactly what Aaron had always wanted to hear. Royce was giving Aaron the opportunity to prove himself right, and Aaron took it.

We exited L1 and Aaron slid the door shut, hanging the cardboard handle-hanger that said *Shhhhh—I'm still sleeping* in lieu of being able to lock the door, which I thought was more than a little ironic. We followed him down the hall. In the rickety space between carriages, muffled by the clanking of iron and the wind whistling through the gaps, I whispered to Royce, "Didn't know you were into feet."

He shook his head. "Junkies usually shoot up in their arms, but if those veins collapse, or if they're trying to hide an addiction, they shoot up somewhere more discreet—the side of their eyes, or in between their toes."

"He's clean," I surmised.

"Drunk? Yes. Druggie? No. Murdered? Definitely."

Aaron unlocked the door to the Chairman's Carriage and swung it open. His shout of surprise cut off my conversation with Royce and we turned to hear him say into McTavish's room, "What the hell are you doing in here?"

# CHAPTER 15

Brooke's hands shot into the air as if we'd come in brandishing guns. The blood didn't just drain from her face, it siphoned down her legs, through the floor and onto the tracks, leaving her with bone-china cheeks and pale, thin lips puckered in surprise.

"These are private quarters," Aaron said.

"This is a crime scene," I said.

"Who are you?" Royce said.

I had been so surprised to see her I hadn't properly taken in the opulence of the Chairman's Carriage. Though it was named so, I hadn't quite realized that Henry's room would be an *entire* carriage. We'd entered into a private sitting room that could easily seat ten or so people. A yellow leather couch ran in a semicircle against the east wall, facing a table piled with some scattered papers. A television was mounted on the far wall. That particular detail stood out the most to me: to be rich enough to afford this cabin but indifferent to the view you were paying for. Another indulgence was betrayed by the small deposit of ash on the carpet by my feet: a flagrant breach of the no-smoking rule. There was a whiff of blueberry in the air, rather than cigarettes, though. The design of the furniture was like any hotel lobby: wood paneling (not fake, as in my room) and gold-trim finishes, even a glittering chandelier. The whole room felt like being in Air Force One.

Royce picked up a half-full bottle of whiskey and whistled.

"Pricey?" I asked. A number on the side of the bottle was older than I was, which answered my question for me.

Brooke's scrapbook was next to the messy stack of papers, and I realized they were strewn not because McTavish had left them in a mess, but because she'd been interrupted going through them. She saw my gaze land on them, and the burgeoning excuse that had been bubbling on her lips transformed as she recognized what I'd said.

"Crime scene?" she said. "You think Henry was—" Her hand shot to her mouth. "Oh my God. Please don't think I—"

"Don't listen to them," Aaron said. "They're just . . . well, they're supposed to be helping, but I'm undecided. No one's accusing you of anything. Except lock-picking, I suppose."

Brooke looked at her shoes. The color bungee-jumped back into her cheeks.

"He gave you a key," I surmised. McTavish had told Brooke that morning it was a shame he'd had to drink his expensive whiskey alone, a hint to an invitation declined. "Last night."

The tiniest of nods. "I wasn't going to go. I wouldn't."

"Why take it then?" Royce asked. It was becoming abundantly clear that he was only able to consider female suspects based on a singular motive—sex—and didn't understand that consent could be given *and* revoked.

"Henry McTavish was my hero," Brooke said. "So, yeah, I was a little butterfly-y when he came up to me last night. That *is* what I wanted to happen. But I wanted it to be as a reader, as a fan. For us to bond over his books, and what they'd given me."

I recalled her question at the panel: puzzling to me but painstakingly crafted to impress McTavish. Simone had said you had to speak to him in riddles and puzzles. *Archie Bench*. She'd come all this way to get the chance to say *I understand your books better than anyone*. It wasn't so shallow as a crush or a seduction.

Her lip quivered as she continued, "And then he comes over, and I'm thinking this is the moment I've waited for. And he leans in—his breath reeks of alcohol—and he presses his room key into my hand. Doesn't say anything. Just the key. The look on his face, like this was some kind of prize. Like I'd earned it." She gagged a little at the memory. "I froze. By the time I'd recovered enough to really process what had just happened, he'd already started walking away. And I'd curled my hand around the key so tightly it almost cut my palm."

"Nice performance, love." Royce gave a slow clap. While he may have had some usefulness in forensics, his psychological insight was lacking: I needed S. F. Majors for that.

"So you didn't come here last night?" I asked, thinking of Royce's female voice behind the door. He'd only *thought* it was Lisa, he'd never actually seen her.

"Absolutely not. I slept in my own room."

"Which is?" I asked, so I could sketch it later.

"The guest carriage."

I waited for more specifics, but she hesitated. I realized I'd just told her there might be a killer on the train. She had every right to be cautious about a stranger asking where she slept.

"N, ah, 1," she said eventually. "Look, I was going to talk to him after the panel. I didn't sleep well. I was worried maybe I'd misread things. I wanted to clear the air with the benefit of sobriety and sunrise. At the very least I had to give him back the key. So I went to the Q and A. But that publisher guy stopped me."

I remembered Wyatt brushing her aside, telling her there'd be signatures after the session.

"And then he had that heart attack and I thought"—her eyes flickered to the side, her first clear lie—"I'd put the key back myself." She straightened, putting her hands on her hips. "I don't know why you're acting like this is an interrogation."

None of us said anything. Aaron scratched the back of his calf with his toe.

"Oh. My. God." She burst out laughing. "This *is* an interrogation. You think you're *actual* detectives. Oh wow. That's too good. Tell me, which one's Holmes and which one's Watson? Wait, let me guess." She pointed at Royce, then wrinkled her nose. "Sidekick."

Royce took a step toward her, but Aaron put an arm out. "I thought we were here to confirm cause of death. Not to hassle the guests."

With the fear that our permission to poke around was about to be revoked, Royce and I launched into a great act of demonstratively looking for clues: bent backs and stroked chins. I inspected the waste bin, which had a wad of bloody tissues in it and a little white card that said *From an admirer*. Brooke's words echoed: *McTavish was my hero*.

Extending from the lounge was a hallway not dissimilar to the regular accommodation halls, leading to four separate cabins. Two of these appeared untouched. The third was set up as a miniature office: a proper writing desk in front of the seat, a lone felt-tip pen sitting on it. The largest room was at the end: McTavish's bedroom, more than double the size of a regular cabin and furnished with an unmade double bed in the middle of the room, a separate armchair facing the window, and McTavish's suitcase open on the floor, tongues of jacket sleeves licking the carpet.

"Where's his typewriter?" I asked, looking around.

"Huh?" Royce shrugged, then lifted the mattress: a predictable place to hide drugs. It was clean.

"McTavish," I said. "Doesn't he write all his manuscripts on a typewriter? He's got the writing desk set up in the other room. No typewriter. No ink."

"Well, he's got a pen, doesn't he?" Royce dropped the mattress, then got on his knees and tried to look under the bed. He fossicked about for a minute, then hauled himself back up, dusting his chest like he'd been exploring a haunted attic and not a five-star train carriage. "The tissues in the bin could indicate a nasal hemorrhage, which is not uncommon among heroin users."

I knew he was lying. There's no way Royce, no matter how long out of the profession he was, could have missed the purpling bridge of McTavish's nose. I'd seen it even before he'd died. Those tissues in the bin hadn't been from using. Someone had given him a bloody nose last night.

But that lie I could stomach. It was the same one Royce had told Aaron back in L1; he wanted Aaron to believe our nosiness was useful, and he also didn't want anyone to steal his limelight. The lie I couldn't abide was that, when Royce stood up, I saw a flash of paper disappear into his pocket. He'd found something under the bed.

Now, destroying evidence is par for the course for a guilty party, and it crossed my mind that Royce had secreted something self-incriminating. But Royce, unlike his books, was also a pretty easy read. I was sure Brooke's needling of him as my sidekick had bruised his ego and he wanted to prove himself the Holmes to my Watson, not the other way around. I suspected he was stealing the evidence merely to beat me to the solution.

We locked eyes for a second and it was clear our marriage of convenience had reached a hasty divorce. I'm sorry to those who love a trope: no bromance here.

"I still need to see the flask," Royce said to Aaron. "It might have trace."

Aaron unclipped the walkie-talkie on his belt and radioed into it. "Cynthia. Any chance you've got the flask that our poor fella was drinking out of?"

"Yeah," Cynthia crackled back.

"Could you hang on to it? Reckon we might need some forensics."

"Forensics? You think—"

"I don't know. But better safe than sorry."

"Sorry, boss. I washed it." Her voice was ditzy, almost deliberately so. I could picture her twirling a strand of hair around a finger. "Was I not supposed to or something?"

Royce rolled his eyes. I'll note that Cynthia was also the one to wash the carpet where the flask spilled out, and given I've already mentioned destroying evidence is worth keeping an eye on, we can consider her a suspect. But I also thought it a bit rich of Royce to criticize her when he had evidence in his pocket. So I'm just pointing that out, because, you know: fair play.

"You're a moron," Royce said, leaning into Aaron's radio. "You've jeopardized the whole investigation."

"I have to press the button for her to hear," Aaron said. "Like this."

"You're a . . . oh, forget it." Royce sighed. Anger is hard to summon twice. "Thank you, Cynthia."

"Who was that?" Cynthia crackled through.

"Alan Royce," Aaron said.

"The jerk?"

"This is a speaker, Cynthia."

It was turning farcical, so I mentioned I was going to take another look at the lounge. Alan wanted to search the two untouched bedrooms again, and I gladly headed back on my own. Brooke was still sitting on the couch. I wasn't sure if Aaron had told her to wait or if she'd just stayed out of curiosity, but I considered it a win: if Royce could hide evidence from me, I could hide an interview from him.

"It's not a good look," I said, picking up some of the papers from the table. "You know that, surely?"

She scratched her right arm, which had a trucker's tan—

sunburned on one arm only—from sitting by the window in her cabin too long, I assumed. "I didn't know it was a murder until ten minutes ago."

I studied the papers in my hands. McTavish's notes had barely any substance to them, and his handwriting was so varied it was possible to chart at which points he was sober and at which he was drunk depending on the legibility. One page said *decapitation— survival? Research* in massive letters. Another: *Morbund. Film meeting. Hugh Jackman. Is this a musical? Ryan Reynolds. Is this a comedy?*

"Come on," I said, tapping the pages on the table. "That's not why you were here."

"Are you playing wannabe detective?" She pointed at me, drew a finger up and down my figure. Pursed her lips.

"You're avoiding the question."

"What do you want me to say? I told you the truth."

"You didn't. And I'm not accusing you of murder, by the way. But he's your favorite author, and he's just finished off a series with your favorite character. And now he's *really* finished with the series. So I'm thinking about what I would do, as a fan, to get one last piece."

"Okay, fine. Well done." She threw a bunch of papers onto the table. One fluttered to the carpet. "I came for a souvenir, okay? Just something, anything, he'd written."

"Like this?" I picked up the sheet from the floor. One of the advantages of my injury was that, even if I hadn't been gloved, I doubted I had any fingerprints, so I tried to use my right hand for anything I thought was evidence. The sheet of paper had a red camel at the bottom, the same as the notepad Juliette and I had in our room. Across the top were the words *Archibald Bench*. Beneath was a series of underline dashes, designations for empty letters, as if he'd been playing a game of Hangman. This was followed by a jumble of letters, then the word *Archie!* complete with ecstatic exclamation mark. Below that was the word *Reich*, underlined. The handwriting was somewhere between the sober and drunk McTavish scrawls, and given it looked like he was trying to solve his own puzzle, I figured it wasn't his at all and had actually fallen out of Brooke's scrapbook. This was how she'd pieced together whatever lay behind Archibald Bench.

Brooke snatched the paper from me. "Perhaps."

"The manuscript's not here," I said. "Which is what you were really looking for."

"I was not." She sold it with the fake indignance of an unfaithful spouse, but curiosity overwhelmed her. "How'd you know that?"

"I heard McTavish deliver it to Wyatt Lloyd last night. It'll be in his cabin."

"So what? I was looking for a novel. Is that so bad?"

"Depends. I was sorry to see your book got ruined. *Misery*, right? Want me to tell you how it ends?"

Brooke put on the shocked air of a courtesan who had just been propositioned. "I would *never*."

"I don't know if you're far enough in to know much about Annie Wilkes—"

"You are drawing a long-ass bow."

This stalled my questioning. I now had three possible theories that involved Brooke. One: she'd been so mad at McTavish for killing her favorite hero that she'd lashed out. Two: she'd been so repulsed, so crushed, by his proposition to her that she'd taught him a lesson. Three: she'd figured out something about Archibald Bench, jotted it in her notepad, and told McTavish what she knew about it that morning at the panel in code. His invite to his cabin might not have been sexual after all, if he thought she knew something she shouldn't. He might have wanted to talk to her about Archibald Bench. Maybe even try to silence her.

Two of those confrontations may have plausibly ended in self-defense. A broken nose and a bin full of bloodied tissues. I wasn't sure whether any of them added up to murder.

The second theory held the most water, given what Royce had in his pocket. But of course I didn't know what that was yet, so neither can you.

"Okay, now it's my turn," Brooke said. "Heart attack, huh?"

"I think it's fairly obvious I suspect otherwise."

"And so far, am I your only suspect?"

"Well, you're the only one inside the crime scene, so by that virtue, sure."

Brooke picked up her scrapbook and leafed through it. It was a collection of articles and photographs, shoddily glued in. Henry McTavish accepting an award. A certificate that had the words *Morbund's Mongrels* on it. She stopped flipping on a yellowed newspaper article and slid the scrapbook over to me.

The first thing I logged was the date: August 2003. Brooke looked in her late teens, early twenties. "Surely you didn't collect this when you were a child?"

"Wasn't even born, mate. You suspect me of being a big enough fan to murder someone but not to photocopy the occasional newspaper from the library? Jesus. You need all the help you can get. Read the damn thing."

*STARS OF THE FUTURE*
*Oliver Wright, 19 August 2003, Edinburgh*

A YEAR AFTER THE PUBLICATION OF HIS DEBUT GLOBAL BEST-SELLER, HENRY MCTAVISH HAS RETURNED WITH ANOTHER IM-POSSIBLE MURDER THAT CAN ONLY BE SOLVED BY HIS RECLUSIVE SCOTTISH GENIUS.

The next half of the piece was a review of McTavish's second book, *Knee-Deep in Trouble*, in which the reviewer's tone, after the initial hook, became much more critical. It was clear he was a big enough fan of the first book to not trash the second, but that was about the only thing holding him back from outright savagery. The review concluded that McTavish's sophomore effort was, in all, a disappointment, and the piece ended with a quick review of two other debut novels, whose authors had appeared on a panel with McTavish at the Edinburgh International Book Festival . . .

I turned to Brooke. "You're joking?"

She tapped the article in response. I looked back down. A small photograph, just an inch square, was squeezed into the column width between the final two paragraphs. In it were three people, merry at a bar. I recognized all of them.

The caption read: *Bestselling crime author Henry McTavish catches up with up-and-coming debut novelists Lisa Fulton (left) and S. F. Majors (right) at the Edinburgh International Book Festival.*

The photo had been taken in a badly lit booth of a badly lit pub—which I mean literally, as according to my research the owner tried to burn it down for insurance purposes in 2015 and failed—but it was unmistakable. McTavish had his arm around Lisa's shoulder, they were both laughing, and S. F. Majors was looking dead straight at the camera. All three had foaming pints of beer in front of them and vibrant, unforced smiles. It didn't seem like they were posing for a newspaper; it had the sense of camaraderie you find in high school yearbooks that makes you wistful for youth.

The three of them, all at the same festival. Twenty years ago. There's that phrase again. And now all on a train together. I knew not to take it lightly.

"Why are you showing me this?" I asked.

"Because if the best you've got is a couple of theories about why *I'm* capable of murder, I thought you'd want to know who actually had motive to kill him. This"—she stabbed a finger at the page—"was taken right after Henry published *Knee-Deep in Trouble,* the second Morbund novel, which tanked. And a year before he published . . ." She unspooled it for me.

"*Off the Rails*," I finished. The third Morbund novel. What Brooke was trying to tell me clicked in slowly. "That's the book that Majors brought up at the introductory panel. The one she said was based on real events."

"Precisely! You see, she has claimed in the past that she first mentioned that story"—with each word, she plugged her finger right on Majors's toothy grin—"at. This. Exact. Festival."

I tried to make the picture flicker to life in my imagination. The clinking of glasses, the whispered gossip, the commiseration over reviews, the bashfulness around better-than-expected sales. A room of people who *get* it. Writing is a dream job, but it is a job, and sometimes it's nice to be around people who share your opinion that the stakes of paper and ink are life and death. Writing is such a solitary act that a room full of communal misery is a tonic that many won't admit is quite rejuvenating. Provided they're not killing each other, of course.

A bunch of writers in a room requires a collective noun that the English language doesn't have. A condolence, perhaps. A sympathy. It's a war hospital for the written word.

I thought back to what I'd originally hoped this trip would be, my dream of hitting it off with McTavish. Now I pictured Lisa, McTavish and Majors huddled together, sharing their dreams and inspirations . . . and ideas.

What had Majors said at the panel? What color was *Off the Rails*? And what had been Henry's answer, complete with gloating smile? *Green*.

Jealousy.

"Majors thinks McTavish took her idea for *Off the Rails*?"

"Bingo," Brooke said. "She's never let it go. Says they got to drinking and sharing, and the conversation was fairly casual, a bit creative. You know how it goes—a bit of *Who are you reading?*, a bit of *What are you working on?* Then a year and a bit later she sees Henry's new book hit the shelves." She mimed a little explosion with her hands.

"How have I never heard about this? I'm not a Mongrel, sure, but I'm enough of a fan to have twigged if any accusations hit the press. How the hell do you know about it?"

"Majors has to be very careful about what she says," Brooke said. "Wyatt Lloyd has been . . . I don't want to say 'threatening,' but I could say . . . aggressively litigious. Besides, if I told you tomorrow I was going to write a novel about Henry the Eighth, I don't dibs that story for myself. It's public, it's out there, so me writing about it doesn't rule out anyone else from having a crack. Come to think of it"—she held up a finger in mock thought—"I reckon someone's been murdered on a train before."

Something McTavish said rang in my mind. *If you knew someone who died or was hurt in a similar way . . .*

"Different question, then. Who's Archibald Bench?"

She burst out laughing. "You're better off barking up the Annie Wilkes stuff."

"What?"

"*Archie* Bench is the reason I wouldn't have killed him. Try harder."

"Okay." I tried again. "Did Majors know the people involved in the real story behind *Off the Rails*?"

Brooke gave a noncommittal head shake. More of a *How should I know* than an *I don't know.*

I turned back to the article. "You kept this, which means you thought it was important. You had your loyalty, of course, to his books. So you're predisposed to believe that he hadn't nicked the idea, I'm guessing. But you believed the rumor all the same?"

Brooke sighed. "Obviously I kept it for a reason. I mean, it's an important biographical incident, regardless of who you believe. Like any good rumor, it's not really public knowledge, but it's not exactly hidden. Most Mongrels know about it, at least. Occasionally it pops up on a podcast. But it's not, like, *news* or anything." This seemed an overexplanation: I'd never heard these accusations before. "And McTavish has always denied it. I always believed him. But . . . you're right, I did keep the article. And now that I've met him . . ." She put a hand on my arm. "You read people's books, and you think you know them. They're having a conversation with you for hundreds of pages, and there's an intimacy there that you develop on your own. I really loved Henry McTavish. And then I got here, and the drinking, the excess, the look in his eyes as he handed me the key . . . Maybe now I think my picture of him was wrong. Maybe now I think he's a man who likes pleasure but doesn't want to have to work for it. And maybe that means I wonder if I should have believed her all along."

I digested that. It seemed a pretty good summation of McTavish—a man who wanted his pleasures gifted to him. Or taken.

"What about Lisa? She hasn't backed up these claims, has she?" I asked. I recalled Majors almost expecting Lisa to stick up for her at the panel, the disappointment when she hadn't, and the friction when Lisa's cover revealed she'd been blurbed by McTavish. That could easily be seen as Lisa choosing a side. Maybe it was even what McTavish had offered her for her silence.

Brooke shook her head, but her eyes looked to the floor.

Royce's words echoed in my mind—*there's more than one way to get a blurb*—until I realized it was too whiny and annoying to be a memory and was actually the real-life Royce, who'd finished searching the other rooms and was leaning against the television casing. He had a smugness to him, like someone who's cheated on the test and knows all the answers. "You talking about Henry and Lisa? They. Got. It. On," he sneered. "Henry said she was a real firecracker of a lay."

Brooke retched at his description.

"Find anything?" I painted on a smile. "Decorum, perhaps?"

"Wouldn't you love to know. And what's going on here, interviewing suspects without me?"

"She's not a very likely suspect," I said.

"That makes her very likely indeed." He waggled a finger at me. "You should know this, Ernest: it's never the least likely, that's too obvious. It's got to be the next along."

"I'll keep that in mind," I said.

"Besides, you probably didn't notice, but I'm quite sharp. She's been reading a bloody copy of *Misery* on the trip." He postured like it was the most genius observation in the world, then turned back to the hallway. "What's taking this bloke so long?" A toilet flushed, answering his own question, but he called anyway, "Aaron?"

Brooke turned to me. "*Misery*'s not about obsession. Not if you look at it from Annie Wilkes's perspective. It's got a much simpler theme." She stood up and, even though Royce wasn't technically blocking her way to the door, managed to get a shoulder into him as she passed. She held up the Chairman's Carriage key and said as she placed it on the table, "Never meet your heroes."

Aaron emerged, patting wet hands on the front of his vest, as the Ghan jolted to a stop. We all swayed in unison with the change of velocity.

"Right," Aaron said, slapping Royce on the shoulder. "Guess that's your investigation over. Thank God for the professionals. Welcome to Alice Springs."

# CHAPTER 16

They made us stay on the train while they unloaded the body. I'd returned to the cabin sheepishly, where Juliette had appraised me, looked at her watch (*You've been gone awhile*) and said, "Had your fill?"

I'd nodded, patted her leg. Path of least resistance.

She might have even believed me had I been able to take my eyes off the paramedics, grunting as they carried McTavish's rag doll body, zipped into plastic, down the steps and onto the platform. It was so mundane, so *practical*, no more the handling of a celebrity corpse than it was hauling a washing machine up a flight of stairs. I've always thought I write things down to help remember them. But there is a part of me that writes to *be* remembered. Watching them wrestle with the body, I realized that it doesn't matter how many names on how many spines of how many books you have, sometimes your legacy boils down to meat in a black plastic bag.

I was about as determined to enjoy myself in Alice Springs as Juliette was determined to distract me from thinking about McTavish. The writers' panels were mercifully canceled for the day, which meant that we had our choice of the activities provided to the regular guests or could simply wander the township on our own. Juliette and I elected to do the latter (Majors told me where to get the best vanilla slice), and then Juliette insisted on joining the bus for a bushwalk to Simpsons Gap, a natural marvel where steep red-rock cliffs had been cleft by weather and time to leave a ravine. I had hoped to bail up Simone with a couple of questions, but I overestimated her proclivity for sightseeing; she'd elected to stay on the train (the bar, we were told, had reopened). In any case, I was quickly taken by the towering view and deep ochre of the rock against the crisp blue of the sky, and promptly forgot all ideas I had about questioning anyone.

I sat in the sand at a point where the ravine was half in sun and half shaded by the ridge, and Juliette put her head on my shoulder, her face half in light and half in shadow. The rocks in front of us had existed for millions of lifetimes. They would be here when our bones were dust and our books were mulch. We were blips. But two blips are bigger than one blip. I think you know you're onto a good thing when you can apologize without talking.

It was nice enough that I only kept half an eye on what everyone else was doing.

Harriet and Jasper took selfies like they were on their honeymoon. Wolfgang chose a high-up flat piece of rock and meditated on it. The book club ladies delighted in spotting wallabies. S. F. Majors skipped rocks across a pool of water halfway down the ravine, where Brooke, intrepid with youth, hopscotched rock to rock as far along the water's edge as she could. Lisa hung back in the shade, telling Brooke to be careful, and, later, helping to apply aloe vera cream to Brooke's one-armed burn. Royce was by the table of drinks the staff had set out, pounding beers. Cynthia kept an eye on us, occasionally yelling how long we had left.

I spotted Harriet and Jasper struggling to get a selfie that captured the whole ravine and walked over to them. "Take your photo?"

I asked. "I assure you I'm a well-trained Instagram boyfriend—there'll be plenty of backup shots. And even retakes without complaint."

Harriet laughed and excitedly handed me the camera. The photos came out well, although I noticed their smiles were a little too tight. Lips fresh from argument. I could tell Harriet wanted me to try again, but Jasper wouldn't let her.

I walked away slowly, just to eavesdrop.

"It's a lot of money," Jasper said. "I can't just say no."

"We don't need it," Harriet said.

"Did you pay for this trip? Trust me. We could use it."

Harriet didn't like that. She sulked off toward the bar. Jasper followed, chanting her name: "Harriet! Harriet?! Harriet?" It was a familiar trifecta to anyone in a long-term relationship, each inflection meaning something different: *Come on; Seriously?; I'm sorry!*

Wyatt hadn't joined us on the trip. I'd last seen him on the platform yelling into his phone; I supposed there was some paperwork to do when an author died. Douglas had also elected to stay behind.

I didn't think of the murder, or of Douglas, again until we pulled in, pink-cheeked and sun-drunk—except for Royce, who was drunk-drunk—and I spotted Douglas hurriedly walking along the platform. It was no coincidence for us to be there at the same time: we'd been told to be back at the train by five P.M. At first I assumed that Douglas was worried about being late. But then I noticed his head was swiveling, checking to see if he was being followed. I watched as he reached a trash can, spun his backpack around and, with one last head-check, moved an object from his bag into the bin. Almost in the same motion he was walking away.

I looked around the coach. People were chattering and jovial, buoyed by the excursion. Juliette was asleep on my shoulder. I was the only one who had seen it.

We disembarked and I made an excuse to divert toward the bin, faking blowing my nose into a tissue and hoping Juliette didn't notice I'd skipped two closer receptacles. Inside the bin were the usual scattered food wrappers and empty water bottles, apple cores and banana peels, but in the middle was a folded newspaper. It seemed an odd object to dispose of so suspiciously. I leaned into the bin and unfolded it.

It surprised me to see a murder weapon.

Not *the* murder weapon, of course. But one that could have only been brought onto the train with murderous intent in mind.

Wrapped up in the middle of the paper was a gleaming silver revolver.

# PSYCHOLOGICAL

# CHAPTER 17

Dinner was at the Telegraph Station, one of the oldest outback homesteads in the country. Halfway along the spine of Australia, it had originally served as a relay post for Morse code messages between Adelaide and Darwin. We writers were traveling the same route as an electron of communication a hundred years ago. The train line may as well have been a telegraph line.

The station itself was a huddle of historic stone cottages converted into a museum with plexiglass blocking the rooms, which featured plastic food on colonial dinner settings. The cottages surrounded a dust bowl clearing that had been gussied up with white-clothed tables as if it were a wedding, tin bathtubs spiked with the necks of white wine and beer bottles so that they looked like sea mines, and a stage where a guitarist and a banjo player were crooning country tunes. The scent of searing meat wafted into nostrils as dinner was cooked on an open flame just far enough away from the guests to tantalize us with how rustic the cooking was, but not close enough to make us feel like we were in the kitchen. We'd been told before the trip to bring one formal outfit specifically for this dinner, so I had on a dinner jacket that thankfully covered up the crumpled shirt

I'd neglected to hang. The sunset was almost offensively golden, photographically perfect. Tripods and binocular lenses clicked into place along the back fence like an army defending the line.

For all the beauty of the sunset, I couldn't take my eyes off Douglas. I don't know much about guns, but I do know the type he had binned—a little snub-nosed revolver, the one where you spin the chamber to play Russian roulette—was, like most guns, illegal in Australia. It's not the sort of thing that one has a ready excuse for carrying around. I had no idea how he'd gotten it on the plane over from Texas, so assumed he'd picked it up in Darwin. Just because guns are illegal in Australia doesn't mean they're inaccessible, of course, and Darwin has a lot of farmland where legal firearms are used, but he'd have to be motivated to find one. And if he had gone to those lengths, why dispose of it without firing a bullet?

Douglas, in contrast to how stressed and furtive he'd appeared at the train station, now seemed relaxed and carefree, dancing with the book club ladies in front of the band. There was a definite air of celebration in him. This isn't as accusatory as it sounds; there was very little grief in the air. Three-quarters of the train didn't know what had happened, and of those of us who did, only a few thought it anything other than an unforeseen tragedy. What I mean is, people were determined to enjoy themselves.

Dinner was flame-grilled apostrophes of lamb chops, with chocolate damper, a bread cooked on a campfire, for dessert. We each had a designated seat; cards had been placed deliberately to separate us from our traveling party, to stoke conversation, so Juliette and I were split up. S. F. Majors, however, was at my table. After mains, when a few people had floated off to stand around the various fire pits or ice buckets depending on their desired temperature, I slid into the seat next to her.

"I don't think we've properly talked," I said, extending a hand. "Thanks for inviting me along to this whole shindig."

Majors raised her eyebrows, looked like she was about to say something, and then gave a half chuckle and shook her head. "This whole 'shindig'"—she rolled the word in annoyance and tossed it back to me—"is an absolute disaster." She rubbed her temples. "If you see Wyatt coming, let me know. I'd prefer to avoid him."

"What happened wasn't your fault."

"Tell that to Gemini's lawyers. Even though Wyatt's about to make his company a literal truckload of cash, they'll want someone to blame. There goes my board seat for the festival too, if not the whole Mystery Writers' Society. We killed Henry McTavish. I'm sure loads of writers will want to join now."

"I thought it was a heart attack." I played dumb.

She slugged back enough wine to endure me. "Sure you do. I'm a psychologist, Ernest, I can read you. Just ask me what you came here to ask me."

She was terse enough that I figured I'd only get one question, so I refilled her wine until I decided on my angle. She didn't seem won over by the gesture but sipped at it all the same. "What's the psychological profile of an obsessive?" I asked. "Like a stalker?"

"Or a superfan," Majors said, not having time for my subtlety. "Adulation is fine, but it's a question of where the line is crossed that makes it unhealthy. It's got more to do with the stalker than the person they're following. The stalker might picture themselves having a certain relationship with this person. A connection that only they see. They insert themselves into a world they aren't actually a part of and justify their actions in very improbable ways. *I was just making sure you were safe by following you home,* for example. It's the inability to distinguish their own desires from those of the victim. Misinterpreting politeness for flirting, welcoming for need. That kind of thing."

"So it's the viewpoint that's dangerous. Because the victim's decisions can feel like they affect, or are even targeted toward, the stalker, even when they have nothing to do with them?"

"Precisely. Say I get my dream job and move across the country. Totally innocuous, totally personal. Someone with that view of me might see it as an attack on *them*. They don't like change."

Change, I thought. Like not writing certain books anymore, perhaps. It was something to chew on. Something else she'd said fluttered up in my consciousness. "What did you mean when you said Wyatt's going to make a lot of money?"

"Oh, bags of it. Henry's books sell, sure, but this will make his last novel a literary event. You know when they dig up half a manuscript from a long-dormant writer, like *Go Set a Watchman* with Harper Lee, or like Stieg Larsson, who died before his *Millennium* series was finished. That's the spin. This is the last one. No more. You better read it. Plus"—she waved a hand—"the rereleases, the new covers, the publicity of a genius"—she basically gagged on this word—"gone too soon. It's a gold mine. McTavish's death is one of the best things that could have happened to Wyatt Lloyd."

"And—"

"Hang on. My turn."

I tore off a piece of damper and stuffed it in my mouth. It was chewy and buttery, like a scone. "Okay."

"This isn't about justice. This is about proving yourself."

"That's not a question."

"Wasn't it? Oh. Well, I'm right. If I can give you some advice . . . You want to be careful about how you look at this whole thing, because right now you want it to be a murder. You want it so badly, you might ignore the real facts to make it fit what you want. And part of that's because you need a story and you've got a hundred grand on the line—"

I threw my hands up. "How the hell does everyone know—"

"And part of it is that you want to prove yourself to the rest of us: Wolfgang, Royce. Those who think you're too commercial or just lucky."

She tilted her glass at me and I refilled it from the bottle in the middle of the table.

"But most of it is that you need to be useful. Because if you didn't survive what happened to you last year to help someone now, why did you survive at all? That's why you wrote the first bloody book. To find some purpose in what happened. Here's your question, then: am I close?"

My silence answered it for her. She nodded: I could continue with my own questions.

"It's quite an eclectic group of people for this festival," I ventured. "Handpicked?"

"I needed a balance of established names, up-and-comers, and headline grabbers. Wolfgang helps get the funding through—grant committees love a bit of pedigree. Though I didn't think we'd get quite so many headlines, per se. I'd say I did a pretty good job, wouldn't you?"

So that was Wolfgang's invitation explained. Royce and I were still the disconnected outliers. "It's got nothing to do with the fact that you, Lisa and McTavish were at the Edinburgh International Book Festival in 2003?"

Her shoulders straightened at this. The wine paused near her lips, and her breath fogged the glass. "I think now would be a very disrespectful time to comment on such matters," she said finally.

"Why'd you invite me then?"

"I didn't invite you," she said cruelly, clearly retaliating for my previous question.

I ignored the barb but wondered: if she hadn't invited me, who had? "You clearly wanted McTavish here. There's a rumor that he stole the plot of *Off the Rails* from you. Any truth to that?"

She bristled. "I'm not about to give you motive. But that's interesting—you do think it's murder?"

"Royce thinks poison."

She snorted at this.

"What?"

"Royce thinks." She used her thumb and pointer on each hand to pretend to draw the words in a box in the sky, the way you'd pretend a title was on a marquee. "The oxymoron of the day."

"He used to be a forensic pathologist."

"Is that what he told you?"

"It's in his bio."

"You know that's worthless, right? You can put anything you want in there."

"But he did work in a lab? He has a degree? You can't lie about that."

"Sure, but he was, like, a graduate or an intern or whatever. Made photocopies, fetched coffees. It's all marketing. Wyatt knew it would sound good so they ran with it on the first book and now, eleven books later, I think Royce's even started to believe it himself."

I'd hinged my entire investigation on Royce's deduction that heroin was the murder weapon, so these words made my stomach plummet. I managed to say, "He's been quite helpful, actually."

"You want a profile on Royce? We don't have time. We couldn't unpack his issues if we had the rest of the train journey. Of course he's interested in the murder, he's finally got a chance to live up to a version of himself that's always been mostly a lie. I *am* a registered psychologist—I've kept up my credentials. Sure, Royce must have had training somewhere, but I'd think twice about letting him diagnose me. Research is just theoretical. You think Lisa hot-wires cars like her character?"

Mentally, I was still trying to salvage the credibility of my evidence. Even if Royce had plumped up his credentials, there was no denying that he'd researched eleven novels (and three novellas, lest I forget), so he must have had a nose for it. He had also mentioned researching heroin specifically for one of his books. Could I trust that? Or was I seeing what I wanted to see? On that, Majors was undeniably correct: I was desperate to be useful.

I opened my mouth to ask another question but she snapped a hand closed in front of me. "Well, that's about all the time we have for today's session, Mr. Cunningham." She spoke in a sing-song voice, breathy and quite deliberate, the way she addressed, I imagine, only her most insane patients. "I think it would be best that we continue your growth exercises another time." She gestured to an imaginary door in an imaginary office. "I'll leave you to make a booking with my receptionist on your way out."

Fires had been lit in steel drums around the circumference of the cottages, and as the band got louder the dust on the dance floor rose with excitedly stamped feet. The stars were magnificent, bright pinpricks in the clearest sky I'd ever seen. Juliette was no longer at her table, and I was looking around for her near the ice tubs when a heavy hand fell on my shoulder. I turned to see Douglas Parsons, rosy cheeked, out of breath, as much tapping me on the shoulder as he was leaning against me to stay upright.

"Ernest!" he yelled with a tone of surprise, like I was an old friend he'd spotted across the supermarket and not someone he'd approached himself.

"Douglas." I nodded, as *hello* felt a little formal, and besides, addressing him by name gave him another notch on the tally, and he was looking a little low at the moment.

"Enjoying yourself?" Douglas said.

"We did the bushwalk. How was your day in town? Get up to much?"

He was almost drunk enough I thought I'd get away with *Shoot anybody?* but I refrained.

He looked up at the stars as if having a religious moment. Eventually he said, "Life-changing."

"I'm glad."

"I've got you to thank for that. That's what I wanted to say. Thank you."

I hesitated, chastened already this trip from accepting apologies I didn't understand, but gave in to his expectant eyes. "You're welcome."

"I mean it, Ernest." He ripped a bottle from the ice like he was unsheathing a sword. A little avalanche of ice cubes toppled from the tub into the dirt. He held the beer out to me. I took it, again not sure what kind of accessory I was obliging myself to become. "I could tell you thought I lied to you the other day. When we met. When I said I was traveling alone."

"Oh." I waved it off. "No, I didn't."

"You did. And it's okay. I get it. I *am* traveling alone, technically. But there's someone else with me, you know, spiritually."

I'll reiterate the rule here that ghosts are not allowed in fair-play mysteries, and I was about ready to write off Douglas as a drunken crackpot, when he went on.

"I used to live out here. I raised cattle back home and wanted a change, and Australia seemed like the best place to use those skills. My partner, Noah, and I would watch this train go past—we could see it from our porch, and he loved it. Would check the schedules and everything. Ever since they turned it into a passenger train, I've wanted to go on it. For him. Well"—he spread his arms—"here we are. All we'd dreamed of."

"But he's not here with you, is he?" I said, though I already knew the answer. Two glasses of champagne. A solitary cheers.

"He's dead."

"I'm very sorry."

"Don't be." Douglas beamed. "That's what I'm trying to say

thank you for. I ran away when it happened. Across an ocean. And I stayed there and tried to forget it all. But today . . . I scattered his ashes. I was able to let him go. After thirty-two *years*. Because of what you've done. I am free!" He looked up at the sky and gave a semi-howl. I noticed droplets of beer clinging to strands of his beard, like dew on a rainforest fern or, less generously, the jaw of a rabid dog. Whether he was ecstatic or lunatic, it was hard to tell.

I thought back to my brief conversation with Douglas. He'd asked me what it felt like to kill someone. He wanted to know if revenge was bitter or sweet. Even given the context of my first book, those questions were particularly intense.

Hang on, I thought. What had he just said? *Because of what you've done.* Sorry to flash back to a sentence literally two paragraphs up, but it's important. Pieces clicked. Three specific events found their correlation.

Douglas had brought a gun on the trip.

Henry McTavish had died.

Douglas had disposed of the gun.

Douglas wouldn't have gone to all the effort of getting a gun just to use heroin for the murder. The only reason to dispose of the gun was if he didn't need it anymore. Which logically meant the man he'd come to kill was already dead. Was he accusing *me* of killing McTavish? Thanking me for saving him the trouble?

"I'm sorry to ask," I said, lowering my voice. "But you said it's thirty-two years you've had Noah's ashes. Your partner—how did he die?"

Douglas's eyes, without embellishment I swear, twinkled. "Oh, you are good. Why don't *you* tell it? So the scene plays better in your book. Like you're explaining it."

I took the invitation. I knew a certain tragedy had happened thirty-two years ago. "Noah was a teacher, I'm guessing."

"Not only that, but a good one. A great one. He knew his kids.

Schools out here, they're different. There's none of that faceless point and learn, it's about getting to know all the kids. Noah could tell something was wrong, but he just had a hunch and a hunch doesn't get you far—especially in the nineties if you're a gay man in the outback, let me tell you. I don't want to put into words what this man had been doing, but some people are monsters. Noah had noticed, though. A girl in his class, usually so bright and happy, had fallen quiet. He finally convinced her to tell him what was happening, and he was going to help her tell the police. I don't know how the guy found out he was about to get exposed, but he did. So he had to think of a way to shut them up. Everyone that knew about it."

A schoolteacher. An abused child. An abuser about to be exposed. Four kids and a teacher killed in a train accident.

"The bus driver," I said. "It was the bus driver. He was molesting the kids."

What had Aaron said? *Bus driver was a bit hard to ask, flat as he was.* Just like the plot of a certain book.

Douglas nodded somberly. "Parked that school bus right up on the tracks. Locked the doors. Noah's ashes are more ceremonial than real. So let me ask you this, do you think you could identify a body from that mess?"

I imagined again those tiny palms against the glass, the plume of dust charging, but this time I saw a lone shadow running from the tracks, sweat-slicked hands slipping off a locked door, as Douglas brought his hands together with a bang.

# CHAPTER 18

The bus driver's name was not Archibald Bench, by the way.

Of course, that was the first thing I googled.

Alice Springs gave me the gift of internet reception, and a freight train crunching a school bus was newsworthy enough to pop right up in a search. I found a list of the dead: four children; a teacher, Noah Witrock; and the driver, Troy Firth. Nothing in the article alluded to accusations being leveled against Troy, or anyone being directly at fault: it was a tragic accident and nothing more. But the story itself, mixed with Douglas's version of it, did hew shockingly close to the plot of *Off the Rails*, the book that Majors had accused McTavish of pinching from her. Swap the parents for the bus driver, a car for a bus, and it was essentially the same method of murder. And the same method of getting away with it.

Troy Firth, unfortunately, is not an anagram of Archie Bench no matter which way you cut it. However, you'll have thought the same thing Douglas did: it's entirely plausible that the bodies were unidentifiable or irretrievable from the crash. It would also be fair to remind you here that Henry McTavish was crippled down his left side. I don't want to lead you up the garden path, but I have already told you some people in this book go by several names. All these thoughts ran through my mind but were too slippery to connect.

Douglas left me to rejoin the dance floor. I passed through the tables. As I walked past Wyatt, he grabbed at me.

"Oi," he said, tugging at my pant leg. "I picked up Simone's scarf the other day. Think your missus left it behind. Let Simone know I've got it?"

That would be a relief to Juliette. I said as much and thanked him. He leaned over and slapped me on the back, but because he was sitting down, it was more a jab to the kidneys. He was incredibly jovial for someone whose author, and I assumed friend, had just kicked the bucket, but I reminded myself that he stood to make a lot of money from the death. He'd seemed quite unhappy with McTavish's manuscript last night when I'd overheard him in the corridor, as it wasn't a Morbund book. I suppose posthumous publicity balanced out the lower value of the content.

"I'll give it back when I see her—it'll give her one less thing to be sour about." Wyatt laughed. "Never likes to lose, that one."

"I think even Simone understands that someone dying doesn't count as losing a client," I said.

"I would pay to see you tell her that." Wyatt gestured over to one of the fire drums, where I could see Simone sitting with Wolfgang. "And she didn't come away entirely empty-handed. I gave her a consolation prize. Not that she'll be signing anyone with it." He snickered at his own joke, though I wasn't quite sure what it was. "Besides, she didn't lose out on Henry because he *died*—no, it's far more humiliating than that. She made her pitch. Screwed you over, by the way. He declined. *Then* he died. Vale and all that." Wyatt did a borderline-offensive sign of the cross that was so wobbly Jesus would need a chiropractor. "Oi!" he yelled again, but this time across me. "Jasper! Champers? Lots to celebrate." He raised his glass and spilled half of it.

Jasper had been on his way to join Harriet, whom I could see on the dance floor. Wyatt's command pulled him into our current, and he grimaced as a glass was shoved into his hand. Wyatt was clearly willing to celebrate his windfalls with anybody who passed him. Like stepping off a land mine, or Indiana Jones switching a golden idol, I sacrificed Jasper to hold Wyatt's attention and scurried off, making my way over to Simone and Wolfgang.

Wolfgang greeted me with a snarl of acknowledgment, and I couldn't quite tell if he was annoyed I was there or annoyed that he had debased himself enough to know who I was. He and Simone each had a long metal skewer, which they were using to toast marshmallows from a bowl nearby. Wolfgang was only lightly singeing his. Simone was letting hers flare into a meteor, the burned sugar dripping into the coals.

"Everyone's in a surprisingly good mood," I said. "Events of today considered."

Wolfgang de-skinned his marshmallow with his teeth. "One less hack, who's complaining?"

Simone laughed cruelly. Yes, I know it's an adverb.

"That's a little cold," I said. "I bet you've never even read him."

"I have indeed," Wolfgang huffed, to my surprise. "His very first. Drivel, of course. Grammatically haunting. Uses commas like cane toads—they multiply on every page—and he's addicted to the bloody Oxford."

I didn't want to get into a conversation with Wolfgang about bad writing, as I would surely wind up insulted, so I changed the topic. "How's your artwork coming along?"

"Artwork?"

"Yeah, your painting, or whatever. *The Death of Literature*."

Wolfgang chuckled dryly. "It's going just fine, thank you. And it's not a *painting*, it's an experience."

"That's worth staying alive until Adelaide for at least," I said.

"If you get that far." Wolfgang's lips transformed into a frown. The fire cast a long shadow of his nose down to his chin, like a slash. "This could be a dangerous journey for you. If I were in your shoes, I'd be concerned."

"Me?" My voice cracked. Was that a threat? Did he know I'd been poking around, playing detective?

His mouth split into a grin, but the type that accompanies a mean-spirited prank rather than an actual joke. "Someone's picking off bad writers. I'd lock your door."

Simone punched him on the shoulder playfully, which seemed, to me, a low amount of physical violence for her 15 percent. She caught my scowl. "Lighten up, Ern."

"It's not a nice way to be remembered, is all."

"Is it not?" Wolfgang scoffed. "You think we look on our dead with fondness? Let me give you a history lesson. The *Washington Post*'s obituary of Edgar Allan Poe said that the announcement would 'startle many, but grieve none.' And he was an *actual* genius. All you crime writers owe him your careers—you talk about Christie and Conan Doyle and forget about Poe."

I was surprised by Wolfgang's knowledge of a genre he supposedly despised, just as I had been by his reading McTavish. It actually made me like him a little more: at least he made the effort to participate in the things he wished to criticize.

He ranted on. "And I'm supposed to grieve some middle-of-the-road Scot because he sold a few books? Please. I show him enough respect to treat him with the disdain a great artist deserves. How do we measure a man? He may be odious and foul, but if his words have value, they will outlive him."

"An ethos you're attempting to live by, I see."

Wolfgang's face did a good impression of Simone's overcooked marshmallow, a sagging melt, before he raised his glass to Simone, ignoring me, and skulked off into the night.

"You're in a bad mood," Simone said, poking the coals. The tip of her silver skewer was glowing orange, flecked with the scorched sugar.

"Don't you think something's going on here?" I asked. "Everyone seems pretty glad that McTavish is dead."

"Just because everyone's glad he's dead doesn't mean someone killed him." Her eyes reflected the flames. Then they lit up of their own accord and her lips curled. "You've got reason to be happy too! You've got your book! That must be a relief."

"Speaking of the book, how does everyone know about my advance?"

Simone kept her poker face, shrugged. "Gossip?"

I knew from experience that surliness was repaid with venom from Simone, so I put it to the side and tried to capitalize on her good mood. If she was pleased I finally had something to write about, I figured she'd be open to helping me with some of the details. "Let's say this does become the book. Help me with the backstory. You worked for McTavish, right? How'd that happen?"

"I did an exchange program to the UK and was in editorial at Gemini. This was back when they were a little floundering thing, before Morbund filled their coffers, but I jumped at the opportunity for a change of scenery. Then Henry poached me to be his full-time assistant after the first Morbund took off."

"Good gig?"

"Better than working for Wyatt. Paid well, good hours. I'd say I got hit on less, but the two of them blur together." She sighed. "God, the early aughts."

"I'm sorry to hear it was so bad back then."

"Back then?" she scoffed. "It's happening *now*. So some of the really bad eggs are 'canceled,' apologize, and slink away for a while—and then they're right back selling more books than ever, on our TVs, filling stadiums. The problem is deeper than that, and every person who sits back and thinks we fixed it because I don't get slapped on the arse at work anymore is ignoring the deep-seated structural issues."

"You seem on good terms with Wyatt," I said. "And you were willing to agent McTavish."

She flicked the superheated glowing tip out of the coals and held it in the air. "It's a brave man who accuses a feminist of double standards, Ernest."

"I didn't mean—"

"I know you didn't. But you don't get to say things like that because you don't have to make those choices. Like I said, men like this go on and on. I've got to play the game as much as anyone. I figure I should take some of their money while I'm at it. *That's* feminism, if you think about it."

I found myself impressed seeing this side of Simone, a glimpse at her vulnerabilities. Her staunch pride and self-confidence had always made her seem so above everything. But I could see now the artifice of what she was doing and the sacrifice of her real self that it was: she had to look hard as nails to go toe-to-toe with people like McTavish and Wyatt.

I thought about McTavish. What had he done that he should have had his comeuppance for? I remembered Brooke's question at the panel, and the note in McTavish's room. What if Archibald Bench was a public accusation, not an attempt to impress? "Did Henry have any, shall we say, distasteful associations?" I asked.

"What do you mean by that?"

"Hate groups? That kind of thing."

"Not that I know of. Why?"

"I found the word *Reich* in some papers."

Simone chuckled. "I love that you're doing codes and puzzles: that sells books. Lots of books. Five stars for effort." She winked, as if she'd just told me something, but I wasn't sure what. "But, no, if Henry was a Nazi, he hid it very well. I couldn't say he was involved with anything like that. Pretty young women were his weakness. And he's not alone in that."

I nodded. "Majors told me McTavish had a fling with Lisa Fulton?"

"Did she now?" Simone looked around and spotted Majors, who was yelling at, of all people, Douglas Parsons in the shadow of one of the homesteads. Douglas seemed clueless, his body language defensive, his hands stretched out in an *I have no idea what you're talking about* gesture. I wondered if they knew each other. "Well, she's always had a grudge against Lisa. Since Edinburgh."

"For not backing up her plagiarism claims?"

I think this was the first time I'd ever seen Simone impressed. "Well, well, well. Maybe you do have a book on your hands. Yes. You've got that right: Majors is adamant that Lisa should have stuck up for her. She insists that Lisa withheld her support because Lisa was with Henry that night."

"So she and Henry have a dalliance, and then she doesn't write another book for twenty-odd years? Is that true?"

"I can't speak to the writing, but they were together." Simone lowered her voice. "It's hush-hush these days. But one of the things about being Henry's assistant was I had all his logins—same password for everything, by the way, so much for codes and puzzles—and I was in charge of his emails, his website. I saw the things he used to send. *Bad egg* stuff. Including to Lisa, after that night."

"Could you get back in?"

"God no. Like I'd remember the passwords. I do remember what he said though. Called her a, if I remember correctly, 'firecracker in the sack.'" She winced at the words, even as she said them. "I'm amazed I lasted as long as I did in that job, come to think of it."

"Why did you leave?"

"I was only there a year and a half. After *Knee-Deep in Trouble*, Henry's second book, sales slipped. It wasn't a great book—second books are tough—and then there was his accident. The painkillers made him fuzzy at the best of times, and I could tell the third was squeezing out of him like a kidney stone. I felt like I had to leave before Henry realized he couldn't afford an assistant anymore. Plus, you know, I saw all the stuff flying around about Majors. I preferred to work on real literature. I scraped together some savings and moved back to Melbourne to start my agency. Obviously a big mistake seeing how popular *Off the Rails* was, given he'd agreed to a contract with bonuses in it to lure me over from Gemini, but, hey"—she pinched my cheek—"I've got you now, don't I?"

"But you still felt he owed you, that's why you wanted him as a client?"

Simone laughed. "You sure do read into things. No, not exactly. I told you the reasons I wanted Henry. He's worth a lot of money—I wanted some. But, sure, maybe subconsciously I thought he owed me a little for the year and a half I spent putting up with him."

"And your opportunity was that Wyatt wasn't happy with McTavish's next book? One wanted to end the series and the other wanted to keep it going. That was the friction between them. Without an agent, I assume Wyatt controls things like film rights and merchandising, and the other stuff that a publisher doesn't usually have their fingers in. That's big money. McTavish was worth more to Wyatt than just book sales."

"Very good," she affirmed. "You have been working hard."

"How'd you feel when Henry declined your offer?"

I thought she was about to skewer me, but she impaled another marshmallow instead. "Where'd you hear that?"

"Gossip."

She sucked her cheeks in. "So. I'm in it?"

"In what?"

"The book."

"I guess."

"You're making me a suspect?"

"Depends on how you felt about Henry's rejection."

"Oh, come on. That's thin. Besides, you can't be that indignant about how everyone's behaving here and not check yourself. As if you aren't a little grateful. A little bit more secure in the inspiration for your next book. It's fallen right in your lap. These murders are *exactly* what you needed. Pretty lucky, huh?" She did a little curtsy. "You're welcome."

"You're welcome?" I repeated. It seemed an odd thing to say.

"For forcing you out of your comfort zone. *You're welcome.*" This time she said it with the slow-motion cadence that people use when they feel they are underthanked, stretching the words like chewing gum.

"You haven't answered my question," I said.

A roar of good cheer sounded from the book club table and Simone turned their way. She gazed at them awhile, then turned back to me. "Here's the truth. People like Henry and, hell, Alan Royce— they think they're the only ones. Truth of it is, there're plenty of people hungrier than they are these days, waiting in the wings. So what if I didn't get Henry to sign on the dotted line? There'll be another Henry. There'll be another *you.* And despite what Wolfgang thinks, there'll be another Wolfgang. And he's got all the prizes in the world, but I've seen his royalty statements." She held up her thumb and forefinger, a tiny space between, like locker room talk. "Now, what I *would* kill for"—she pointed at the book club—"is one of those Erica Mathison books. I *know* it's another first-name last-name book, but those numbers . . ." She whistled. "Wyatt's gotta be happy with that."

"First-name last-name book?" I asked, confused.

"You know, you put the full name of the character in the title?

Put a number next to it too, if you want to get real flashy. It's the trendy thing right now. *The Eleven Orgasms of Deborah Winstock*, *The Five Lives of Erin O'Leary*, *The Four Cousins of Barbara Who-Gives-a-Toss*. They're everywhere. You should consider it for whatever this"—she spun a finger at me—"turns out to be."

"I'll think about it." I saw Juliette at last, over by the camel rides, talking to Harriet. "I've just spotted Juliette, if you'll excuse me. Oh, and Wyatt has your blue scarf. He'll give it back to you. Thanks for the chat."

Simone grabbed my arm as I turned to leave, squeezing it just a little too tightly. "You're onto a good thing here, Ern, and it's great to see you thinking and writing again. I'm proud of you. I am. And I want you to write this book. But just, you know, leave me out of it, would you?"

It felt like a demand rather than a favor. I nodded, more out of obligation than agreement, but it seemed to please her.

"Attaboy. Also, if this is going to be a book, you'll need to spice it up a little. It doesn't *all* have to be true. Chuck in some romance. I've got that list you gave me on your structure. It seems the trip's been following it pretty well so far. Setting up all the suspects and their motives is great, but you probably need a little *action*." I was surprised she'd even kept my rambling note, let alone was taking it seriously. Her eyes shone with excitement. "What you need, my friend, is a second murder."

She wasn't wrong. We are not too far from the sixty-thousand-word mark, which means I am due another body. Not that the real world is beholden to my schematic for writing fiction, but it had, up until now, felt like it was sticking to my desires for this book a little too closely. I chalked it up to cosmic luck.

I turned over Simone's words in my mind as I waved at Juliette. The box in my pocket rubbed against my leg. I couldn't summon up another body—in fact, I'd much rather have prevented it—but romance I could do.

Simone had been surprisingly candid; I felt I'd learned a lot about McTavish. What I wouldn't know until later was that she had just lied to me. Twice.

The Two Mistruths of Simone Morrison, if you will.

# CHAPTER 19

*Romance I can do.*

I chanted it like a mantra in my head as I marched up to Juliette, until I realized I was so determined that I was literally marching. I tried to turn it into a more casual saunter but just ended up making myself wobbly enough to look saddle-sore.

"Had a few?" Juliette chuckled.

"I spy my husband actually," Harriet said, in a way that meant she knew we'd argued recently. "Better stop him before he goes the same way." It was a tactful exit, swiftly made.

That left Juliette and me alone. She'd taken the dress code seriously and looked beautiful in a knee-length orange dress. It was creaseless, carefully hung. We were under the clearest starlit sky I'd ever seen, partway through one of the world's great rail journeys, in the middle of a natural wonder of a desert. It should have been perfect. Instead, the remnants of our argument hung over us, brighter than the stars. Despite our day at the ravine, I still had yet to actually *say* I was sorry. I wished I had some marshmallows to keep my hands busy.

"Hey," I said.

"Hey."

Fair enough. She wanted me to earn it.

"What were you talking about?" I nodded back to Harriet.

"Men."

"Oh. Good things?"

As any shacked-up men reading this will know, sometimes your questions answer themselves.

"I'm sorry if I got carried away," I said.

She took a deep breath. "If?"

I tried again. "I'm sorry. I got a little carried away."

"That'll do." She smiled, took my hand. Tilted her head back. I followed her lead and we stood for a while, side by side, looking into the night. "And I didn't mean to be so negative. I'm glad you're excited. I'm glad you've got the potential for another book. But I also want you to be here with me. If you spend too much time looking for clues, you'll miss the stars."

"What if the stars are the clues?" I asked.

"You're right. Sagittarius did it."

I didn't know which set of stars was Sagittarius, but I searched for a moment anyway. "I love you, you know that?"

"I do. I love you too."

My hand felt for the box in my pocket, massaging it through the fabric. "I'm thinking we could spend more time together."

"This is a nice start." She thought I was still apologizing for running off and playing detective.

"I meant every day."

"We're stuck on a train together. I think we'll get a lot of each other."

"Well, we haven't seen all that much of one another in the first half of the trip."

"And whose fault is that?"

"I wasn't talking about . . . Look, I'm trying to say something else. I'd do anything for you."

"And I'd do anything for you, Ernest. Are you feeling okay?"

"You're my blip."

She looked down from the stars and sized me up. "What the hell are you talking about?"

I dropped to one knee. Whether that's because I didn't know what else to do or because it was going so badly my balance gave out is still with the jury.

"Oh my God," she said.

"I know we haven't really made the most of this trip. I've been distracted and we haven't seen a lot of each other. I couldn't join you on the gorge excursion, and then I stayed up while you went to bed early . . ." I paused. I'd had a thought.

"This is a pretty long prologue for a man who doesn't like them," Juliette said.

"Did you go straight to bed last night?"

Her mouth formed wordless circles for a few seconds. "Is that the question you got down on one knee to ask me?"

"No, spur of the moment. It's just, when you say you'd do *anything* for me—"

"Oh my God." This was a very different *oh my God* from her first. "Are you . . . *interrogating* me?"

"No. Sorry, I want to ask—"

"I don't care about what you want to ask, I care about what you did ask. You're checking my alibi?"

"It just popped into my head."

"Did it." It wasn't a question.

People over at the dining tables had noticed I was down on one knee. I could tell they were starting to turn and watch; too far away to hear our words, it looked like it was going better than it was, and they clutched together in groups of excitement. Whispers carried on the wind, sounding like waves breaking on the shore.

Okay, look. I'm not proud of what's about to happen. But

I promised you the truth, stupidity and all, so I've resisted the urge to edit myself into a more, shall we say, debonair position.

"I'm not seriously a suspect?" Juliette said.

"I mean, everyone's a suspect."

"Are you?"

"Well . . . no."

"Why not?"

"I'm the narrator."

She went to throw her hands up but then realized too that everyone was watching us, and instead held them with quivering restraint by her sides as she pulled on a fake smile. She spoke behind her teeth. "That's bullshit and you know it. Just because you're writing it down doesn't give you a special pass. This is real life: it doesn't follow the *rules* of a detective novel. You waltz around like you're invincible, and it's going to get you killed. Royce is writing it down too, genius, I bet he's not the villain in his book."

"I'm just asking questions. This case is important."

"Case? *Case?!* You're not a detective, Ern." She shook her head. "I knew I shouldn't have come." Tears splashed down her cheeks and she wiped them frantically with the back of her hand. Annoyingly, this got a cheer from one enthusiastic member of the crowd who mistook it for happiness. A camera flash went off.

"You didn't want to come?" I asked, surprised by how much that hurt.

"I don't know how to explain this to you. You'd been in a funk ever since the murders. I get it, I do. And you thought this book you wrote defined you, gave some kind of meaning to what happened. You defined yourself so much through it. I thought it would give you a bit of confidence back, coming here. And you don't even take five *seconds* out of your day to appreciate it."

"Appreciate what?"

"*You* weren't invited on this festival, Ern. I was."

It was as if the stars had been shut off. My vision started getting blurry, dark. My conversation with Majors flashed through my mind: the way she looked when I thanked her for the invite; *I didn't invite you.* "But Majors—"

"Invited *me*. A bit of quid pro quo for the endorsement she wanted. I said no, and suggested you instead. I thought you needed it, I thought it would help you feel valued. And instead, I've been relegated to a bit part in the Ernest Cunningham Show, like I'm a side character in my own story. You keep saying I'm waiting on my next adventure, but when have I ever told you that? I might like to open up a new resort. I might like to write another book. But you've never asked, because we're always talking about you. And I *know* that what you went through broke you, and I know it's been hard to work through. But *my* home burned down last year. I lost *my* livelihood. And yet I still gave this invite to you. I'm not twiddling my thumbs 'waiting on my next adventure,' I'm waiting for *you*. But now I see that this might be all I am to you. Just a part of your story." She took a breath. "That scares me."

"I'm sorry," I said, simply because I didn't know what else to say. I'd never even been invited on the trip. She'd made this huge, unspoken gesture for me and this was how I'd been treating her? Shame sat hot in my stomach. My knee was feeling the hardness of the dirt. The murmur of the crowd was growing; they were starting to think it was the longest proposal they'd ever seen. Proposing is the opposite of sex in terms of desired durations: the faster the better.

"It's too late for sorry," Juliette said. "You thought I did it."

"I didn't—"

"Even for a second. Even that it crossed your mind. That's enough." She sniffed. "Humor me. Why would I have done it?"

Now, it is a great virtue to understand when a question is rhetorical. This is a virtue, I've learned, that I do not possess.

I should have left it.

I definitely should *not* have listened to Simone's voice in my head: *As if you aren't a little grateful . . . It's fallen right in your lap.*

"You might have wanted to help me . . ." You're willing me to stop, but unfortunately, I do not. It sounds just as stupid now as it did then. ". . . write the book."

She looked at me like I was a waiter who'd gotten her order wrong. "You think that's motive for murder?"

I don't know why my mouth was still moving. I winced as I said it. "And he gave me that bad review."

"That is some really outdated sexist shit, Ern. Not all women kill just because their boyfriend's pride gets a little dented." Now she was laughing. "*I* murdered Henry McTavish because *you* got a bad review. Wow. You really do think this is your story."

"Please, Juliette," I took a deep breath. "I'm sorry. I wasn't thinking. I was nervous. My tongue has a mind of its own. Please. Just let me start again."

I pulled the box from my pocket, opened it and held up the ring.

The crowd cheered.

# CHAPTER 20

She said no.

# CHAPTER 21

It's a little more complicated than that.

In terms of dud proposals, accusing your girlfriend of murder partway through has got to be an all-time clanger. I said before that *only an idiot* would accuse Juliette of being the murderer. *This* idiot, as it turns out.

"I'm going home," she said. I was still on one knee, the ring in the air. My hamstrings were straining; I hadn't planned on being down for this long. Tip for anyone proposing: do some squats first.

"What? Now? You can't just leave."

"It's not a school excursion. I can do what I like."

"But the train—"

"I'll get a motel tonight, fly home tomorrow."

"Please."

"It's not a *no* no. It's just a not now."

"Not now," I echoed. "When?"

"You've got a lot of things to figure out between here and Adelaide. And I'm not talking about a murder. Once you know whose story this is. That's when. But now"—she grabbed my hand

and pulled me up—"let's save ourselves some embarrassment. Everyone's watching. We should give 'em a show."

She kissed me, and there were whoops and hollers and camera flashes and her lips were cold and dry and pressed against mine flatly as if we were posing for the paparazzi. She even put her hips into it, kicking a heel into the air.

Writing this out now—that kiss frozen in time thanks to both these words and the photo Lisa Fulton emailed me before she . . . well, we'll get to that—I am once again considering Juliette's question: whose story is this?

It's no spoiler to tell you that I'm writing this all down because the guilty have been discovered and dealt with. This leads to the cardinal rule I keep sticking to so doggedly, that because this is in first person, I have survived the events of the story. But just because I'm writing it doesn't mean the story's mine, or that it's over. I could write this sentence, for example, just as someone kicks in the door to my Adelaide hotel room and puts a bullet in my brain. It's not the writing that tells the story, it's the reading.

Words on a page aren't a legacy until they're read.

So what if I'm writing this down and the story is still going?

I was subjected to a carnival of backslapping on my search for a drink, only to find an oasis in Jasper Murdoch, holding a glass of champagne out to me like those hooks that catch fighter jets on aircraft carriers. If he thought it was strange that I was toasting on my own, he was too polite to say it.

"I think we're sharing congratulations," he said as I necked the glass and plonked myself down at his table. He misread my dejection and refilled my glass. "Mate, I get it. I remember when I proposed to Harriet. Felt like I'd run a marathon."

"Doesn't get any easier the second time around," I said.

"Oh." He hadn't known about my previous marriage, which also meant my last book was on his bedside table, unopened. He blushed slightly, then offered, "Surely easier than divorce."

I raised my glass sarcastically. The champagne was going straight to my head. "Cheers to small achievements, I suppose. You're better at romance than I am. I saw the petals by your door the other night. That was your room, right, next to Wyatt? Smooth moves."

"Except it gave Wyatt the sniffles." Jasper laughed. "That's all Harriet anyway." He put on her Irish lilt. "*Brighten the space.*"

I examined him. "How do you do it?"

"Do what?"

"Not take it all so seriously."

Jasper sighed. "Is this still about Henry?"

"If I said it wasn't, would you believe me?"

He tilted his head in acknowledgment. "Writers are normally better liars than you are."

"I'm quickly learning."

"Bad reviews are part of being a writer. We all get them. I got one once, wrote to the reviewer. Then I married her."

"No way! Harriet?"

"Yeah, she was an arts journo, way back." He nodded. "Look, there's no secret to it. Do you write this stuff for people to read, for people to enjoy or to have your name in lights? That's all it comes down to."

I'd been emboldened by my chat with Majors to try a psychological profile of my own. This train was jostling with egos and blurbs and legacies, and Jasper seemed too nonchalant about being *known* among it all. Harriet clearly disagreed. But maybe it wasn't humility. Maybe it was necessity. I remembered Wyatt, whom I'd barely seen crack a smile this whole trip, wanting a celebratory drink with him, and this bolstered my confidence in my deduction.

"That's easy for someone to say who doesn't have their name on their covers," I said.

Jasper's smile had fallen so far he had to retrieve it. Eventually he mumbled out, "I don't know what you're talking about."

"Of course you don't." I winked.

I saw Jasper wrestle with it, and then accept my discovery. "Just don't tell anyone. I'm serious. It's only worth anything because no one knows."

This is far from my finest deduction. Veronica had a personalized signature in her copy: *To V!* A copy that I knew had been bought in Darwin, at the beginning of the train ride. It could only have been signed in the last three days. There was no other solution: Erica Mathison was on the train.

"You are killing it," I said. "No wonder Wyatt was smiling. You were here to hash out a new deal. Seems you've got something to celebrate?"

"Me? Yeah. Harriet? She'll come around." He read my expression. "She's happy for me, of course. She'd rather I publish under my own name."

I remembered them arguing about money. It made sense now: Harriet was disappointed that he was just doing it for the money. She wanted him to do it for himself, and she'd been trying to convince him it didn't matter if they took a hit financially. She wanted him on the other side of those panels they'd come here to watch.

"But I have been published as myself. It's not all it's cracked up to be. And I'm happy, especially if Wyatt keeps doubling my advance. Sometimes I think it might be nice . . ." I realized he was staring across the yard, where Harriet was dancing in the dust, arms above her head, swaying in the throes of the music. "Then again, I've got better things to put my name on." He pointed at her. "That right there, that's what you've got to look forward to. We're trying to adopt.

My name there, handed down to their kids and so on, that's going to outlast any book."

"Yeah," I muttered, staring at my shoes.

He turned back to me. "It's nice to have someone else to talk to about this for once."

"Seeing as we're being honest, I think I might have stuffed things up with Juliette."

"That's gotta be a record. You got engaged twenty minutes ago."

"I guess I'm a better liar than you think I am."

"Why the hell are you sitting here drinking with me, then?"

I stood up. "That is an excellent point." I extended a hand and put on a toffy formal accent. "It's been a pleasure to meet you, Ms. Mathison."

He laughed, great relief in his voice. His secret out, the burden gone. He squeezed my hand, mimicked my poshness. "I prefer Jasper Murdoch, if you please."

# CHAPTER 22

You'll have to read Erica Mathison if you want a race to the airport and a romantic climax (plus a tryst in the toilets, if those types of books are anything to go by), because not ten minutes after I'd left Jasper, we were all being shepherded onto the buses headed back to the Ghan. I was told Juliette had already gotten a taxi from the homestead into town. She wasn't answering her phone; I tried the whole ride back. On the platform, Aaron looked nervously at his watch, sucked his teeth and said, "I'm sorry, sir, she asked me not to tell you where she was going. We leave in five minutes."

I looked around the platform, hoping Juliette might suddenly appear, mind changed. I noticed there were no police cars in the lot anymore.

"Are any officers joining us for the second half of the journey?"

Aaron seemed surprised. "No. Why would they?"

"Protection?"

"What would they be protecting us from? They've taken the body, and you and your pal said yourselves there's no foul play. Listen, I know it's been a tough night. But you're either on the train or you're staying here."

The lights of the township cast a dim halo into the night. My vision for what this trip could be had crumbled: it was all a dream. It was a choice between the train and door-knocking every Alice Springs motel room until dawn.

Writing this all out in hindsight, it's so easy to see I've gotten a few things wrong so far, both deductive and emotional, and here's another one.

I chose the train.

# CHAPTER 23

The first thing I did back on board was commit a crime.

Theft, specifically. Everyone was in a good mood from the food and the grog and most were kicking on in the bar carriage. Douglas asked Cynthia to make him a cup of tea, complaining that the binned kettle in the hallway was of no use. I made my way there for a drink too, intending to drown—no, that wasn't severe enough, waterboard—my sorrows. However, as I walked in I saw Alan Royce, legs splayed the way stockbrokers sit on public transport, and I pinwheeled immediately back into the corridor. It wasn't that I was avoiding Royce, it was that he'd changed his clothes.

The Ghan has limited locks on the doors, remember, and so I swiftly ducked into Royce's room. Sure enough, he remained allergic to putting things away: his crumpled jacket from this afternoon lay on the bed. On the ground, piled like they'd been literally stepped out of, were his trousers. Jackpot.

I know. It's not a nice thing to do, even to a man like Royce. But I think, after the events of this book are all printed, he won't really be in a position to press charges over something so small as burglary. Not after what he did.

Afterward, I meandered my way through the carriages down to the back of the train, where there was an outdoor smoking deck. It was tiny, suitable for three or four people at most, with a wrought-iron fence to stop guests tumbling off the back, and a small awning. The clanking of the train was loud here, mechanical and foreign against the quiet of the desert night. The symmetrical tracks whizzed out from under the carriage, our journey perfectly measured by their line, meter on meter unveiled as we picked up speed. I watched Alice Springs, and everything in it, fade into the distance.

Then I unfolded the piece of paper I'd taken from Royce's pocket. The one he'd secreted away while searching McTavish's room. It was a check. Well, half a check. It had been burned, starting in the bottom right corner, the flame devouring all the identifying details except the bank's header and the amount: $25,000. I recalled the ash on McTavish's floor and my assumption that he'd flouted the no-smoking rule. This is one of the places where I had been wrong.

The door opened behind me and I stuffed the check back in my pocket as I turned to see Lisa Fulton. She was wearing a floor-length sapphire-blue evening gown, which was almost too fancy for the *formal evening* dress code on the itinerary. The hem had been splashed up with dirt and dust from the farmyard, and she had a slight bruise just above the elbow on her right arm, which was enough to make me glad I'd skipped the rowdy dance floor.

"Congratulations," she said, sheltering a cigarette from the wind and flicking a lighter.

It took me a second to deduce what she was congratulating me for. I could still see the dim glow of Alice Springs retreating behind us.

"Thank you, we're so happy."

"Happy enough that you're traveling on your own?"

I thought I'd have a little more time before people noticed Juliette hadn't boarded the train with me. I tried to think of a fast excuse. "It's all a bit ad hoc. We thought we might do it quickly. Like, next weekend quickly. Lots to organize." Lisa didn't look like she bought it, so, as with all teetering lies, I simply built it up. "Besides"— I laughed—"a few too many dead bodies for her ideal holiday."

"Weak. There's only one."

"Surely one's enough."

"Depends where you holiday. I took a photo of you proposing, by the way. Give me your email and I'll flick it to you while we still have reception." I obliged, and a minute later, the reception growing more sluggish as we moved, my phone dinged. The photo looked properly romantic to the unknowing—starry night, the glow of the marshmallow fires—but all I could see was the strain in my jaw. The glisten in Juliette's eyes.

"It's very . . ." I hunted for the word, shot it out of the sky. "Memorable. Thank you."

"You're welcome. Now, what's this I hear about you and Alan thinking Henry's death was suspicious?"

This was much more comfortable ground for me. "I think the circumstances invite a certain level of inquiry. And I think a lot of people had reasons to dislike McTavish."

"A lot of people?"

"Well, everyone."

She turned away from the tracks and sized me up. "Me?"

I hesitated. "I heard McTavish was an old flame."

Her hands kneaded the grate. "More a candle than a bonfire. It was very short-lived."

"You left an impression on him, though—he gave you that blurb. And you were the only one to skip his panel the next morning."

"It's all been a bit overwhelming." She sighed. "Anyway, I'm glad I sat it out."

"It was gruesome. You're lucky you missed it."

"Good research, I suppose."

"I wish people would stop saying that."

She was fiddling with the filter of her cigarette now, clearly uncomfortable, but she hadn't yet left. It was like she wanted me to ask her something. Like Jasper's truth: desperate, in a way, to get out. Or she wanted to see how much I knew. I was happy to play that game.

"Royce heard you in McTavish's room last night."

Lisa snorted. "Royce is a drunk."

"So you weren't in his room? Majors I doubt he'd let in. Harriet's got an Irish accent, Cynthia and Brooke are too young, and Simone's too loud. I have a feeling even an inebriated Royce hasn't mixed up all those voices."

She was silent.

I took the burned check out of my pocket and showed it to her. "I wonder if this is about enough to buy an endorsement?"

Lisa laughed it off, but I could tell she was a little surprised. "If you think I'm earning enough from book sales to ladle out twenty-five grand on a blurb, you are barking. Besides, that amount wouldn't even flutter Henry's heart."

"Maybe there's other ways to pay."

She made a sour face. "You got that from Royce, didn't you?"

I stared at the tracks. I had indeed recycled that from Royce, and it felt nasty on my tongue even as I said it. "Yeah, I'm sorry. That's not me. You want to tell me something though, that's why you followed me out here. And you're the first person to practically ask me to question them. Maybe I'm asking the wrong questions. What is it you want to tell me?"

This was a better tactic. She took a deep breath. "I didn't kill him," she said. "But tomorrow you're going to think I did. And I guess I just wanted to say that to somebody. I assume you're writing this down for a book. Will you put it in, exactly like that?"

"What's going to happen tomorrow?"

"That would be the wrong question."

"But you were in his room?"

"If it'll make you happy, yes, I went there to thank him—*with words*—for his endorsement. Royce was bashing on the door so I had to stay there until the two of you left. That's it."

I considered for a second. "You didn't hit him? There were bloodied tissues in the bin."

"No."

"Let me pose a scenario. You go to his room to thank him for the endorsement, with words." She nodded. "But maybe words aren't enough. Maybe McTavish wants a different sort of thanks. We all know what he was like. Maybe he grabs you by the arm, firmly enough to leave a bruise, right there, just above the elbow. Maybe you crack him in the nose. It's not murder. So why hide it? Am I close?"

She turned to go. I reached out to her but stopped myself. I didn't want to be the man who grabbed at women. "I believe you," I said. That turned her on her own. "McTavish was a sleaze. Whatever you're worried about tomorrow, maybe we can get ahead of it? Help each other?"

She didn't answer, but I could tell she was grinding her teeth by the wriggle in her cheek.

"You've got legal expertise—that actually might come in handy."

That cracked a glimmer of teeth. An almost smile. "Is that what you've been doing? Royce on forensics? Majors on profiling? Me on law? Wolfgang on, what, being an asshole? All our specialties combined into one super detective? Like a Mighty Morphin Power Ranger?"

I blushed. "Sounds stupid when you put it like that."

"It is stupid. We're writers. I haven't practiced law in . . . Hang on, what's Majors's profile of me, exactly?"

"Jilted lover," I said.

Don't worry, your memory's not dodgy and you haven't skipped any pages. Majors hadn't given me a profile of Lisa. I thought I could provoke a reaction if I made one up. It worked.

"Selfish piece of—" Lisa seethed. "Don't listen to her. She's got it in for me."

"Why didn't you back her up about Edinburgh?"

Lisa was so incensed, she had forgotten I was probing. "I couldn't, and she knows that. Jeez. It's not like she was on the witness stand. A year later when *Off the Rails* comes out"—she snapped her fingers—"suddenly it's my problem. This is ridiculous." She looked back at me. "I didn't kill Henry. People only kill for one reason: love. I didn't love him. Far from it."

"People kill for two reasons," I said. "Love and money."

She shook her head. "Maybe people kill for the love *of* money. But it all comes down to love." She opened the door. The warm light of the carriages spilled onto the deck and gave us a better view of the tracks rushing under us. "Hell, like you say, everyone's got a motive. Maybe everyone did it."

"I think that's been done before."

"Nothing beats a classic." She closed the door behind her.

# CHAPTER 24

It would be a cliché and untrue to say my bed felt empty without Juliette, seeing as it was a bunk bed.

But there was something missing all the same. She'd left in such a hurry, or was so keen to avoid me, that she hadn't come back on the train to collect her things. Her clothes still hung on the hangers, her toothbrush still by the sink. The cabin felt deserted in both senses of the word.

I procrastinated before bed, neatly folding her clothes and zipping up the bag, laying it on the top bunk. I resisted the urge to check the pockets for any small vials. I wanted to, but her words hung heavy in my mind—*Even for a second. Even that it crossed your mind. That's enough.*

My phone's reception had continued to deteriorate, and by this point clung to a thread. I sent a text to Juliette. And an email. And another text.

Then I tried to squeeze some backstory googling in. I know, it's lazy detecting. But cut me some slack. Mystery writers these days always have to find a way to take away their crime-solvers' phones because otherwise the reader sits there the whole time thinking,

*Google it!* My Golden Age compatriots didn't have to work around this, there was no *Oh no, Sherlock Holmes can't access his* Encyclopaedia Britannicas *because someone lost the key to the library!*

I started, because I was losing faith in Royce's medical pedigree, with the symptoms of heroin overdoses. Google begrudgingly (or perhaps that was just me) confirmed the symptoms in Royce's favor. Next I searched for "Henry McTavish limp," which didn't get me much (except for reviews of his second book, his worst received, where *limp* was used adjectivally), and then for details of his accident, which proved more fruitful. An image of an unrecognizable, purple-faced and heavily bandaged McTavish shuddered onto my phone screen like it was an incoming fax. Surgeons had to almost entirely re-skin his leg. This was in 2004, between the publication of his second and third novels. How had Simone put his writing of the third novel? *Kidney stones.* Recovering from an accident like that, though, no wonder it had been tough.

Still nothing from Juliette. I began to wonder if I was in internet range but not messaging reception—I'm not really sure if that theory holds up technologically, but it succeeded in making me feel momentarily better until my phone dinged and disproved it. Disappointingly, it was a text from Andy.

"*I've got my list of suspects. Statistically speaking, it's most likely to be the ex-husband.*"

I sent one back: "*Yes, that sounds reasonable. Jealousy. Anger. All good motives.*"

Andy messaged quickly. "*Great. Problem is she doesn't have an ex-husband. She does have a husband though.*"

I replied: "*If she doesn't have an ex-husband, why is one on your list of suspects?*"

There was a pause while Andy, bless him, tried to think.

"*Apparently it's likely,*" he replied.

I texted: "*Apparently?*"

"*I fed in all the details here*"—he sent me a link—"*and that's the most probable.*"

I clicked the link, which took me to ChatGPT, the open-source AI software that had taken the world by storm, much to the consternation of universities everywhere whose students were using it to write their essays. While it was indeed an impressive piece of software, it was quite a scary proposition for both those whose careers were typing words and those who'd seen *The Terminator*. You could put anything to it, and it would spit you out a response, from "Write me a five-hundred-word essay on ancient Egypt" to, in Andy's case, writing the bio on his website or "Who robbed the old lady's flower shop?" Of course Andy was into AI; he's able to maintain a straight face while using the word *fungible*, plus he can declare that crypto is the future while arguing he's been shortchanged coins at a café. I was tempted to type in "How do I call my uncle an idiot but make it sound constructive?" But I didn't think AI would have the plethora of curse words I required.

I texted him back: "*AI is no replacement for the human brain, Andy. But humor me. What are Skynet's other suspects?*"

The good thing about insulting Andy is that sometimes all you have to do is set him up to do it to himself. He replied: "*Undercover FBI agent . . . And then a satanic death cult.*"

There was a pause, then Andy texted again. "*Okay, point taken. Night.*"

My internet lagged out, then blipped in. I turned my attention back to my research. This time I went to the Morbund's Mongrels forum on Reddit. The most recent post was titled *The Dawn Rises—Spoiler Discussion*. I had half expected the news of McTavish's death to break, but evidently it hadn't filtered out yet.

I scrolled through the thread. People were discussing the latest release, and many were anguished about the end of Detective Morbund. One post drew my attention:

*MongrelWrangler22 (admin):*

*Oh no, you guys. Morbund is my LIFE. I'm actually literally lying here screaming. I'll have to get another copy, because this one's stained with tears. If this is the end . . . I don't know what I'll do . . .*

The user was an administrator, which would fit someone involved with the Mongrels in an organizational role: president, perhaps. It did sound an awful lot like Brooke to me. I scrolled through the replies, a mix of commiserating with MongrelWrangler22, outright denials that Morbund could be dead and one alarming post saying *All we need to do is get to McTavish. I'm sure we can . . . convince him . . . with the right motivation,* next to a little emoji of a hammer.

I got tired of the deluge of comments and instead clicked on MongrelWrangler22's profile. The avatar was a cartoon version of Morbund himself, I assumed, given his rugged Scottish appearance, and the location was listed as Australia, but other than that it was anonymous. All of MongrelWrangler22's recent comments were neatly listed below though. I clicked one at random:

*Can I just say something? I love these books because I feel like he's speaking to me. You know? Like they are written just for me. A bedtime story or a special treat. I know you guys all love the books as much as I do, but that's how it feels when I'm reading them. Like it's me and him. Let me know why you read the Morbund books. Would love to hear from everyone else* ☺

What had Majors said about obsession? That it's the ability to center another's experience on yourself? This matched it to a T.

I clicked back to MongrelWrangler22's profile page and opened the most recent comment, just to see if it mentioned the Ghan. The comment had been posted three days ago in the *Dawn Rises— Spoiler Discussion* thread:

*Stand down. I repeat. Stand down. I can breathe again.*

**Archie fucking Bench!**

The comments that followed were variations of *Who's Archie Bench?* and *I don't get it, what's the big deal?* but MongrelWrangler22 hadn't posted since then. Conveniently, the timing of the post fit neatly with stepping onto an outback train with limited phone reception. I couldn't see how it would be anyone *but* Brooke.

*Stand down.* Was that a figure of speech, or literal? Everything's literal on the internet these days, like literally everything, so it was hard to tell. Stand down from what?

On a whim, I tried "Wolfgang art project." But the search was too vague, and I was subjected to pages and pages about his namesake: the famous Austrian musician. I wondered if Wolfgang spoke German, and if he could help me with *Reich.* Next I tried all combinations of Wolfgang's name and the words *writer, art, interactive* and *experience.* All I got were hits like this very festival, with the same line repeated at the end of every bio: *His next project is an interactive art project titled* The Death of Literature.

A fleeting thought whisked across my mind—*Just how interactive is your project, Wolfgang?*—and was gone.

My phone was struggling. I typed in one last Hail Mary search, which took five minutes to load and so I knew it was the last bit of twenty-first-century help I was going to get. But this one wasn't clue-hunting, it was simply pure curiosity. The article was from the *New York Times* in 2009 and was titled "Crime Debutant Jasper Murdoch Can't Match It with Crime Fiction's Best" by Harriet Sykes, freelance writer from Melbourne, Australia.

Honestly, on reading it, I was surprised he'd married her. It was an absolute pasting. Although the review didn't have too much to say about the book, it was dogged in comparing Jasper to the literary heavyweights of the genre—career authors, multimillionaires. Harriet couldn't quite accept that he wasn't up to their level, and she razed him for it. *Murdoch wishes he could write like McTavish, and there are glimmers of potential in his work, but alas, he falls short of the high mark set by the Scottish favorite.*

No wonder Jasper didn't write crime anymore. But I remembered the look in his eyes as he'd watched Harriet dance. If this review had led them to cross paths (I imagined him plucking up the courage to write this reviewer an email, perhaps offering a coffee so he could explain what he was trying to do with the novel, or maybe downing half a bottle of white wine and cavalcading in with a thesaurus's worth of inventive and invented curse words), he probably didn't mind it one bit. I reread it through the lens of Jasper's hippie zen-ness and it didn't sound so cruel. On scrolling, I also saw Harriet was the writer of McTavish's oft-used *NYT* blurb—"unputdownable and unbeatable: McTavish is peerless"— pulled from a review of his fifth novel in 2006.

I sent another text to Juliette and was momentarily excited by the immediate ding in return, until I realized it was a red exclamation mark claiming the message could not be sent.

I put the phone away and shut my eyes. But Jasper's voice stayed inside my head. Except now he was saying something else: *especially if Wyatt keeps doubling my advance.* I remembered Wyatt on the phone at the station. Trying to authorize a deal term, perhaps?

It had glanced off my notice at first; I'd assumed Jasper's new deal was for an Erica Mathison book. But if this review held weight, if Jasper's writing really was Dollar Store McTavish, then his own fiction would always be just an imitation. Even the success of *The Eleven Orgasms of Deborah Winstock* wouldn't have papered over that feeling, that he was a wannabe relegated to a permanent second place behind a better author. One way to beat the comparison, perhaps, was to remove it entirely.

I fell asleep thinking two things:

Henry McTavish hadn't wanted to keep writing the Detective Morbund books.

And perhaps, to Wyatt Lloyd, McTavish-lite was better than no McTavish at all.

# CHAPTER 25

I had no idea how long I'd been asleep, but I knew from the bashing on the door whose inelegant fist the knock belonged to, so I wasn't all that surprised to see Royce standing in the corridor. What did surprise me was the line of people behind him.

"Come on," was all he said, shuffling off to assault the next door before I'd had a chance to wipe the sleep from my eyes. He kept moving along the line, like a prison warden waking inmates.

I slid into the conga line between Simone and Wolfgang. Everyone was in pajamas: I was decent in a faded band T-shirt and tracksuit pants; Simone wore a matching purple silk shirt and trousers, *SM* embroidered on the breast pocket; and Wolfgang, most surprisingly, was in full-length blue-and-white-striped flannel pajamas. I'd assumed he slept in a three-piece suit. S. F. Majors was behind Wolfgang, still in the finery she'd worn to dinner, which meant she had either taken the time to get dressed or not yet gone to bed. We shuffled along to the next door. I checked the time: three A.M.

I tapped Simone on the shoulder. "What's going on?"

"Royce has solved it," she whispered. "Wants us all in the bar carriage."

"What?" If I'd had a drink, I would have spat it out. "*Royce?*"

"It's not like you didn't have enough chances. Damn it, Ernest, you were supposed to get there first."

"Well, what's all this then?"

"Don't be bitter. You know you've got to get all the suspects together to do the grand reveal. That's what you'd do, isn't it?"

"I know how a denouement works," I said, sulking.

"De-noo-moh," Wolfgang said from behind me, ladling the French over my mispronunciation like syrup. "Not dee-now-ment."

"Merci," I growled, refusing to turn and face him. Up ahead, Lisa slid out of her room, closing the door quickly behind her lest anyone see inside, and joined the line.

A heavy hand clapped me on the shoulder. Wolfgang again. I couldn't see his face, but I could feel his grin burning into the back of my neck.

"Looks like he beat you to it, old chap. Your book will be second fiddle now."

Royce's audience was both sleepier and smaller than he'd anticipated. We slumped over the chairs and couches while Royce stood by the bar, pulling on his suspenders and doing a head count. The writers were all there, though not many others—only Harriet, who must have been roused by the procession past their room (I imagined a scissors-paper-rock between Harriet and Jasper on who'd go check out the commotion), and Simone. Jasper, Douglas and Wyatt were absent, as was the cult of Erica Mathison. Aaron's and Cynthia's rooms were on the opposite side of the restaurant, and it appeared Royce hadn't woken them up: he mustn't have thought they were important.

Royce seemed hesitant to start; his finger kept tapping the air as he added us all up again. Wolfgang eventually stood to leave, which made Royce cut his losses and clear his throat loudly.

"I'm sure you're wondering why I've gathered you here, especially at this late hour," he said. It seemed rehearsed.

There was a general murmur of disagreement, as we all knew exactly why we were here. That did little to deter Royce from his script.

"This may surprise some of you, but Henry McTavish *was* murdered. And somebody in this room"—he faltered—"on this train, sorry, is the murderer."

It was a revealing stumble. Royce hadn't wanted to start speechifying because someone important to his theory was not in the room. That included Jasper, the book club ladies, Wyatt, Aaron, Cynthia, Douglas and, I suppose, Juliette. Royce may not have known she had gotten off the train. It would also have included Brooke, but she walked in just as I had this thought, squinting tired eyes at the group as she tried to figure out what was going on. She sat down next to Lisa, who seemed annoyed to have a seating buddy and tilted away from her.

"Get on with it," Simone said.

This only rattled Royce further.

"You want some pointers?" I couldn't resist heckling. "I've done this before."

"Would you just—" He squeezed his fists by his sides and took a breath. "Thank you, Ernest. I'll be fine on my own from here." He rummaged in his pocket and, in a small defeat, pulled out his notebook, from which he unclipped his Gemini pen and used it to trace his position in his speech. "Many of us here had reasons to dislike Henry McTavish. Several are probably glad he's dead. But there is only one . . . oh, yes, just one"—this was definitely written alongside the phrase "dramatic pause"—"person who would actually go through with it."

Simone yawned loudly. Red was crawling up from under Royce's collar.

"Let's look around. We have the fellow novelist who thinks Henry stole one of her ideas. We have the literary agent who wanted a piece of McTavish's earnings and was left at the meta-phorical altar." He wriggled the pen at his accused, both of whom scowled. To be fair, so far Royce's theories were reasonable; I'd considered both of them. "We have the literary writer who hates commercial fiction."

"That's seriously the motive you've got for me?" Wolfgang snorted. "I didn't kill him."

Royce paused, thought a moment, then moved his pen across the notebook in a clear horizontal line. It seemed as easy as dis-agreeing with him to be crossed off Royce's suspect list.

"Then we've got the struggling writer." His pen landed on me. "Desperate for a new scenario for his second book. Maybe he's created it for himself. There's a bit of money at stake, too. Maybe someone else wants him to succeed, someone close to him, like—" Royce's head swiveled, clearly looking for Juliette.

"She's sleeping," I said. Lisa shot me a look, as if surprised I'd lie. I put both hands on my cheeks in mock surprise. "Unless . . . unless . . . maybe she's off murdering people," I gasped in breathy discovery.

"If you're not going to take it seriously—"

"The struggling writer is taking it *very* seriously." I furrowed my brow dramatically.

"Am I a suspect?" Lisa put up her hand. "Tell them why I'm a suspect, Alan."

"Well, I hardly think an ex-girlfriend—"

"That sounds very likely, actually," Majors said. "From a pro-filing angle."

"You strike me as someone for whom twenty years is enough water under the bridge," Royce said to Lisa through his teeth. He was almost too deliberately keen to move away from her possible motive. "So I don't think you're a very viable suspect."

"Can I go to bed then?"

"No." Royce's lips fizzed with spit. "I haven't told you—"

"I've got to give you credit, Royce," Wolfgang broke in. "Your words are normally so good at putting me to sleep. This is surprisingly entertaining."

"What about you?" I asked. "Why aren't you a suspect?"

"Henry was, uh"—Royce faltered—"my friend."

"What do you think, Majors?" I asked.

"I think a close personal relationship probably makes it more likely, if we're profiling."

"You were furious he didn't give you that endorsement quote," I said. "You told me he owed you, big-time."

"I did not." Royce paled.

"You did. You were blind drunk at the time. I caught you going to visit him to give him a piece of your mind. Maybe you gave him a piece of something else instead."

"Can everyone just *shut up for one*—" Royce took a breath. "This isn't how it goes. Okay? I go around the room, I deconstruct your alibis and then I reveal the killer. There's not normally this much heckling in a denouement."

"De-noo-moh," Wolfgang and I said in unison.

If the Ghan were a steam train, Royce's ears could have powered it. "There's only one person with real motive. That's where the clues point. Someone who visited Henry in his room, who was close enough to him to spike his hip flask. Someone who was upset by the amount of money they were about to lose on Henry's next book. Someone who offered Henry a check for twenty-five large to retcon the series ending. Henry turned down the offer—he burned that check in front of our killer. Bet you didn't know I had that clue, did ya, Ernest?" He patted his pockets, looking for the burned check to show off, which he, of course, couldn't find.

I hid a smile.

"They fought, which gave Henry a bloodied nose. This person realized Henry's next book would be twice as marketable if he was dead than if he was alive. That someone was . . ."

Just quickly, if it helps see who's close to 106, I'll interject with a name tally:

- ~~Henry McTavish: 286~~
- Alan Royce: 220
- Simone Morrison: 96
- Wyatt Lloyd: 90
- S. F. Majors: 86
- Lisa Fulton: 83
- Wolfgang: 77
- Aaron: 59
- Brooke: 56
- Jasper Murdoch: 55
- Harriet Murdoch: 50
- Douglas Parsons: 35
- Book Club/Veronica Blythe/Beehive: 26
- Cynthia: 25
- Archibald Bench: 24
- Erica Mathison: 11
- MongrelWrangler22: 6
- Troy Firth: 3
- Juliette: EXEMPT
- Noah Witrock: EXEMPT (by virtue of being introduced past halfway, too late to be a killer in a fair-play mystery)

Majors has really come around the outside here to bump up the ranks, and there's a bit of a move from the back of the pack in Aaron, Jasper, Harriet and Brooke, all climbing up a notch or two to pretty much dead even. Royce has tipped into the category of "too obvious," and besides, why stage this grand reveal if he was really the killer? A few look primed to overjuice the tally, but consider that Wolfgang's only put on a meager thirty-seven since the last count and anything can happen. And remember to add multiple identities together.

Okay, interlude done. I'll let Royce finish his sentence . . .

". . . Wyatt Lloyd!"

There was a silence as we all digested it. Though there was more head-scratching than gasping. On pure statistics, having now used his name ninety-two times, Wyatt's (ninety-three) definitely in the mix.

"Does that work?" Brooke asked skeptically, breaking the silence.

I was running through the clues in my head. Wyatt definitely had motive; Royce was right about the financials. But I'd heard them arguing in *Wyatt's* cabin, not McTavish's, though Royce didn't know that. So the burning of the check would have happened there. I was also certain Lisa had given McTavish the bloodied nose.

"Of course it bloody works," Royce snarled.

Simone had a hand up now. "I don't know if it does. Where'd you find the check?"

"Twenty-five's not really going to move Henry's needle—his advances must be in the six figures," Wolfgang said.

"Did Wyatt have bruised knuckles?" Majors asked. "I didn't notice them."

"LISTEN!" Royce bellowed. "I am telling you exactly what happened. Henry McTavish was murdered, and Wyatt Lloyd is— without a skerrick of doubt in my mind—*definitely* the killer."

Not even a millisecond after he'd finished speaking, there was a scream from the tail carriages. No one spoke or moved for the next few seconds. Then Jasper burst into the room, gasping, and said:

"Wyatt Lloyd's been killed."

# LEGAL

# CHAPTER 26

The book. The blood. The body.

Wyatt's room was carnage. The mattress of the bottom bunk was flipped out of place, the sheets ragged, the pillow knocked to the floor. A bloodied handprint was smeared on the bathroom door. On the table under the window lay a fist-thick stack of paper. Underneath, between the table and the bathroom door, sat Wyatt Lloyd.

Wyatt was propped between the corner of the wall and the bathroom, his head slumped. Blood had flowed from his neck down his shirtfront, forming a morbid red napkin, and pooled on the floor between his legs. He was wearing blue satin boxer shorts and a formerly plain white T-shirt: it seemed he'd been in bed before he was attacked. More so than the gore and the death, the fact that he was in his pajamas seemed the most undignified. A blood-soaked piece of fabric was wrapped around one hand: Simone's blue scarf.

The cause of the blood was sticking out of his neck: the stem of a Gemini Publishing pen. I remembered Royce waving his at me, the razor-sharp tip. It was easy to picture it plunging into the soft flesh of Wyatt's neck, him flailing, hand against the bathroom door, grabbing at the nearest piece of cloth to try to stop the flow.

We squeezed around the door frame, none of us willing to step into the room. It was a jostle of heads to get a good look, as we overcrowded the thin corridor. Royce was at the back of the pack, hopping to get a view; he seemed annoyed that his number one suspect had turned into a victim. Jasper, after alerting us, had gone to fetch Aaron.

Simone shoved me aside, looked into the room for five seconds, and then spun back into the corridor.

"Eurgh." She buried her head in her hands. "What a waste."

"I know, he didn't deserve that." I put an arm around her.

She picked it off like seaweed. "That scarf's dry-clean only."

She took off, shaking her head.

"Excuse me? Can I see?" Royce was still trying to get his nose in the room; due to his stature, all he could do was push against the forest of shoulders. "Come on!"

"You'll contaminate the crime scene," Lisa said, turning around.

"I think you'll benefit from my medical expertise," he huffed.

"That's in doubt, seeing as he was supposed to be your killer."

"Maybe he couldn't live with the guilt," Royce protested. "Did himself in."

"Stabbing yourself in the neck with a pen doesn't seem a reliable method of suicide," Majors said. "Besides, I don't think many people tear apart their room and desperately try to stem the bleeding if they've done it to themselves."

"Let me examine the body and I'll tell you."

"Royce." I couldn't resist. I moved my body slightly more in front of the door. "I don't think you should be examining anything here. I'm told your whole background is a myth. You were never a pathologist, you were just an intern. Your bio's as inflated as your ego."

"You were happy to take my advice when it suited you," he shot back. "I have studied for decades! I have two degrees. I went to the same university as Arthur Conan Doyle, I'll have you know.

That's my bona fides. And," he complained, "the *Sunday Times* said I had a very good grasp of realism."

The *Sunday Times* had clearly not met Royce face-to-face.

"Well, in keeping with your actual experience in forensics labs, if we need a coffee I'll be sure to let you know."

Royce was shaking. "If you continue to treat me with such disrespect, I'll . . . I'll . . . I'll withhold my diagnosis on the cause of death."

"He's got half a pen jammed in his throat," I said. "I think we'll figure it out."

At this, Royce stormed off, forcing Brooke to step into the kitchenette alcove as he passed. She joined the back of the group, but Lisa put her hand on Brooke's shoulder and guided her away. "It's pretty gory in there," she said. "You're too young to see this."

Wolfgang, in the end, was the first to enter the room. He stepped over Wyatt's legs and peered at the paper on the desk, thumbing through the top few pages. I followed him in, looking around the room for more clues, but, given its size, I'd already spotted most things of note from the doorway. I couldn't decide whether the room had been torn apart in search of something, or whether it had been the chaos of the deadly struggle. Wyatt's bag was zipped on the floor. If someone was looking for something, they hadn't searched all that hard.

Over Wolfgang's shoulder I could see the top page of the stack on the desk: a manuscript with the title, typed in neat typewriter font, *Life, Death and Whiskey*. Then the words *First draft* and our departure date from Darwin, which meant he'd finished it, or at least typed the cover page, on the first day. Underneath, hand-scrawled in blue ink: *by Henry McTavish*. The story told itself: McTavish had finished the manuscript, signed it and handed it to Wyatt, and that had kicked off the argument I'd overheard on the first night.

"It's not a Morbund novel," Wolfgang said, looking up from the manuscript. I painted on some surprise: he didn't know I'd heard Wyatt complaining about exactly that. "But it's also not crime. It's, well—it's literary fiction." He raised his eyebrows. "It's not that bad."

That this was perhaps the first compliment I'd heard Wolfgang ever give did not escape me. It seemed to surprise even him.

"McTavish was writing literary fiction?" Majors said.

"I mean, it's still McTavish. He'll never shake all his foibles—a writer's prose is like a tattoo. Some habits die hard. But he's improved in some areas." Wolfgang seemed to realize he was being kind, because he chucked in an "I suppose."

I thought about Simone pinching the air at Wolfgang's sales. No wonder Wyatt was upset about the novel. It wasn't just a departure from McTavish's well-known character, it was a shift to a potentially lower-selling genre. But it was an interesting shift, and one that humanized McTavish a little in my eyes. Even he, after all those books he'd sold, wanted to be taken seriously.

"Lisa," I said. "Time for you to flex. Who owns *Life, Death and Whiskey* now? Legally?"

Lisa thought for a second. "It's still owned by McTavish, really, even if he's dead. Copyright is generally the creator's death plus seventy years. So yesterday plus seventy, I suppose."

"But Wyatt was going to make money out of this—that's why Royce thought he was behind the murder. McTavish delivers an out-of-genre book, so Wyatt knocks him off and suddenly its value skyrockets. Right?"

"Yes, but only from the increased sales," Lisa said. "Wyatt's right to publish the work wouldn't have changed at all. He either has a contract, which he will now hold with McTavish's estate, or he doesn't have a current contract, and that means he has to buy it from the estate."

"Henry was a lifelong bachelor," Wolfgang said. "No family."

"So where does the copyright land?"

"There will either be beneficiaries in the will," Lisa said, "or I suppose it would go to probate, and they'll find a suitable recipient."

"And people can claim they are suitable recipients, right?"

"Yes, that's what probate means—they manage all that." Lisa shrugged. "But in Henry's case, who could?"

"Long-lost brothers, et cetera et cetera," Wolfgang muttered, nose still in the pages. "They'll come out of the woodwork when there's money involved."

"And Wyatt's not a suitable claim?"

"Not based on being Henry's publisher, no."

"They have a long relationship though," Majors said, over by the vanity mirror and small cupboards. "It's not crazy to think Wyatt could have been the beneficiary of Henry's estate. Lifelong friends might make their way into a will. It gives Wyatt motive, again, for murder. But motive for murdering Wyatt—well, the person most likely to benefit would be *second* in line. Hey, that pen in his throat has Gemini branding on it. Where do you get one of those?"

"Publishing gift," I said. "Royce has one."

"He had it during his little speech," Wolfgang said. "Dare I say, he made a great effort for us to see it in his hand." I pictured Royce picking through the gathering, making sure the pen pointed at every one of us. It was a sharp insight.

"McTavish probably had one," Lisa said. "Did you see a similar pen in his suite?"

I shook my head. The only pen I'd seen was a felt-tip. Then again, I hadn't been the first one there. What had Brooke said? *I came for a souvenir.*

"And you," Wolfgang said. I had to follow his gaze to see who he was looking at. Lisa. "Before you changed publishers."

"Maybe I have one somewhere," Lisa said. "Buried in a box at home, no doubt. I was published by Gemini a long time ago."

"Convenient," Wolfgang said.

"What about this?" Majors was pointing at the cupboard, where two wooden boxes were lined up next to the miniature safe, which was open and empty. She cracked one box. Inside, atop a white silk cloth, lay a Gemini pen. She checked the other, similarly stocked. I'd never realized, but the case for a fancy pen looks very similar to a coffin. "Maybe there was a third."

"What the hell are you all doing?" Aaron asked from the doorway. Jasper and Harriet hovered behind: they must have fetched him.

"Investigating," I said.

"Thinking," Lisa said.

"Reading," Wolfgang said.

"Out. Out. Out!" Aaron ushered us into the corridor and shut the door. "I can't believe you're making me say this, but could you not play games around a dead body?"

"It's not a game," I said. "If there's a killer on this train, we want to find out who it is before they get another one of us."

"Another one?" Brooke whimpered.

"How soon can the police get here?" I asked Aaron.

"We're in the middle of the desert—they can't."

"Send a chopper," I said.

"They're all occupied, water-bombing the bushfires." He was chewing his lip. "None spare." That *bastard* bird, I thought to myself.

"Let's head back to Alice Springs," Majors said. "What's that, six hours or so?"

"Oh, I'll just pull a U-turn then, shall I?"

"Well, stop the train and call a bus," I said.

"This is still a working freight line. We have to reach our stops so the freight trains can overtake us."

"Well, change the blooming freight schedules," Wolfgang said. He was scarily intimidating in full flight, even in his striped pajamas; he towered over Aaron. "I want off this junk heap *right now*."

Aaron finally snapped. "Listen! *None* of you are detectives, or police. Just as we did last time we found a body, I'm going to ask you to go back to your cabins and wait. We'll stop at Manguri, where an officer will come on board, we'll let the freight train that's behind us pass us, and then we'll hoof it straight to Adelaide."

"What about Coober Pedy?" Lisa asked. "That's supposed to be next on the itinerary."

"It's a small town, but it's at least a thousand people, right?" I added.

"We're not stopping at Coober Pedy," Aaron said, "we're stopping at Manguri, which is the closest point on the train line *to* Coober Pedy. Manguri is not a full station: it's a platform in the middle of the desert designed for freight to pass us, which we have no choice except to head to unless we want to be barreled into from behind. There's forty kilometers of mine shafts between us and the town. Trust me: the best plan is to pull over at Manguri, let the freight pass us, and then we'll go directly to Adelaide. I'm hoping to get there about twelve hours before our original arrival time."

Wolfgang was already marching off. "Well, I'm *hoping* not to die," he called over his shoulder. "I'll take my meals in my room, please."

Aaron put his hands out flat, as if to exaggerate that he had nothing better for us. Cynthia arrived with a chair and sat it down in the corridor. It was clear this was on instruction: she was a guard.

Adrenaline faded and the time started to sink in; it was almost dawn. It felt strange to say good night, so oddly formal but also not quite enough for the situation. Phrases like "sleep well" hummed with the hidden meaning of "stay safe." "See you tomorrow" became a dark question. But we said our pleasantries anyway, slowly splitting off to our rooms. Lisa was the last one left as I reached my door. Her room was closer to the bar, which means she'd deliberately followed me past her room and down to mine.

"What do you think?" she asked. "Love or money?"

"It can't just be money. Everyone with the financial motive to kill McTavish doesn't have the motive to kill Wyatt." I was thinking of Jasper specifically; my late-night rumination that he might have wanted to remove the competition seemed misguided now. To kill McTavish to secure a book deal had made enough sense to make him a suspect in my mind last night, but it gave him possibly the *least* motive to kill Wyatt, who he'd just struck a deal with. "How did you know this would happen?"

Lisa furrowed her brow. "I didn't say that."

"You said that something would happen and I'd think you were the murderer. Perhaps you expected the body to be found later in the morning. Maybe Jasper blew it by discovering it early. Is that what you meant?"

She looked both ways. The darkened corridor was empty, the shadows of trackside foliage whipping across her face in a flickering roulette wheel. She leaned in, lowered her voice. "Is that really the type of question you want to be asking when we're all alone?"

"You've got to sell it a little more if you want to sound threatening. Put some shoulders into it," I said. "Besides, you followed me here. I've been thinking about what it means to write all this down. You want to make sure you're in this book, to be a large enough character to have your story written. That's why you're going out of your way to cause a scene. I don't think you're a killer, but there's something you want me to say for you."

Her cheek twitched.

"You can't defame the dead," I went on. "If that's what this is about." When she remained silent, I probed, "I didn't know Wyatt published you."

"Wyatt published my debut. The book about the car thief. It's not like I'm hiding it. Anyone can look that up. I changed houses for this one. Purely a business decision"—she held a finger up—"before you get ahead of yourself."

"I wasn't."

"I believe that even less than Aaron's reason keeping us on this death trap." She leaned in closer still. "Here's that legal expertise you wanted from me. I've worked with law enforcement enough to know how they work. They could *easily* bus us into Coober Pedy. It's small but there's a hotel, a tiny airport. But you introduce more links in the chain—a bus to town, for example—and the weaker it gets. Right now we're sealed up tight. No one on. No one off."

It dawned on me. "They wouldn't."

"They would. They don't want this killer to get away, and so they've locked us in with them. All the way home."

# CHAPTER 27

Don't walk backward in Coober Pedy, so the saying goes.

Coober Pedy is famous for two things. First, the unforgiving heat, which forces much of the one-thousand-person township to live underground. Their houses are burrowed into mountainsides, with rock-walled living rooms like nuclear bunkers from the 1950s. Front doors are either entranceways carved into cliffsides or hatches in the very ground. Surprisingly, given the first, the second thing the town is famous for is not vitamin D deficiency but opal mining. Even more uniquely, given the riches beneath the earth, it's not entirely overrun by a multibillion-dollar mining conglomerate; rather, it's largely mined by a mix of industrial operations and hopeful prospectors. Rumor has it the town is filled with secret millionaires who choose to project an exterior of poverty in case people suspect their plots are valuable and move in on their dig.

Opal mining is a simple matter: dig hole, check hole, leave hole. Coober Pedy mandates that mine shafts are to be left open, the mound of excavated dirt left beside the shaft. This serves two purposes: preventing people from falling through an improperly filled mine shaft, and declaring that a site has been explored.

The consequence is that the desert is pockmarked with dig sites, mine shafts and mounds of dirt. Though Coober Pedy was nowhere in sight from the station at Manguri, where the train now stood still, these excavations peppered my view like an ever-expanding asteroid belt. Each dig is often only a meter from the next, with drops of varying depths and lethality. So the general guidance is to watch your step. Hence, never walk backward.

I wasn't in too much danger of falling down a mine shaft, given that we'd been confined to our rooms for the rest of the journey. I didn't envy Aaron and Cynthia's duplicates down the other end of the train, where nonfestival guests wouldn't know about either McTavish's potential murder or Wyatt's definite one, and would just be annoyed about having their once-in-a-lifetime trip cut short.

I looked out the window at the thousands of termite-hill mine shaft markers. I was trying to determine, among the many theories, motives and suspects, where the truth was. Solving a crime was much like opal mining. Dig hole, check hole, leave hole. If I'm honest with you, I thought I'd solved enough of it to rule out four suspects by this point, and I needed only a single piece to eliminate the rest. I just had to dig one more hole.

A Land Cruiser four-wheel-drive kicked up a plume of dust, weaving through a track cut between the opal plots, and pulled up alongside the train. The car wasn't marked as police, and neither was the man who got out, but it was clear that this was either an officer or a detective. He carried a small backpack and wore a wide-brimmed hat that was floppy with regular use, the complete opposite of the straight-from-the-packet tourist gear that Douglas wore. The man wore a beige set of ill-fitting farmer's clothes and had a moustache thick enough that I figured he'd grown it to stop flies from getting in his mouth. He leaned back through the Land Cruiser's door and spoke into a two-way radio mounted on the dash, then walked across to the train and rapped on the side of the bar carriage.

The corridor was so silent—the other guests being better at following rules than I was—that leaving my room felt illicit. Having spent three days in motion, rattling tracks underneath us, the quiet was even more profound. Murder seems exciting in fiction, but it's a roller coaster of adrenaline in real life, and sometimes you need a moment alone. This was the mood of the carriage: everyone withdrawn and reflective.

Cynthia was asleep in the chair outside Wyatt's room. I tiptoed past her.

In the bar carriage, Aaron was chatting to the police officer when he spotted me. His arm went up immediately, finger pointed. "No," he said. "No. No. Not this again. Not you. We have professionals now. Back to your room, please."

"I want to know what's going on," I said.

"Is this the amateur detective?" The policeman's moustache twitched with a smirk. "Who's been helping out?"

"He's not helping," Aaron said firmly. "They've been running amok, if I'm honest with you."

"Ernest." I crossed the bar and offered the policeman my hand. He shook it. "Detective Hatch."

"Please, Detective," Aaron begged. "This farce has gone on long enough. I don't think we should be enabling this further."

"I needed to talk to Ernest at some point, it may as well be now. I'm sure his contributions will be valuable."

I couldn't help but puff my chest a little. *My contributions would be valuable.* Damn right they would be. The detective put one hand on my back and shepherded me into a seat. I could tell, even through my shirt, that he had thick, rough hands. He looked settled, unrushed: I figured he planned to travel with us to Adelaide and then catch the next train back to Manguri to pick up his car.

"Tell me what you know, partner," Hatch said, and I'll admit to a little flutter of excitement at *partner*.

"Well, Henry McTavish collapsed in the middle of an event yesterday morning. We suspect poison. Possibly heroin, though we're open to other theories."

"We?"

"Alan Royce and I."

"Ah, the one who used to be the pathologist?" Hatch held both hands clasped in front of him. I figured he was one of those detectives whose mind was electric enough not to need notes. A real Morbund type. He nodded slowly. "Well, you've got that right, we think. Heroin. According to the bloods."

*What do you know*, I thought, *intern or not, Royce has come through.*

"So what else?" the detective asked.

"Most people here had some reason to do McTavish in," I said. "I'd say it ranges from dislike to strong hate, depending on the suspect. Starting with S. F. Majors, for example. She thinks that McTavish—"

"Yeah, yeah." Hatch unclasped his hands and waved my explanation away. "Let's talk about all the facts before we get into theories. What about the second murder?"

"That was earlier this morning. We found Wyatt, McTavish's publisher, stabbed through the throat after the train left Alice Springs. Now, that makes it tricky: arguably Wyatt had the most motive to kill McTavish, as he stood to make a good deal of money out of the increased posthumous value of the next book." I described to him the behind-the-scenes of why McTavish's last words—literally, his handwritten name on the cover page likely the last mark he left on the world—would increase in value for a publisher. "But who has the motive to kill Wyatt? Well, if we look at our suspects again, we could think about Lisa Fult—"

"Yep. That's excellent work. Yep."

"I haven't really told you my theories yet."

"We'll get there, we'll get there." He reached into his breast pocket and now took out a notebook. He clicked his pen, then spun it around his knuckles like a poker chip. "Now, Wyatt Lloyd. You found his body once you were on the move. Well, Jasper did. He's in the room next door, said he could hear everyone traipsing past and, once he was awake, could smell blood. Did anyone see Wyatt leave the dinner at the Telegraph Station?"

"I didn't," I said. "I can't speak for everyone else. Would you like me to follow that up in my next interviews?"

"Let's take it one step at a time. Before we assign anything more to your caseload." *Click, click.* The pen spun. "So no one's seen him since the dinner. It's conceivable he died before you left Alice Springs?"

"I don't think so. The blood looked fresh . . . ish."

"Fresh-ish?" He rolled the word around like it was a different language. "That's Royce's medical opinion?"

I cleared my throat. "Not exactly. I decided Royce was a bit of an Achilles heel, so I thought it best if he kept his distance on this one."

"That seems like a reasonable decision. Take tire-kickers out and use your own, extensive, experience." He lingered on the word *extensive.*

My smugness was rapidly eroding. I realized his phrasing—*caseload, partner*—was the same you'd use to send a child down to the shops for some ice cream. *Now, I've got a veeery important mission for you, Deputy!*

"And so the medical consensus of Wyatt's time of death was developed"—he swirled the pen in the air—"how, exactly?"

"It was fairly obvious."

"Yes. Fresh-ish. Very good."

"Are you taking the piss?"

"No, Mr. Cunningham, I'm taking this very seriously." He wrote something down. "So it's conceivable that Wyatt Lloyd was murdered before the Ghan departed Alice Springs."

"I suppose. I mean the blood *was* fresh."

"Ish."

"Yes," I relented. "He could have been dead awhile. I don't know."

"Ah."

"Look." I leaned forward. "Did you want my analysis of each suspect? I've conducted several interrogations."

"Interrogations? Impressive."

"In my opinion—"

"I think we'll stick to the facts for now"—he smiled—"Mr. Cunningham."

"You're not interested in my take on this at all, are you? You were just buttering me up."

His teeth showed through his bristles, like a white tiger glimpsed behind a thatch of jungle. "No. I don't need your shambolic theories, and I could do without your theatrics. I just need you to help me ascertain some facts regarding the timelines."

I turned to Aaron. "I'm not going to sit here and be patronized while there's a killer loose on this train. Let me help you."

"You're perfectly safe. The killer's not on the train at all," Aaron said. "The arrest was made at Alice Springs."

"That's enough, thank you," Hatch said firmly, but Aaron had already given away too much. Hatch turned back to me and I realized: even if he didn't care for my deductions, he needed me to tell him *something*.

"You arrested someone? Who?" I flicked through the Rolodex of everyone I'd seen since boarding the train. I swore I'd seen the others board. Maybe with the exception of Wyatt. Had he really been killed before we left the station? I knew Hatch put little stock in my medical opinions, but even he would likely admit I could tell the difference between fresh and dried blood. "I don't understand who else you could have arrested in Alice Springs." I turned to Aaron. "I don't think we're safe at all."

"She's in custody," Hatch assured me. "You're safe."

"She?"

Hatch's eyes shrunk with his mistake. Suddenly I understood. Why he'd wanted to talk to me. Why I hadn't gotten a call or a text message back before I lost phone reception. Why he'd been worried about Aaron telling me too much.

I blanched. "You've got to be kidding!"

"Juliette left the dinner before you. Did you see her again before departure?"

"That's ridiculous." I made to stand.

Hatch put a heavy hand on my shoulder and pushed me down. Despite his ill-fitting clothing, he carried some serious bulk, and his strength surprised and overpowered me. "I need you to answer the question." He squeezed slightly. "And it's not ridiculous. Juliette was the wearer of the scarf that a dead man had wrapped around his fist. Unless you can explain that away, I need to know if you saw her between dinner and departure."

"You've got it wrong. The scarf is Simone's, Juliette was just borrowing it."

"So Juliette gave it back to Simone, then?"

"Well . . . no . . . but she left it behind at breakfast." A memory struck me. "Wyatt picked it up! Because he recognized it was Simone's. He told me he was going to give it back to her."

Hatch set his eyes on mine. "So the only person who can back you up that Juliette was no longer in possession of the scarf is a dead one?"

"It's the truth," I pleaded. "And no. I didn't see her after the dinner."

"But she left before you, right? Caught a cab. I've talked to the driver already—he dropped her at the station in Alice."

I was shaking with incredulity. "Maybe because it's the center of town? Her bags were still in the cabin, untouched. She didn't get back on."

"Or that's what she wants you to think. Why would she leave the train? People dream of going on this trip and she leaves early? Unless she's running from something."

This question was acidic. Hatch must have known the real reason she'd left. Juliette would have rationally explained her motivations when they'd questioned her. Surely.

I'd had enough. "Can I go now?" I asked firmly.

Hatch released the pressure on my shoulder and replaced it with a gentle pat, the type a doctor gives a child getting a needle: *See, it's not that bad*. "Sure. Thanks for your *expertise*."

I couldn't resist having the last word as I stood up. "My fiancée is not a murderer."

"Fiancée-*ish*, though," Hatch snarled. "Isn't it?"


I didn't entertain it. Not even for a second. It didn't cross my mind.

Juliette was innocent—she had to be. And that piece of blind faith, which Juliette had so wanted me to have twelve hours ago, one knee in the dirt, awoke something new within me. A Golden Age detective doesn't really *need* characterization or motive, so to speak: intellectual curiosity is their raison d'être. It's enough for them to scratch an itch, to solve a puzzle simply because it's there to be solved. I'd started in that place, merely curious at the piecing together, not invested in what the answer might mean. My motives had broadened—I'd wanted to build my book out of it—and then, Wyatt's death being so much more violent than McTavish's, plot seeking had given way to fear. But all these motives—curiosity to cashing in to safety—are selfish ones. It's exactly what Juliette had said about whose story I thought this was. Mine.

I pictured Juliette sitting on a cold aluminum bench in a holding cell. The detective act was no longer a charade. I didn't just want to solve this, I *had* to. Fast.

I had this revelation as two things happened simultaneously. The first was that Aaron's voice floated over the intercom, announcing the tracks were clear and we would depart Manguri for the final stretch to Adelaide in five minutes. The second was that I noticed that Detective Hatch's Land Cruiser had a broken window, and a shadow was sitting in the driver's seat.

I darted from the room. I didn't have to go all the way to the bar to bump into Hatch, who was peering into Wyatt's room, tutting as he examined the scene. Cynthia, now awake, stood up as I approached. Hatch turned around and put an arm out, blocking me.

"I think you're better off in your cabin," he said. But I could see through the gap between his arm and body, and I saw enough to confirm what I'd suspected. "Come on, mate," he added. "This is better done with lawyers and courts now."

I was tempted to snap at him, "Somebody's stealing your Land Cruiser," but instead I put my hands up in surrender and backed off apologetically. I did my best to look casual as I headed to my room, but my legs itched to run and I settled into a stiff-legged speed-walk. I quickly checked that Hatch had turned around as I approached my room, then skipped past it and kept going to the carriage divider. Once I was through the door, I let my legs fly. I ran through the remaining carriages full pelt, just about bouncing off the walls of the tiny corridors, until I was finally at the back, where I wrenched open the door to the smoking deck.

The heat of the desert hit me like a wall. The white glare made me wince. Then the engines of the train rumbled to life and, with a clank, we started to roll: Adelaide bound. I looked out over the end of the train, where the ground beneath had turned into a conveyor belt. The speed increased, from a walk to a jog to a run. The ground started to blur. I couldn't hesitate any longer.

I was done digging holes. It was time to find some opals.

I gripped the iron railing and vaulted over the fence, landing with a crunch in the middle of the tracks.

# CHAPTER 28

I didn't have time to think about the consequences of the train pulling away into the distance, leaving me without shade, food or water, forty kilometers of barren desert between me and the nearest town. Or the fact that I was on my own chasing a potential murderer and, not only that, but on foot, while they had a vehicle. I was acting on instinct and adrenaline alone.

I suspected they'd steal it at some stage, I just hadn't known when. But then I'd seen the shadow sitting in the Land Cruiser and remembered Cynthia being asleep, and I knew it had happened. A quick glimpse over Hatch's shoulder into Wyatt's room was all I'd needed: the table by the window was empty. *Life, Death and Whiskey* was gone.

I sprinted down the tracks—the movement of the train had taken me past the Land Cruiser and so I had to head back to it. The rattle of the Ghan faded, and now I could hear the revving clunk of an engine that someone was desperately trying to hot-wire, sweaty fingers slipping off the wires as they saw me coming. I was maybe fifty meters from the vehicle when they gave up and stepped out into the desert, looked at me for a second and then ran across the road and into the opal fields.

"Lisa!" I yelled. "Wait!"

I peeled off the tracks and into the fields myself, past a gigantic skull-and-crossbones sign that read: *Warning: Uncovered mine shafts, do not enter on foot.* I dashed past it. Lisa was ahead of me, the distance shrunk by ten or so meters. I kept an eye on her while trying to keep my gaze down. All around me the ground opened up into gaping wells, mounds of dirt beside them. Lisa was being slightly more cautious around the mine shafts than I was, so I was closing in on her.

"I know what happened!" I yelled. "Please. Let's talk about it."

Lisa didn't stop. And so I kept running, weaving between the holes and the dirt and gaining, step by step. Closer. Closer. I focused on her back as the distance closed. Thirty seconds and I'd have her.

My left foot slid sideways. I looked down and saw cascading silt pouring into a deep black hole. My arms pinwheeled as I regained my balance. I stood for a second, peering into the hole, breathing deep relief.

When I looked up, Lisa was gone.

I whipped my head around but she was nowhere to be seen. The entire opal field was desolate, empty. Mounds of dirt surrounded me like statues. Spindly insect legs of cranes and drills rose up in the distance against the bright blue skyline. I listened. No footsteps.

She couldn't have outrun me so quickly; my rebalancing had only taken a couple of seconds. Had she fallen? I figured I might have heard a scream. She had to be hiding, must have ducked behind one of the dirt mounds. She might even be moving from mound to mound, circling back to the car. Or sneaking up behind me. I imagined hands on my back and spun around. Nothing. Just me and hundreds of silent mounds.

I edged forward, now prioritizing silence over speed and peering behind each mound as I passed it. "Come out, Lisa," I said. "The Ghan has left. It's just us here."

I kept moving forward, in a wide sweep, giving myself as broad a view as possible of the backs of the dirt pillars. And then I spotted an elbow. It was indistinct, about three mounds down to the left of me—Lisa had indeed been moving back toward the car, hopping mound to mound while my head was turning. I'd only caught the barest glimpse. I took a sideways step to get a better view.

The saying should really be to never walk backward *or* sideways in Coober Pedy, but it wasn't really the right time to be pedantic. This time I'd taken a heavier step, straight in the middle of the shaft: open air. I pitched forward immediately, my whole leg in the hole. My chest hit the rim, and the air was knocked out of me. My other leg slid in after. My hands scrabbled for grip, but there was nothing but gravel, tiny shards of dirt and stone that shredded my fingertips, ripping my nails on my gloveless hand. I tried to yell but couldn't draw breath. My feet paddled air underneath me. I tried to ground my forearms on the rim, but they kept slipping as gravity dragged me down. I had no idea how deep the hole was, but even if the fall wasn't enough to kill me, surely, out here, I'd never be found. A broken leg and a week to die, down in the dark. I hoped I died on impact.

I heard footsteps, running. It was hard to tell where they were coming from over my thrashing. My scrabbling got more desperate. But all I was doing now was dislodging more and more dirt, creating, unwillingly, an almost perfect funnel for me to slip down. I could feel blood on my fingertips, sticky and warm. *There goes a second set of fingerprints.*

I slid backward another couple of inches and knew I was gone. Red dust was in my hair, my eyes, caked in my mouth. Bite the dust, huh? Tears rolled down my face. I wondered if I would be able to see the sky from the bottom, or if I would die in the dark. I thought of Juliette, alone in that cell. I wondered if she had a small window, if she would look up at the same sliver of blue that I might see from the pit, and it made me feel not quite so alone.

I fell.

# CHAPTER 29

A hand clamped around my wrist.

A violent jerk rippled through my shoulder. The drop halted. I looked up. Silhouetted against the sun was Lisa, legs splayed, heels gouging into the earth on the rim of the pit. We hung there for a second, me dangling in the hole. She was a strong enough counterweight, due to our relative positioning, to stop the fall, but not to get me back out again. I dug my knees into the wall and grappled up it, and somehow we overcame gravity to spill me over the top and onto the dirt. I rested my cheek against the ground, marveling at my breath. Lisa sat, knees up, her wrists balanced on top.

"Thank you," I said.

"I didn't kill him," Lisa said softly. "Either of them. And because I'm not a killer, I'm not about to let you fester in the bottom of one of these." She wiped her nose with the back of one hand. Her hair had been whipped around by the run. "But I don't suppose you believe any of that."

I rolled onto my back, still catching my breath. Jagged rocks dug into my neck. This is what's missing from action scenes in novels like this; sometimes everyone involved needs a bit of a break.

"I believe exactly that, actually," I said, propping myself onto my elbows. "And I know what he did to you. In Edinburgh, two thousand and three. This supposed fling isn't the truth. He raped you."

"He didn't—" I thought she was about to deny it, but then something squeaked in her throat. "He didn't stop." She locked eyes with me. "I tried. I really did. McTavish told everyone I'd wanted to. I was the young hopeful newbie, he was the older big shot. It was so hard to be believed. They all thought I was starstruck. It wasn't like that."

"It's okay."

"I've never told anyone this. But Majors was at the bar, before we all split off. I'm pretty sure, deep down, she knew something was wrong. I went to her, begged her to back me up. But she stayed quiet for the same reason I ended up silencing myself. You wouldn't understand. I want to be known for the art I made, for my words and my voice, not for the mark some man left on me." She sighed. "Of course, at first I did want to speak out. Even if it was on my own. I wanted justice. I'd tried to fight him off and had scratched him on the cheek, so I had his DNA under my fingernails. But would you believe it? There was a bloody admin error and they mislabeled my test. By the time they found it, it was inadmissible because no one could be sure it hadn't been tampered with. Wyatt threatened me, said he'd bury my career, and by then I thought I had no other option, so I signed an NDA. There was money too. But if I'm honest, it had become my word against his, and signing seemed like the only path out. And I . . . needed the money." Her jaw set hard. "How'd you figure it out?"

"A few reasons. Wyatt published your first book, and you moved away from him for the second, which hints at a falling out of sorts. Of course you wouldn't want to work with the man who had enabled Henry McTavish to get away with what he had. But that only becomes clear once the rest clicks into place. My agent, Simone, used to be McTavish's assistant. He has a certain . . . shall we say *tone* to his interactions with women."

"That's one way of putting it."

"He's an outright sleaze, if you prefer. But that's conjecture. As is the reason I suspect that you and Majors refused to support each other's accusations after Edinburgh. You were there together, after all. Surely each of you saw *something* that might help the other."

Lisa had told me this herself: *It's not like she was on the witness stand*. Without Majors, Lisa lacked a character witness. And with her physical evidence ruled out, there was no chance for a criminal proceeding. "Majors could have been a second voice, changed the your-word-against-his narrative, but she didn't come to your aid. A year later she realized that McTavish stole her idea for his new book, and her only evidence came from that very same night. You were a witness to the conversation when Majors told McTavish her story. She turned to you, but by then you'd already signed your own NDA. Besides, you must have been too hurt to back up her story. Am I close?"

"I don't blame her." Lisa tossed a rock into the pit, watched it disappear into the dark. I didn't hear it hit the bottom, which made my stomach quiver. "She didn't have much of a choice. They would have ruined her career. And I would have had to break my NDA to back her up. But it hurt. So I guess I chose not to help her too. The number of times I've seen it." She shook her head. "The world can't stomach two strong successful women in the same place, so we have to hate each other, we have to compete. That's how people like Wyatt designed it. I've got nothing against her, I just . . . let Wyatt and Henry win. Even if I didn't know that was what I was doing at the time." Another rock sailed into the abyss.

"That's the key to how I knew," I said. "Wyatt wouldn't have taken losing your new book to a new publisher too easily. And McTavish was a bitter soul. So they cooked up a stunt. Of course, your new publisher would have been delighted to see the Henry McTavish quote on the cover, even with the caveat that you weren't to see it before this trip. I thought at first that you were overwhelmed when you saw the quote, but you weren't: you were horrified. Because that's the exact word Henry used in a message he sent you. Simone's his old assistant, and Royce is a perv, but I heard the same word from both of them. *Firecracker*. So by putting that word on something that was supposed to be yours, they marked it. Forever. A humiliation only you would know."

"This all sounds like a pretty good reason to kill both of them," Lisa said. "You still have no reason to believe me, so why do you?"

"I figure seeing the quote was the final straw. You marched into McTavish's room and told him you didn't care about the NDA and that you were done keeping his secrets. He wrote out a check for twenty-five thousand dollars, tried to pay you off, the same as he did before, but you burned it in front of him. The world's changed: you hoped people might listen to you this time. You were done. Was that when he grabbed you?"

Lisa nodded. "Yeah."

I sighed. "I'm disappointed. I thought we had a bit of truth-telling going on. Why bother lying?"

Lisa swallowed thickly. She'd stopped throwing rocks into the hole but was peering down it like jumping in was a viable way to get out of the conversation.

I kept on. "Henry didn't grab you. He was crippled down his left side; his left hand was always clutching his cane. If he was going to reach out and grab you, he would have done it with his right hand, so if you were in front of him, which you'd have to be to hit him in the nose, he would have grabbed your left side. Your bruise is on the wrong arm."

Lisa sucked her teeth.

"It's okay," I continued. "This isn't an accusation, I'm just trying to get all the pieces on the board. You were always going to hit McTavish, that's why you went there. You headbutted him straight in the nose. Partly because it felt good, and partly because you could pocket a bloody tissue. You gave yourself the bruise so you could claim it was self-defense if McTavish dared to pursue the injury, but that was just insurance: you knew he'd stay quiet, given what you were talking about. What you really wanted was the tissue. Well, the blood on it, anyway. Here's where it gets tricky."

Lisa laughed, but it sounded shaky. "Why would I want a bloody tissue?"

"You had a child. *His* child. You kept it. That's why you took the hush money in the first place, because you were pregnant. Now, fast-forward all these years, you wanted his DNA to prove it. It's taken you two decades to write your second book, partly because of how you felt about the industry—how hard it was to trust anyone with your work, with your life, again—and partly because you were raising a kid on your own. Staging a fight is fine and all, and you walked away with what you wanted: the DNA. But then McTavish dies and you realize that you might be the prime suspect. There's the history between you, and now there's also physical evidence of a violent altercation. And now you've got even clearer motive, because the copyright in all his books, including the new one, should go to his estate. And your child *is* the estate. Or at least that's supposed to be what the DNA test will prove. So you pinch the manuscript to protect it, and hope that by the time anyone realizes you're gone, we might have caught the real killer. Your only problem was that hot-wiring a car in real life is far more difficult than just researching it. And, of course, that you had to leave your daughter behind."

Lisa paled so much I think she got immediately sunburned.

I stood up, dusted my knees. "Let's put your car thieving to the test, because you need to help me get back on the train. Then Brooke can tell me her side of the story herself."

# CHAPTER 30

It took twice as long as it should have to walk back to the Land Cruiser. Even on flat, safe ground we walked like we were crossing a river on loose stones. I checked every spot I put my foot twice.

"I thought I'd hidden it so well," Lisa said. "I didn't want Henry to know."

"Like mother, like daughter," I said, pointing to her bruises. "Wrong arm."

Her shoulders rose. "He hurt her?"

"No. Brooke's right arm is sunburned. The festival punters are all in carriages on the east side of the train—they paid for the tickets so they get the sunrise views. The writers are all on the west, so we get the sunset. Each cabin only gets sun half a day. If she was sitting by the window in a guest cabin, where she's supposed to be, she should have had sunburn on her left arm, not her right. If she'd just been burned outside, it would be across both arms evenly. Which means she's been staying in a writer's cabin. That, and it was pretty obvious she was lying about her cabin number when I asked her. She's someone's plus-one."

Lisa chuckled. We'd reached the Land Cruiser. I brushed flecks of broken window glass off the seat and hopped in the passenger side. Lisa crouched by the driver's footwell, alongside the dislodged panel and dangling wires she'd been fiddling with before I gave chase. "Gosh," she said. "All that out of a sunburned arm."

"Not just the arm," I said. "When Royce woke us all up, you made sure to slip out of your cabin quickly, so no one would see anyone else was inside. Royce only deliberately woke the writers, but of course knocking on your door woke her as well. Her curiosity got the better of her and she followed you. That's why she was last to arrive, and why you were annoyed to see her when she sat down next to you. Then there was her fascination with McTavish, which didn't quite fit her age; it just took me a while to figure out if it was psychopathic or not. Plus you guided her away from Wyatt's body. You told her to be careful when she was skipping rocks in the canyon. You gave her aloe vera cream to use on her sunburn. That all points to a motherly instinct. That and the fact that she was in the Chairman's Carriage looking for the manuscript."

"Very good," Lisa said, a cable in her mouth.

"And she knew too much about that night in Edinburgh, when she was conceived. She held on to a copy of the article with you all in it, for one thing. But she knew a lot about Majors's plagiarism accusations too. She brushed it off as being public knowledge, but that's not true: there's barely been a proper plagiarism accusation on this trip, it's all veiled threats. The only way Brooke would really know about what went on that night was if someone who was there told her." Brooke had told me, when I thought she was talking about Majors: *I should have believed her*. But she'd been talking about her mother. "You told her to try to discredit McTavish."

"She was fascinated by him—Henry himself, sure, given all his success, but it was mostly the idea of a father in general. She hit her teens and she had questions. I knew she would. I'd been spending a lot of time thinking about what to tell her. I couldn't lie to her, but I also couldn't bring myself to tell her what he did to me. I hoped that telling her about Majors would be enough for her to know he was bad news without me telling the whole story. I thought I'd never have to, that he was an ocean and a lifetime away. I thought she'd never meet him."

"But she wanted a father figure, and so she built one herself. Out of his books," I surmised. I'd been thinking back to S. F. Majors's interpretation of obsession: *The stalker might picture themselves having a certain relationship with this person. A connection that only they see. They insert themselves into a world they aren't actually a part of.* In this case, the connection was more literal, but the interpretation still held. MongrelWrangler22 had posted that they felt like he was speaking directly to them. *A bedtime story.* To Brooke, reading the Detective Morbund books was like talking to her dad. No wonder she didn't want them to end.

"I indulged that. I figured it was harmless, healthy even. A bit of an outlet. Like I said, he was supposed to be a continent away."

"Until this trip."

"Exactly. Ouch." Lisa sparked the cables against her fingertips and shook them, just as the engine sputtered and then roared. She hoisted herself into the driver's seat and patted the dash. "Research pays off after all."

Then we were moving. The only road at Manguri was the one bending away to Coober Pedy, so Lisa drove off-road parallel to the train track. The ground was flat enough to accommodate the train but ragged enough to jostle us roughly in our seats. The Ghan was a speck on the horizon ahead.

"When you were invited here, I imagine she would have begged to come with you?"

"Desperately. But I wasn't having it. I wasn't even going to accept the invitation—I certainly didn't want to be anywhere near him. But she really wanted to finally meet him. We had a huge blow-out, screaming-the-grout-from-the-kitchen-tiles type stuff. And I told her, in the heat of the moment, what he'd done. That he'd raped me."

"And she still wanted to come?" I said, despite already knowing the answer. *I should have believed her.*

"It made her want to come even more. You must understand, I didn't sit her down and gently tell her the reality. I screamed it at her across the room." Lisa took her eyes off the tracks, where the back of the Ghan had gotten closer, turning from a blurry lump to glinting steel, to read my face. "You clearly don't have kids. Or if you do, not girls. She was livid, accused me of saying anything to get her to not go. She's a smart girl, she wouldn't have let anger override common sense, and she knows what men are capable of. But you've got to understand, she had this picture of him in her head. Her father. The writer of her favorite books, the teller of her bedtime stories. He'd been speaking to her for years through Morbund. She couldn't replace that image she'd built so easily."

"I imagine she'd have found a way to come without you, then."

"She told me if I didn't take her, she'd pay her own way. Sell her car if she had to. I figured I was better off here protecting her."

"Looks like she wasn't the one who needed protecting."

"She wouldn't have killed them."

"I don't think you believe that."

My conversations with Brooke flashed through my head. Her sucking up the courage to introduce herself to McTavish. Him pressing his room key into her hand. The image of him that she'd built, in denial of her mother's warning, crumbling in front of her. The key, squeezed so tight it cut into her palm. The note, which must have been originally attached to the whiskey: *From an admirer.* McTavish whispering to her: *It's a mighty fine drop to drink alone.* Her telling me in the Chairman's Carriage: *Never meet your heroes.*

Lisa's knuckles whitened on the steering wheel. The man who raped her and the man who had covered it up were both dead. I didn't have to say it.

Lisa would have had the same thoughts I did. I knew exactly why she had left Brooke alone. *Even for a second. Even that it crossed your mind.* Love doesn't make you invincible to doubt. I knew that as well as any. Lisa knew that by leaving the train she would incriminate herself with the appearance of guilt, and it might give her daughter a head start.

Lisa had sought me out, told me what she had, in the hope that I would write it down. And that one day her daughter would read, and understand, what she'd done to save her.

The funny thing was, Brooke believed her mother capable of the very same crime. That was why she'd been at pains to introduce me to Majors's possible motives: to distract me from her mother's. Each protecting the other.

"Why take me back?" I asked.

"Because you've solved it. Haven't you?"

I nodded, but with the bouncing of the Land Cruiser it was a bit more enthusiastic than I'd intended, so I added, "Almost."

"And you *don't* think it's her. I can tell. So maybe she needs you." She floored the accelerator and the engine whined. "That's why I'm going to get you back on the train."

I'd been so focused on her I was almost surprised when I looked up and saw the back of the Ghan filling my view. Lisa was nudging eighty, and she pulled up alongside it, dropping to seventy and holding close. From the outside, the calm meditative *clack-clack* was gone: the train kicked up an absolute clattering roar as it moved.

"You came after me not because you cared that I'd taken the manuscript," Lisa shouted over the noise. "And not because you thought I was a murderer. You came to ask me something. And you haven't asked me yet. You've just been telling me what you already know. Train's coming up. So you'd better ask."

"Majors. Is she telling the truth?"

"Seriously? Is that it?"

"You were there that night. I think she told McTavish a version of the story that *wasn't* the true story from the papers. That's the version he stole for *Off the Rails*. Right?"

"You jumped off a *moving* train to ask me that?"

"I had to know for sure."

"You already do. Have you learned nothing about Henry McTavish? What he does?" She was nodding. "This is a man who takes from women. He took my body. And he took her mind."

# CHAPTER 31

It is much more difficult hanging out of a car window than they make it look in the movies, let alone jumping from one.

I had one hand on the side mirror and one hand on the roof as I maneuvered my way out of the car. The window didn't wind all the way into the sill, so the glass dug into my thighs. The wind roared in my ears, the tires kicked dust into my eyes and my cheeks stung with the peppering of bugs. I squinted against the wind at the Ghan. Lisa was aiming for the smoking deck; she had the Land Cruiser as close to the tracks as she could go without hitting them. The deck was too high to jump onto easily, but I was pretty sure I could grab on to the fence and climb over.

We edged forward, now side by side. The fencing was just past my fingertips. I levered one foot up on the windowsill, found purchase, and tensed my legs.

"I'm going to jump!" I yelled to Lisa. "Keep it steady."

Her mouth moved, but I couldn't hear her reply above the wind and the train. I hoped she'd heard me. I reached an arm out toward the railing, took a deep breath and . . .

. . . the car jerked wildly underneath me, braking and swerving at the same time. I tilted dizzyingly sideways, face down to the blur of red dirt underneath me, before snapping back the other way, crunching a rib into the door frame. And then the back of the Ghan was rapidly approaching. We were going faster than it was, and I whipped my head inside just in time for the *whoosh* of the carriage to rattle past the window, shearing off the side mirror in an explosion of glass.

"Sorry. Telegraph pole," Lisa said.

I looked out the back window to see a large column, shrinking behind us, by the tracks: she'd had to swerve around it. "Bit of a heads-up next time?"

"I did say not to jump."

I looked at the train beside us. Lisa eased off the gas and drew back to the smoking deck again, this time a little behind it. I snuck a look at the speedometer. Fifty now. The train had slowed down slightly. "We might need a new plan. These heroics are a bit beyond me."

Lisa thought for a second and then wrenched the wheel hard toward the tracks. We bounced over the rails, a shower of sparks flew out behind us, and then just as quickly she pulled the steering back, settling us exactly in the middle. The tracks ran between the wheels; we were now directly tailing the train.

I nodded, impressed. "That's a better plan. Keep an eye on the speed. It seems to be slowing down slightly."

"Thirty-eight," she said.

I levered my way out of the window again, except this time instead of trying to jump sideways, I grappled my way around to the front until I was crouched on the bonnet. It's not exactly the high-speed stuff of action films, given that we would have been able to perform this stunt in a school zone. My legs were jellied all the same. If I fell, the fall might not kill me. But if I went underneath the Land Cruiser, or if I got jammed between the car and the train, or if I went under the train itself, I figured I'd be a goner no matter the speed.

Lisa nudged forward. I heard a satisfying crunch of metal on metal; this was as close as we were going to get. It wouldn't be as simple as walking across: it was hard for Lisa to match the speed, so the gap varied from nonexistent to terrifying as the Land Cruiser wavered forward and back. I adjusted myself to a runner's starting position, keeping one hand in touch with the windscreen.

That was when my phone rang.

More specifically, I felt it buzzing in my pocket. We must have hit a sliver of reception. I dug the phone out and answered without looking. "Juliette?" I yelled.

"No, mate. Andy. You busy?"

I considered the crumpled front of the Land Cruiser, nose to tail with a speeding train, the wind whipping past as I hunched on the bonnet. The Ghan sheltered me from much of the wind's noise, so I could just hear Andy over the chaos. "It's not a great time," I said. "If I'm honest."

"I'll be quick. It's about Margaret."

A car horn beeped, and I saw Lisa's exasperated and incredulous expression, two hands thrown up in the universal gesture for *What the hell?*

"Who's Margaret?"

"The robbery I'm working."

"I thought you said her name was Poppy."

"No. I said she *sold* poppies."

"You didn't. I told you that specifics are important here, Andy."

Lisa beeped again, long and slow. I held up a finger. Her mouth formed a word that's not fit for print. Turns out Andy's actually quite important. I told you that's a thing in these kinds of books: two disparate cases coming together.

"Jesus, Andy. You and I are working the same case."

EVERYONE ON THIS TRAIN IS A SUSPECT

"Huh? You've got a case?"

"Couple of murders."

Andy tsked in annoyance. "You've always got to have one better, don't you?"

I ignored that. "Your robbery. You think it's a junkie, right?"

"Yeah! That's what I wanted to tell you. Break-ins are like a *thing* in the flower industry. Because some of the plants, you know, they have opium in them. Which is basically heroin. You can boil it out."

"Poppies," I said.

"No, her name's not Poppy. I told you, it's Margaret."

"Poppies have opium in them, Andy."

"Yes, that's what I was saying. It's this place's specialty—" He dropped out, then came back on. "Weird, huh? What's this got to do with your murders?"

"I think your thief is my killer."

"Bit of a leap?"

I looked at the smoking deck, where I'd have to jump. "Tell me about it."

"No way." Andy's enthusiasm accelerated from slow dawn to shouting. "Did I solve it for you? Did I?"

He hadn't. I already had most of it worked out after my chat with Lisa, but I was in a generous mood. Maybe it was the adrenaline. And he had given me a great clue last night. So I said, "Yeah, Andy. You solved it."

"Yes! That's going on the websi—" He cut out.

Lisa beeped again, this time two sharp bursts—*bip-bip*—and I turned my attention back to the train in front. The noise of the wind was even less now. Lisa honked again, I assumed to hurry me up. The gap between the bonnet and the railing wobbled but stayed small. This was my chance.

I stood up, strode across the hood and jumped.

*

I overcooked it.

I had expected my jump to take a half second longer given the speed, but I crashed into the railing immediately. Stunned, I slid a little before I found purchase on the fencing, clutching it tightly while I caught my breath. The wind buffeted me less here; it was quieter. I actually laughed. A spasmodic response to surviving. Who'd have thought, when I started this journey, that I'd be hanging off the back of a speeding train? Now all I had to do was pull myself over the railing.

I didn't dare look down, as I didn't think I could stomach seeing the ground blur past, but I shot a look back at the Land Cruiser, expecting it to have peeled off in a cloud of dust, Lisa and the manuscript for *Life, Death and Whiskey* free.

The Land Cruiser was still behind the train. But that wasn't the most surprising part. The most surprising thing was that Lisa was no longer in the driver's seat. Neither was she clambering over the bonnet. She was standing beside the car, in the dirt.

Wait. *Standing?*

I looked down. The ground was there all right, but it wasn't moving.

So much for clinging to a high-speed train. No wonder my jump had slammed me into the railing, that the wind had lessened. Lisa's beeps had been telling me not to jump, that the train was coming to a stop. I must have made the jump when we were at walking pace. Now here I was, clinging on for dear life, and the Ghan was completely stationary.

Sheepishly, I clambered over onto the smoking deck. Lisa grabbed a satchel from the backseat and followed.

The back door opened, and Aaron stepped out. "What the hell are you two doing out here?" he asked.

To both my surprise and his, I hugged him. "Thank you. Thank you. You stopped for us."

"What is that on the tracks?" He looked at the Land Cruiser, aghast. "What were you doing?"

"We were trying to get back on."

"*Back* on?"

"That's not why you stopped?" Lisa said. "You didn't see Ernest go all Tom Cruise?"

"What in blazes are you talking about? I didn't stop for you." He took a second to properly absorb my appearance: bug-splattered cheeks; dirt-caked chin; wind-whipped hair. He took in the Land Cruiser again and his jaw dropped as if on a hinge.

"You had to stop?" I hoped someone else hadn't died. "Why?"

"Cows on the tracks." He shook his head in disbelief. "It's not a bloody action movie."

# CHAPTER 31.5

I'm about to solve it.

Well, I've already solved it. I'm about to explain it to everyone. Like Royce tried to. Except I'll get it right.

You know how these grand reveals tend to work. According to my writing schematic—which the events of the last few days have been keeping scarily close to—we've just crossed the "All is lost" moment (I almost died, twice!) and that means it's time for it all to come out.

So I thought I'd pause here and give you, you know, one last chance to put your guesses in. This page is the last page where you get to brag about figuring it all out before I do. If you want to grab a pen and paper and have one more crack at Archie Bench, this is the spot for that too.

Also, I want you to know that, over the next couple of chapters, six people are going to use the phrase "I didn't kill anybody." Such repetition is not a fault of my creativity, it's just what happened. I told my editor, who wondered if I could mix it up, that she could raise her concerns directly with the people who spoke those words, but I don't think she was all that interested in hunting down everyone involved, let alone visiting a jail cell and a morgue.

Okay, back into it.

No more stops. Express to Adelaide.

- ~~Henry McTavish: 337~~
- Alan Royce: 246
- Lisa Fulton: 149
- ~~Wyatt Lloyd: 138~~
- S. F. Majors: 106
- Simone Morrison: 106
- Wolfgang: 94
- Aaron: 80
- Brooke: 71
- Jasper Murdoch: 63
- Harriet Murdoch: 53
- Douglas Parsons: 37
- Cynthia: 31
- Book Club/Veronica Blythe/Beehive: 29
- Archibald Bench: 26
- Erica Mathison: 12
- MongrelWrangler22: 8
- Troy Firth: 4
- Juliette: EXEMPT
- Noah Witrock: EXEMPT
- Detective Hatch: EXEMPT

# LITERARY

# CHAPTER 32

Now it was my turn to bash on the doors, rousing the writers and several of the guests. Mysteries tend to have a lot of waiting around for everyone except the detective, and everyone was in various states of lazing, counting the minutes to Adelaide. Majors was listening to a podcast. I had to wake Royce. Jasper and Harriet were playing Travel Scrabble. Douglas was not in his room. Wolfgang was writing in a Moleskine notebook and was skeptical when I asked him to meet us in the bar, muttering that he'd seen this already on this trip. Simone was marking up a contract. She scanned my bloodied, dirt-caked self and then patted me on the shoulder and said, "Perilous third act, I see."

Brooke flung her arms around her mother, before seeing me and dropping them, concocting some stammering half story about how they were friends and she'd been waiting in the room.

"Jig's up," Lisa said, and hugged her back. "He knows. It's okay."

Brooke eyed me warily, untrusting.

"I solved Archie Bench," I said, as a peace offering.

"Well, aren't you clever," Brooke said, taking off toward the bar. "This will be fun."

Everyone was either curious or bored enough to follow me. Even Aaron had given up objecting. The only guests I didn't retrieve were the three women in the Erica Mathison book club, Veronica Blythe and her two friends. Not because they weren't important—they are but because I didn't need them there in person.

Inside the bar carriage, Cynthia was wiping down the coffee machine, and Detective Hatch was, conveniently, interviewing Douglas. Hatch stood as we all entered. "Hold it!" His protesting was futile against our advance into the room. "I am still conducting interviews. I require you all to stay in your rooms."

"Haven't you heard?" I said. "This is a writers' festival. We've actually got one last speaking event. I'm announcing my new book. It's called *Everyone on This Train Is a Suspect*."

Simone gave a little fairy clap of excitement.

"The festival is canceled," Hatch interrupted, indignant. "No more panels."

"I'm the festival's director," Majors said firmly. "And I say we have another session planned. Right now. Festival's back on."

Hatch flopped back into his chair. Waved a hand as if to say, *Get on with it.*

"Actually," I said, "don't kick back too quickly. I am going to need your help a little."

Hatch sighed. "What?"

"Do you have a gun?"

"No. Taser."

"Okay. How many pairs of handcuffs do you have?" I pointed to his backpack.

"Two."

"That'll have to do." I thought for a second. "First things first, I need you to arrest Alan Royce."

# THE SEVEN DEDUCTIONS
# OF ERNEST CUNNINGHAM

# CHAPTER 33

"I didn't kill anybody!" Royce protested.

"I'm not cuffing anyone simply because you say so," Hatch said.

"I didn't say arrest him for *murder*," I said. "I think it's got a technical name. Obstruction of justice? Evidence tampering?" I addressed everyone now. "Henry McTavish committed a vile crime, and Wyatt Lloyd and Alan Royce helped him cover it up."

The color vanished from Royce's cheeks. People were staring at him now, trying to figure out what he'd done. S. F. Majors looked at the floor. I turned to Lisa. I didn't want this to be any more painful for the Fultons than it needed to be, but they deserved justice for what Royce had done to them, and that meant laying out all the facts. "May I?"

Lisa gave a stiff nod. Brooke held her arm tightly.

"Edinburgh, two thousand and three. McTavish and Lisa did not, as has been attested, have a fling. He raped her." The silence in the room was thick. "It was your word against his, Lisa. You didn't stand a chance against the money and power behind McTavish, namely Wyatt. But you had forensics. McTavish's DNA under your fingernails was supposed to be your proof that you'd tried to fight him off. Until there was a stuff-up, a simple admin error, which meant the evidence was inadmissible. With no one willing to be a witness for you, Wyatt offered you a deal. Some money to stay quiet. Take the check and sweep it under the rug. You accepted because not only did McTavish force himself on you, he fathered your child. Brooke is Henry McTavish's daughter."

I'm pleased to report there was a little gasp at this.

"Though you'd never met him, Brooke, you idolized your father through his books. You couldn't wait to meet him. You didn't really believe your mother when she tried to warn you away from Henry. And then you got here, and he was everything Lisa had told you he was. It broke your heart."

"That sounds like much more motive to commit murder than I have," Royce exclaimed. "Her father, and then the man who helped him get away with it." He thumbed at his chest. "Inn-oh-cent!"

"I didn't kill anybody," Brooke said.

"You have motive, of course," I replied. "Everyone here does. But if you were the murderer, for those reasons at least, I'd suggest that Royce would probably have been killed by now too."

"Are you threatening me?"

"No, Royce. I'm saying that if someone is killing off people involved in covering up the rape of Lisa Fulton, you'd be a very likely target."

He squeaked something that sounded like *don't* but I was low on pity.

"You were never a full-fledged pathologist, not like it says on your bio. You were an intern in a lab. This was in Edinburgh, right?"

Royce hadn't told me this directly, but he had bragged that he'd gone to the same university as Arthur Conan Doyle, which is, indeed, the University of Edinburgh. So it wasn't too much of a leap to guess his internship had been in the same city. "But you had dreams of being a writer. Your work sat unread on publishers' desks, even though you submitted it *four* times to Gemini. Until Wyatt picked it up. So along Wyatt comes one day, offering you a book deal that most writers would dream of. And he just wants a little favor. Swap the labels on a couple of vials. That was the deal you struck, wasn't it? You cover this up for Wyatt, and he publishes you as the next hot new thing. It makes sense: why else would Gemini have changed their mind after four rejections? Your job description would have been in your bio. Wyatt must not have believed his luck. And the timelines work: your first book published in two thousand and four. But now your sales are dropping, Wyatt was losing interest, and you decided a blurb from Henry would fix it. You were humiliated that Henry had endorsed Lisa over you. You told me yourself that McTavish *owed* you."

Snot ran out Royce's nose. I'm not going to bother with his dialogue, but I'll tell you that *blubbering* and *groveling* are suitable descriptions. Between mucus bubbles, he admitted that everything I'd deduced was true. Hatch leaned forward with interest.

Harriet spoke up. "So that's three people in a secret cover-up, and two of them are dead? And yet Alan *isn't* the killer?"

"His big accusation was certainly a distraction," Wolfgang said. "To do that whole song and dance accusing someone who he knew was actually dead. It would be a way to take the heat off."

"Thank you both. But Royce didn't do it. Mainly because he's a coward. He sides with and hides behind others. This is not a bloke who carries the knife. But destroying a victim's chance at justice, just for a book deal, that seems pretty cowardly to me." I looked at Hatch. "You can cuff him now, if you like."

Hatch held up the cuffs to Royce. "I don't have jurisdiction for an international crime that may or may not have happened. But it will probably help your cause later if you cooperate now."

Royce nodded. His arm was al dente as Hatch cuffed him to the chair's armrest, sitting like it was boneless. He looked resigned to what he knew was coming. I'd say it was a fall from grace, but grace was probably a few stories too many above Royce for him to have a proper splat. The next thing he'd write would be an apology on Twitter, which is a format reserved for the sincerest of apologies.

"Despite his conclusion being wrong, Royce actually laid out some reasonable motives for the rest of you," I continued. "But, Lisa, this was why he refused to consider you a suspect in his summation." I recalled her trying to bait him into it: *Tell them why I'm a suspect, Alan.* "He was discounting a completely viable path of inquiry because he knew that if he unpacked your motive, his involvement could be exposed."

Majors crossed the room, tears in her eyes, and hugged Lisa.

Hatch cleared his throat. "Does it usually take this long?"

All the crime writers in the room said simultaneously: "*Yes.*"

"I have to go through everyone's motives and alibis publicly," I said. "It's basically a requirement of the genre." I lowered my voice in a conspiratorial whisper. "And my literary agent is here, and given all she's done—behind the scenes, so to speak—to bring this book to life, I think she'll want a proper ending. She'll want me to really milk it."

Simone squirmed in her seat. I enjoyed that too much to elaborate just yet, so I turned instead to S. F. Majors.

"One thing Royce had right was your motive. That same night in Edinburgh, you told McTavish your idea for a novel. A year later, his new book *Off the Rails* was published and it had the exact same plot. And that boiled in you. Because not only was it your idea, it was your *story*. Wasn't it?"

Majors was chewing her lip. She shot a glance at someone else. I'll get to who in a moment.

"You attended a regional primary school, didn't you? It's in your bio. You used to reread the only three books in your school library, which speaks of a very small school to me. You know Alice Springs—

you recommended the best bakery to get a vanilla slice. You grew up around here."

Majors nodded.

"That school bus that was hit by the Ghan, I am guessing that was from your school. I don't think you survived the crash though—no one could have. I think you missed it entirely."

"I was sick," Majors said. "Any other day my parents would have bundled me up with tissues and painkillers and sent me off, but I never liked sports on Wednesdays, and so I hammed it up. I could've gone." Her voice quivered, and I felt a wave of empathy: the *why me* I'd struggled with so much myself. "The girl . . . in my story, if that's where you're going with this . . . her name was Anna. She was my best friend. If you care to know."

I knew it was like pushing a rotten tooth with your tongue to her, so I turned my attention to Douglas. "Let's talk about how the two of you met. Your partner, Noah, was a teacher at the school, and he died that day in the crash. You told me that the driver of the bus, Troy Firth, had been inappropriate with a student. Anna, as we've just learned. Noah had convinced Anna to come forward. To stop that from happening, Troy parked on the tracks and locked all the doors."

"He killed five people," Douglas said. "Four kids."

"The accident makes local news, it's a tragedy, but nothing more. Normally such a story would fade into the past, but not here. Because a version of the story gets retold and lives on in one of the most popular crime novelists in the world's third book. But *Off the Rails* is not just a retelling of the accident, it's the *real* story—someone staging a murder as a rail accident—a story which only a few people knew. A victim's best friend"—I nodded to Majors—"and her teacher's partner. But there's one crucial difference: in the book, the murderer gets away. If you believe it is a *true* story, you might believe something crazy. You might believe that *Off the Rails* has a hidden meaning: that Troy Firth is still alive."

All the women in the room sized up the men: Wolfgang, Royce, Jasper, Douglas. Even Aaron didn't escape the scrutiny.

"That's where you come in, Douglas. You brought a gun on this train." This drew a murmur. "Don't worry, Hatch. The gun's in a trash can at Alice Springs. Douglas, you asked me a question about revenge during our first panel. You wanted to know what it felt like to take a life. You set foot on this train ready to kill someone."

"I'm not—"

"I know you're not Troy Firth. But you were looking for him."

I let that sink in.

Simone gasped. "Troy Firth is *Henry McTavish*. His injury."

"Sorry to be the editor," Wolfgang said. "But is that plausible? Majors knows the man who molested and murdered her best friend is walking around still alive, and she doesn't turn him in to the cops?"

"It's not plausible at all," I agreed. "The timing's out, for one thing. That could be a plot point straight out of any one of our books, but it's not real life. The problem is: it's exactly what Douglas believed. He thought *Off the Rails* was the true story of how Henry McTavish got away with multiple murders. He convinced himself McTavish was Firth, and that *Off the Rails* was a confession. Because there was *just* enough truth in the book to make it seem convincing, after all. But it was truth that McTavish stole, not knowing the consequences, from Majors's story."

Majors cleared her throat. "The idea for the book came about because I *thought* I saw a man that looked like an older Troy Firth, many years later. That's it. A fleeting glimpse that triggers a random memory. That's all we hunt for, Hatch, if you don't understand. Writing is merely piling up the sticks and the grass and then hoping a tiny flicker sets it all aflame. Like all the best ideas, it just snapped into focus as a story. *What if* I'd just seen Troy Firth? That's what I told Henry in two thousand and three. My *idea*. But it had details of Anna's story. Real details. Enough to convince Douglas that it was really true. But then he approaches me at dinner after the first panel, where McTavish and I argued over *Off the Rails*, and he thinks I also suspect what he does. I tell him he's mad, that my grievance with McTavish lies elsewhere, and that the plot is fiction." I remembered them whispering, excluding Royce from their conversation. "And then I let him have it at the Telegraph Station the next night. Troy Firth was a terrible man, but he's been dead a long time. Douglas let his desire for vengeance blur fiction with what he *wanted* to be the reality."

I focused on Douglas. "That's why you thanked me and tossed the gun after McTavish had died—you *had* come here to kill him, and you thought I'd just done it for you. Majors was yelling at you at the Telegraph Station because she thought you'd acted on your suspicions and killed him. Of course, you were dead wrong. Henry McTavish is Henry McTavish: where in his biography would he find time to drive school buses in Australia? And Troy Firth died in the crash. McTavish got his injuries in a hit-and-run. That's documented. But the fact that you came here believing otherwise, and willing to kill for it—well, that's true."

"I didn't kill anybody," Douglas said, looking around the room. "Just like I told you. I picked the gun up in Darwin with revenge in my heart, sure. But I changed my mind, after what you said. About the toll it takes. I skipped the bushwalk to scatter Noah's ashes, and I let it go."

"Legally speaking, I didn't kill anybody either, remember," I said. I believed that Douglas's intent and actions were separate. Of course, forgiveness was easier when McTavish was already dead, but Douglas had had plenty of opportunities to shoot him on the first day and hadn't. Maybe Majors had put just enough doubt in his mind, and I'd helped him realize that true justice isn't simply revenge. Either way, he'd come to his senses and binned the revolver at Alice Springs station. "At the formal dinner, you looked like you'd been set free. I didn't understand at the time, but I do now."

"You've solved a lot of half crimes," Hatch said, folding his arms. "But I was promised a *murderer*."

"Right. Before I start this next part, I just want you all to remember the murder weapon used on Wyatt."

"A pen," Hatch said.

"Not just any pen," I corrected him. "A Gemini Publishing pen. A gift to all of Wyatt's authors, which extends to, as I understand it: Royce, McTavish, probably Jasper, and Lisa, for her first book. Plus Simone, to whom Wyatt gave a pen yesterday." I had recalled Wyatt's snarky words at dinner: *She didn't come away entirely empty-handed. I gave her a consolation prize. Not that she'll be signing anyone with it.* Wyatt wouldn't have been able to resist the opportunity to patronize Simone, handing her a pen with a *Better luck next time* frown. "And, of course, Wolfgang."

"Wolfgang is published by HarperCollins, actually," Simone said.

"Wolfgang." I turned to him. "Just how interactive is your art project?"

# CHAPTER 34

Wolfgang brought his hands together in a slow, droll clap. "You think you're very clever, don't you?" He stopped clapping and spread his hands. "The floor is yours. Entertain us."

I didn't hesitate: I'd been looking forward to this part. "Ever since I saw the name of your project, *The Death of Literature*, I knew it had to encompass some kind of humiliation of the establishment. Because you believe that your works are art, and anything else is . . . What did you call a *writer like me*?" I did air quotes as I reminded Wolfgang of his words on the panel. "Ah, yes. Pulp. And who's the very embodiment of pulp fiction at the moment? Well, one might say the Scottish crime sensation Henry McTavish. Another might say Wyatt Lloyd himself, specializing in publishing commercial fiction, including not only McTavish but also Erica Mathison."

Wolfgang yawned. "Royce tried this on already—you're going to need a little more than that."

"Clearly your project was designed to humiliate Wyatt. You couldn't resist gloating over dinner on the first night, and Wyatt was mortified by what you'd told him. He yelled at you that what you were doing would ruin him. Then he tried to buy you out. I assume you declined?"

"The price of preserving literature isn't one that can be paid by men like him."

"Exactly. So the question becomes: what could you possibly have done that would ruin Wyatt Lloyd? The answer is simple. You've invited three people on this train journey: two art curators and a book reviewer. All three of them are reading *The Eleven Orgasms of Deborah Winstock* by Erica Mathison. All three of them have fresh copies, bought in a bookshop in Darwin. One copy is newly signed, from a reclusive author who never does appearances. All three of them, respected intelligent women, think it's absolute genius. Why? Because Erica Mathison *is* your art project."

If you're playing along at home, you'll know Wolfgang was at 94 mentions, and Erica was on 12. Added together as per my rules for aliases, that puts him on a certain magic number.

"Oh, you're much better than Alan," Wolfgang said with a smirk.

"That's why you have a Gemini pen," I said.

Wolfgang made a great act of pulling off an invisible mask from his chin to his forehead. His eyes sparked. "You're looking at Erica Mathison. Wyatt didn't know it was me. I set it up through a company, with an international account and a PO box for him to send contracts or whatever."

"Or a pen."

"Indeed. My plan was to sell him the most basic, abjectly dreadfully written pulp"—his wet lips popped with disgust on the P—"and he lapped it up. Like a dog. Then he made it into one of the year's biggest bestsellers. Proving my point: true art is undervalued, and commercial art can be concocted."

"You didn't exactly mind the commercial aspect, though, did you? Simone told me your sales are likely miserable. And yet you pulled up to Berrimah in a two-hundred-thousand-dollar Jaguar. You're not exactly Robin Hood."

"The spoils are part of the point," he said, sneering. "It's irony. I can explain it to you if you like."

"You can justify it however you want. For the record, I think you're a hypocrite. But you are a man of convictions, and the point of the experiment was always to unveil it. That was what you were telling Wyatt over dinner: who you really were. You were also telling him that you were going public. That's why you invited these influential tastemakers, people whose opinions you respected. You let them in on the joke, signed their books, basked in their adulation of your genius." The comments that had so appalled Simone, from the supposedly respected professionals over such a trashy novel—*genius . . . true vision . . . a revelation*—now made sense.

I paused, glanced around the room, then turned back to Wolfgang. "But none of that's *quite* ruinous—that's what I couldn't understand. Your thesis could be to set out to prove that anyone can write a bestseller. Sure. Mario Puzo reportedly did that with *The Godfather*. Or maybe you wanted to highlight the financial excess that some books, some writers, receive. But at the end of the day, none of that matters. Millions of people are still going to read Erica Mathison. Wyatt might be embarrassed, but Gemini's profits must be through the roof. *The Death of Literature* demanded something more dramatic."

Erica Mathison was supposed to be a huge middle finger to the establishment; she was supposed to take them down a peg. Veronica Blythe had said this herself to Simone: *It's people like you who could learn a lot from this book*. I was pacing now, working my way into my deductions. Aaron had slowly moved to the back of the crowd. He'd finally cracked his professional veneer, pulling up a stool at the bar and unscrewing the cap from a bottle of vodka.

"Erica Mathison isn't real. But here's the kicker: neither are the books she wrote."

At this, Wolfgang's smugness dropped for the first time. He knew I had him all figured out.

"It was never as simple as writing a book that you consider beneath you. You created *The Eleven Orgasms of Deborah Winstock* using a computer program. Artificial intelligence wrote it for you. That's why you were reading a textbook on AI coding the other morning, *The Price of Intelligence*. AI is open source now, everyone can use it. Hell, my uncle used ChatGPT to write his website. Why not use AI to write a book? You said yourself on that panel that in fifty years books like mine will be written by machines. And that"—I jabbed a finger at him—"*is* dramatic enough to prove your point. Wyatt Lloyd's new bestseller was written by a *computer*. He'd be livid. It's almost worth killing for."

"You'd be surprised how easy it was," Wolfgang said. "I just punched in what I needed to happen in each chapter. The algorithm spat it back out. It took me all of a single day. The writing wasn't perfect, but Wyatt's team cleaned it up in edits. He was so titillated by this debased concoction, his judgment so blurred by dollar signs, that he ignored all the red flags. He didn't even care we didn't meet. Voilà. That was the point of the whole thing. Commercial fiction is a recipe. True art can only be made"— he pointed at his forehead—"here."

"If I understand correctly," Hatch interrupted, now leaning forward like an overeager schoolchild, no longer objecting but fully invested, "this gives Wyatt motive to kill Wolfgang. Not the other way around."

"Exactly," Wolfgang said. "Not only that, but I *wanted* everyone to know. That's why I invited my guests. It was going to be in the papers as soon as we hit Adelaide. I told Wyatt to his face. This was always a secret I intended to tell. I didn't kill anybody"—that was, if you're counting, the fifth of six times this phrase will be used—"to cover it up."

"You're right," I said. "I did wonder if the money might have been enough to make you change your mind. Now that you'd enjoyed the financial success that had eluded your career so far, would you kill to keep it? But I don't think you would. And you gave me the biggest clue of all to the real killer."

"At your service," Wolfgang said dryly.

"No joke. You actually *liked* someone's writing."

Wolfgang grunted, perhaps offended by the accusation of positivity.

"I'm talking about *Life, Death and Whiskey*. When you flicked through it in Wyatt's cabin, you thought McTavish's writing had improved. Right?"

"A little," Wolfgang scoffed.

"Yes. *Literally*. You thought *Life, Death and Whiskey* had the *smallest* of improvements. You thought his first book, the only one you've read, was bloody awful. Littered with Oxford commas, you told me. You also told me writing is like a tattoo. No one can shake their little tics. An Oxford comma is one of McTavish's habits. The answer's been looking us straight in the face."

Given we were down to discussing literary technique, most of the writers in the room had figured it out by now. Hatch still needed a little more explanation, so I went on.

"It's in the bloody title! *Life, Death and Whiskey* omits the Oxford comma."

I'd like to apologize quickly. I'm about to break one of the fundamental rules here. Turns out there are ghosts in this book after all.

"Henry McTavish wasn't writing his own books anymore," I said. "Jasper Murdoch was."

# GHOST

# CHAPTER 35

A ghostwriter. It was as simple as that.

It should have been so obvious that McTavish wasn't writing his own books anymore. The timeline of his publications alone told enough of the story. His first book was a worldwide bestseller and his second was a flunk, which had made his confidence plummet. Coupled with his painful recovery from his accident—*I could tell the third was squeezing out of him like a kidney stone*, Simone had said—this had meant he'd had to steal from S. F. Majors just to get the third one done. But that wasn't a trick he could use twice. Brooke had summed it up perfectly in the Chairman's Carriage: *Maybe now I think he's a man who likes pleasure but doesn't want to have to work for it.* He'd needed another way to write the books.

"I thought you'd bought the Erica Mathison story," Jasper whispered.

"As I told you last night, I knew you weren't writing for yourself. You looked a bit worried that I'd figured it out at first, but at the time, of course, I thought you were Erica Mathison. You seemed relieved when I told you this, which I thought was a natural response after holding such a big secret for so long, but it was really because you thought your secret was still protected. After all, the scheme only has value if no one knows about it, as you told me. You were only too happy to confess to being Erica when I prompted you, not knowing Wolfgang was the real thing, to keep me off the scent. But, even if I was wrong about that, the clues are the same. The way you act is all developed from never being in the spotlight. And Harriet's always trying to boost you up, make you recognize those achievements. That frustrated you—I assume the confidentiality clause in your contract is drum-tight, and so that was why you often tried to quiet her. You told me Harriet wants you to write under your own name, and maybe once that was your dream too. Your first novel came out in two thousand and nine, and the *New York Times* review compared you unfavorably to McTavish, whose books you were also writing. Despite the fact that Harriet had praised the fifth McTavish book, one you wrote, in two thousand and six, so highly that the blurb is still used on his covers. There's that tattoo simile again—your voice is not something you can hide. You sound like you, and you can't shake it, even though the world believes that *you* is someone else. But that review, that was what broke you. That was when you stopped pursuing your own voice and decided you were happy at the back of the room. You also did something no writer should ever do: you responded to the review."

Simone physically winced. Jasper had told me this himself: *Bad reviews are part of being a writer . . . I got one once, wrote to the reviewer.*

"You told Harriet the truth in your response, didn't you? That you thought her review was unfair because you *were* Henry McTavish. I'm assuming that confession led to your first meeting."

Harriet nodded as Jasper explained. "I wanted to apologize. She thought it might be a great scoop, and I needed to beg her to keep it quiet. We got coffee. And, suddenly, such little things didn't matter anymore."

"She's your biggest supporter," I said. "Has been since she discovered you were the real McTavish, trying to give you the credit that even she, back in that review, hadn't given you. So while you're trying to shrug off the attention, Harriet could never resist the occasional flattery. Or a dig at the truth. She asked McTavish on the panel where he got his ideas. She told me you'd sold *just as many books as McTavish*. An easy enough statement to pass off as a general brag, but she was very specific: your sales *were* McTavish's sales. And when I asked her if she was a fan of McTavish, Harriet said she was a big fan of his *books*. Not of the author. Of the books. Your books."

Jasper turned to glare at Harriet. I remembered his anger when she'd told me these things, the friction between them. She wanted him to take center stage, but he was happy, or so he said, in the wings. Harriet squeezed his shoulder. Hard to tell whether it was in fear or apology.

"But the clues didn't just come from Harriet. McTavish writes all his books on a typewriter, one single copy of the manuscript, supposedly to protect against spoilers, but really he doesn't want the metadata of the true author to exist, evidence of the computer it's written on. Supposedly he finished *Life, Death and Whiskey* on the train and hand-delivered it to Wyatt, but he doesn't have a typewriter in his room. And, of course, there're Jasper's callused hands—from working on an old machine. There's also the panel, back at the very start of this."

I recalled McTavish slurring, slightly drunk, confusing *The Night Comes* with *The Dawn Rises*, brushing off not knowing which book came first: *There are so many release dates and formats and countries to keep track of it's easy to get muddled.*

"McTavish didn't even know what book he was supposed to be talking about on the panel. Not only that, but he didn't even seem to properly understand that the series was ending." I'd gotten this the wrong way round: I'd thought McTavish was upset at Wyatt for pushing him to keep the Morbund series going, but in reality he probably hadn't even known Morbund had died in *The Dawn Rises* until that first panel. I remembered him glaring at Wyatt. "I assume he had a word with Wyatt about that little surprise. He'd been so hands-off he didn't realize his cash cow was coming to an end. But, Jasper, that was your ultimatum to Wyatt. No more Morbund, until he published your own novel: *Life, Death and Whiskey*. And then when you gave it to Wyatt, he didn't want it. Because Wyatt needed to smooth things over with McTavish, he went back on your deal: he *needed* a new Morbund from you. I heard you arguing."

*It's in your contract. More Morbund*, Wyatt had said. *Why change it after all this time?* Once I'd realized my error about Erica Mathison, I figured that it wasn't McTavish in Wyatt's room. After all, I hadn't heard the distinctive *thunk* of McTavish's cane. Just plain old, regular footsteps.

"Wyatt thought I was going to give him another Morbund novel," Jasper said. "Even though *The Dawn Rises* was supposed to be the finale. The only way I could get him to agree to me killing off Morbund was by pitching it as a publicity stunt. Big sales for the final—so to speak—book, and even bigger sales for the comeback. I really hoped that if I gave it time, if I put something fantastic in front of him, he would come around. Or maybe I could convince him that if I just had a year off the Morbund books, I could do both." He sucked his teeth. He was angry now. "He didn't read more than a page."

Harriet massaged Jasper's shoulder. It fit with what I'd deduced. *You promised me you'd bring him back*, Wyatt had said. *I know, I know. Archie Bench. Real fucking cute.*

"Wyatt could have just gotten another ghostwriter though," Hatch said.

"No one's as good," Harriet said. I agreed with her: the DNA of the Morbund books was as much Jasper's as it was McTavish's. He'd written most of them, after all. Wyatt would have seen him as irreplaceable.

I went on. "That's why you put Archie Bench in the last book—that was your promise to Wyatt. To the sharp-eyed fans, including Brooke, who told me Archie Bench was the reason she *wouldn't* have killed him. Archie Bench is an anagram for *Reichenbach*. As in Reichenbach Falls, the famous waterfall Sherlock Holmes died falling over. Only he didn't stay dead: Conan Doyle brought him back, safe and well. Which is, of course, another reason I knew McTavish didn't write it. I found a piece of paper in his notes, written on Ghan stationery, where he was trying to solve the anagram himself after the panel. Why would he need to solve his own puzzle if he was the one who'd come up with it?"

Brooke smiled at this.

"Jasper"—this was Hatch now—"how did you react when Wyatt declined your book?"

Jasper sighed. "I said I'd blow it all up. I'd out myself, McTavish. The whole thing."

*Don't threaten me*, I'd heard Wyatt say through the door.

"And there's one final clue," I said. I didn't technically need this, I had more than enough confirmations of Jasper's ghostwriting, but given Simone had gone to so much effort to set this up for me, I might as well give her the finale she desired. "Simone, you knew about all of this, didn't you, all the way back when book three was finally delivered? You knew that *Off the Rails* was plagiarized, you would have been privy to Majors's accusations, and negotiations with Jasper had begun for book four. You told me you wanted to work on real literature. That's why you left that job."

Simone, surprised that the conversation had turned from Jasper to her so quickly, stammered, "Y-you get a stink on you, it follows you around. I wanted out before the dominos fell."

"But they didn't, and you watched Wyatt and McTavish grow rich off a secret you held. You wanted your slice, which meant convincing McTavish to sign with your agency, so you tried a little bit of old-fashioned blackmail. You told me that the way to get through to McTavish was by speaking to him in codes and riddles, and you did exactly that."

That was what she'd told me: *To get his attention, to impress him, you have to use his own tricks. He loves codes and riddles and wordplay and all that Golden Age stuff.*

"Just before we got on the train, you logged in to his Goodreads social media profile, the one Wyatt had always begged him to use—because although Goodreads wasn't around when you worked for him, he only ever used the one password, even though you told me you didn't remember it—and left five individual reviews as Henry McTavish."

Simone's objection doused itself before it got out of her mouth.

"McTavish was confused when Wolfgang suggested he was an ally in disliking my writing, even though he'd supposedly just given me one star. He'd never used the platform before, and these were his only reviews. That was why you wouldn't talk to Wyatt about taking it down. Because it was a code. A threat for McTavish."

I'd seen it in Royce's notebook, almost perfectly stacked, and I felt a fool for not figuring this part out sooner.

*Ernest:* ★ *Ghastly*

*Wolfgang:* ★★ *Heavenly*

*S. F. Majors:* ★★★ *Overblown*

*Me:* ★★★★ *Splendid*

*Trollop:* ★★★★★ *Tremendous*

"You were spelling a five-letter word in code. That's why Wolfgang's two-star review is incongruous with the word *heavenly*, and Majors's *Overblown* is a bit harsh for three stars. The star rating dictates the letter placement in the code word. Using the first, capitalized, letters of the reviews in order, it reads GHOST."

Up by the bar, Aaron took a long swig of the vodka straight from the bottle. Cryptology is not for everyone.

"Of course, McTavish doesn't actually use his Goodreads, but you knew Wyatt would tell him. And McTavish was savvy enough to piece it together, given his skill at codes. And because it couldn't have been Wyatt, he'd have suspected you were the most likely to log in to his accounts. So you made your pitch. He must have invited you to his carriage for privacy—I smelled your blueberry vapor in his room. But the threat of exposure wasn't enough to persuade McTavish to sign with you. All you got was a red face and, from Wyatt, a consolation pen. But then he died, and you figured I might write about it. You told me that the more complex, the more cryptic clues there were, the better it would sell. You tried to make me think about the reviews too, drawing my attention to them at the dinner—*five stars for effort*. You were pointing to Jasper as the killer all along. If I figured it out, you won in two ways: I'd have a better shot at another bestselling book, and I'd take Wyatt down a peg in the telling. Too bad he died before he could see his name in print. Right on schedule, it occurs to me."

Simone folded her arms. "Maybe some of that's true. But I'm not killing people so you can write your stupid book, Ernest. And I only gave you one star because I thought you could take it. I didn't realize you'd be so fragile."

"You don't know me very well, do you?" I said.

"Doesn't mean I hurt people." She was the last of the group to say "I didn't kill anybody." She marched over to the bar and snatched Aaron's vodka from him, swigged it and put it on the counter. "Can you just arrest Jasper already?" she appealed to Hatch.

Hatch took a step toward Jasper, having heard enough to

convince him. Jasper shuffled backward, but he was hemmed in by the bar itself. He had nowhere to go. Harriet took his hand in sympathy.

"The problem is," I continued, "Jasper *did* agree to a deal with Wyatt. Wyatt doubled his ghostwriting advance so that *Life, Death and Whiskey* could be McTavish's posthumous novel. If he has motive to kill McTavish, he doesn't for Wyatt. Jasper didn't do this."

Before I could say it aloud, the murderer revealed themselves. If I'm honest, it was sort of disrespectful: they spoiled my big moment. The detective is supposed to announce the solution while everyone slowly turns to look at the culprit. But by the time she'd grabbed the vodka bottle from the bar, smashed it and held its ragged mouth at Simone's throat, all eyes were already on Harriet Murdoch.

# CHAPTER 36

"Harriet?" Jasper said to me, confused. Then turned to her. "Harriet?" As in, *Is this really you?* And then back to me for a final, "Seriously. Harriet?" His incredulous chanting of his wife's name did my tally count a real favor.

Harriet had Simone in strength, age and size. She'd spun her into a tight grip, forearm clutched against Simone's chest. The rest of us, Jasper included, backed away. Though several of us could have taken her one-on-one, the jagged shards of the bottle dimpling Simone's neck held us at bay.

"I'm sorry, Jasper," I said.

"Tell them it's not true," he begged her. "Tell them. Or that you didn't mean it. It was an accident. Please."

Harriet didn't say anything. A drop of red beaded on the broken glass, trickled down the inside of the bottle. Simone was bug-eyed. Her hands were fluttering at her sides: *Stay back*. Hatch made a pantomime show of putting his Taser away in the hope Harriet might relax.

"It was no accident. Harriet boarded this train with a plan and a bag full of stolen flowers and was ready to kill with them. But, if

I'm honest, I think she was still working up the courage when she got on the train."

"Sorry, the murder weapon is *flowers*?" Hatch said.

"Opium poppies can be used to make heroin. You can make a tea with them. They're grown in Tasmania for pharmaceutical purposes—you can't buy these kind of flowers in a shop. Addicts often try to steal them to make their own drugs. Of course, you know all this, don't you, Harriet? What you *don't* know is that the person whose poppy farm you stole from was a quaint old lady named Margaret with a penchant for justice and terrible taste in low-budget detectives."

"Tasmania?" Jasper said, staring at his wife like she was an abstract painting.

"I knew you'd started your trip there," I said. "You said you'd taken the chance to drive Australia top to bottom while you finished *Life, Death and Whiskey*. And you accidentally gave Wyatt seasickness pills instead of hay fever tablets. The only way to drive Australia truly top to bottom is to put your car on the ferry across the Bass Strait from Tasmania to the mainland: hence the pills. Wyatt, who had the room next to you, got terrible hay fever on that first day. That's because your room, your clothes, were coated with pollen from the poppies Harriet had stuffed in her bag. I saw the petals in the corridor too, but I assumed it was some romantic flourish."

Harriet took a step backward, toward the restaurant carriage. Simone stumbled with the movement, and the jagged edge of the glass drew a longer line of red across her neck.

"I did it for you, Jasper," Harriet said. "That stupid review I wrote, I saw what it did to you. It snuffed out your ambitions for anything more, made you happy in the shadows of someone else's career. You know how that makes me feel? Knowing I led you to believe that you were nothing more than another man's name? I'm sick of seeing my words—*peerless . . . ,*" she seethed, "*unbeatable*—on every fucking cover. Those words should have been yours. They *are* yours. No. I wanted to put it right. You should have your own name. Your own success. Your own *legacy*."

"And McTavish was in the way of all of that, wasn't he?" I said. "Because even though Jasper had tried to finish the series, killing Morbund off, Wyatt was never going to let him out of it. Wyatt didn't want *Life, Death and Whiskey*; why accept a Jasper Murdoch novel when he could be getting more McTavishes? And so McTavish had to go to clear Jasper's way. But that *still* wasn't the final straw, was it?"

Harriet shook her head.

"Like I said, you didn't know if you could go through with it. But the tipping point, the thing that changed you from hypothetical to murderous, is so simple. It's a beer coaster."

I remembered Jasper approaching McTavish, introducing himself. McTavish had signed the beer coaster *To Jasper Murdoch*. Harriet had read it aloud. *Wow. That's a keeper.*

"He didn't even know your name!" Harriet yelled. She maneuvered, forcing Simone to fall in step with her, into the small corridor beside the bar, toward the door to the next carriage.

Jasper, Hatch and I kept gentle pace, one step forward for each of her steps back.

"The things you've done for him. The money you've made him. And he thinks you're some fanboy who wants an autograph? *An autograph?*"

I kept going. "You brewed the opium tea in the little kitchenette at the end of the carriage. That's why the kettle was in the bin, because you didn't want anyone else on the train accidentally dosing themselves. You mixed the tea in with a bottle of whiskey—top-shelf stuff, the kind that McTavish wouldn't be able to resist—and left it in front of his door so he'd see it in the morning, adding an anonymous card: *From an admirer*. McTavish thought it was from Brooke, whom he'd propositioned the night before, not realizing she was his daughter. That's why he offered to share it with her that morning, just before he died; he assumed she'd know what he was talking about."

I'd heard him say to her: *It's a mighty fine drop to drink alone.* "Now, you didn't mean for his murder to be so dramatic. You thought he might have a nightcap, die in his sleep. Or, even better, drink it after the journey, when you wouldn't even be close to him. Unfortunately, McTavish is an alcoholic. He got stuck in straight-away, filling his flask with it."

The bottle pressed deeper into Simone's neck.

"Harry, please—" Jasper said.

"Easy, Harriet," I said. I hardly had to explain her own crimes to her, but it seemed my talking was distracting her from any throat-slitting, so I kept going. "The thing is, you still might have gotten away with it. It was a good plan, after all. The only problem was McTavish's death had the opposite effect to the one you wanted.

"This was supposed to *free* Jasper. But suddenly *Life, Death and Whiskey*—the book Wyatt hadn't wanted while McTavish was alive—was valuable. You hadn't unshackled Jasper at all, you'd clamped another chain on him. Because, whether he's writing as himself or not, just like your *New York Times* review said, Jasper writes like McTavish. And so Wyatt knows he can pass *Life, Death and Whiskey* off as McTavish, so he doubles what he's been paying previously for the Morbund books, so he can buy this, now post-humous, novel. A *literary* McTavish." I knew now when I'd seen him on the phone at Alice Springs, he'd been rustling up the ap-proval for enough money to do the deal. "And Jasper is more than happy with the money, so he gladly accepts. He just wants his work out there, no matter whose name is on the cover. You were arguing about him taking the deal at Simpsons Gap.

"You're furious. You did all this so Jasper could make it on his own. You go to talk to Wyatt that night. I don't know exactly how that conversation went, but I think I know how it ended. He tells you that he owns Jasper and there's nothing you can do about it. To make his point, he takes out his Gemini pen and writes with a flourish on the cover page, on Jasper's opus: *by Henry McTavish*. The only handwritten words on the whole typescript. It was a final insult that you couldn't take. You grabbed the pen out of his hand and—"

"You're free," Harriet said, interrupting me. Her back was against the carriage door. She had eyes only for Jasper. Love, Lisa had said, would be the motive. Love indeed. "Your whole career everyone's looked at you a certain way. You deserve so much more. They deserve everything they got. I love you so much. It was for you."

Jasper was crying. "This wasn't for me, Harry. Don't say that."

"I love you."

"Don't say that."

"I love you." She faltered. I've looked enough killers in the eyes to know this moment. Their eyes almost physically unglaze. It's like waking up from a coma. "Jasper? I love you."

"Harriet . . . I . . . I . . ." Jasper could barely get the words out. "I don't even recognize you."


The movement was minuscule, but I saw the tendons in Harriet's arm flex and knew she was about to use the bottle. I lunged forward. Harriet saw me move and pushed Simone at me, which in the tiny corridor was like a ten-pin bowling strike: everyone went down. Harriet ducked through the door between carriages.

We untangled our limbs. Hatch was groaning and holding his wrist. Simone seemed okay; the blood on her neck smeared away and did not replenish. She pushed me back. "I'm fine," she growled. "Stop her."

I dashed into the restaurant carriage, Jasper close behind me. It was empty.

"Where the hell is she going to go?" Jasper said.

The sound of breaking glass came from the next carriage, accompanied by the howl of wind rushing into the train. We burst in to see leaves fluttering in the air, glass on the carpet under the closest window. I stuck my head out and saw Harriet's foot disappearing over the rim. She'd scaled the ladder that was on the outside of each carriage. I looked back at Jasper and pointed to the roof. The wind was a tornado in our ears.

Hatch staggered through the door behind us, wincing as he cradled his wrist. He tapped me on the shoulder, handed me his Taser. He wouldn't be able to get up the ladder. I nodded, pointed to the end of the carriage, where I'd remembered the sign: *To Stop Train Pull Handle Down.*

I'd already far surpassed my desired number of moving vehicles to stand on top of—the ideal number being, of course, zero—but, much to both my personal disappointment and the disappointment of anyone making a movie out of this book on a tight budget, for the second time that day I pulled myself out of a window.

I climbed the ladder quickly, adrenaline masking the pain in my still bloodied fingertips. On top, I could barely open my eyes against the wind. Harriet was a blur, even though she was only meters from me, hunched over like a cat. The wind rocked me backward, and my shoes slid on the corrugated roof. That's why Harriet was crouching: I was catching too much of the wind. I dropped to my belly and slid forward.

I felt a tap on my ankle and looked behind me: Jasper had made it up the ladder. I gripped the Taser tightly, pressing it into the roof as I dragged myself forward. The train didn't seem to have slowed at all. *How long does it take to pull a lever?* Surely Aaron had been on the radio to the drivers, too. But fourteen hundred tons doesn't stop on a dime, I figured.

Suddenly, something hit me in the wrist. I saw enough through the squinty blur of wind to make out a shoe, and the Taser went skittering across the roof. I'd love to tell you it teetered on the edge, perilously balanced, so a stretched-out hand could grab it at the perfect moment, but while thrillers often contain fight scenes that are laden with luck, this book has one thing most don't: physics. The Taser wobbled and fell over the side.

I clutched the air in front of me, hoping to grab Harriet. My eyes were getting used to the wind, and her blur had started to take shape. She looked like she'd turned around. In fact, I could see her well enough to watch as she raised the broken bottle and brought it down firmly into my shoulder.

The bleeding was immediate, and serious. It felt like a bucket of water had been tossed over my back. I tried to grab her but realized I couldn't move my right arm. I felt my skin pucker as she pulled the bottle out. Saw her clamber away. So much for a big fight scene. I was getting light-headed. All I could do was lie flat and hope the wind didn't blow me off the train before we came to a stop.

I felt a hand on my shoulder, then hot breath on my ear. Jasper, leaning close.

"Use my name," he said. "My real name."

Then he was moving ahead of me. He widened his arms as he approached Harriet, and she dropped the bottle. I couldn't tell what he was saying to her. She wiped her face with the back of her hand. And then Jasper made his move.

He hugged her.

It was a tight embrace, tight enough that their hearts would beat against each other's chests. Like a soldier home from war. Harriet nuzzled her face into Jasper's shoulder. Maybe, for a second, they forgot everything around them: the wind, the blood, the death, the pain. They just held each other.

Then Jasper rolled them both over the side.

From: ECunninghamWrites221@gmail.com
To: <REDACTED>@penguinrandomhouse.com.au
Subject: Epilogue

Hi <REDACTED>,

The epilogue is proving tricky, mainly because it hasn't happened yet.

I'm supposed to catch you up on the bits after the climax, and that's easy enough. There are not all that many opal mines left to fill in. Royce has been arrested for covering up the rape. Douglas Parsons, to my understanding, has been fined for illegal possession of a firearm. Lisa Fulton sidestepped criminal charges for grand theft auto, but Hatch grumbled that she owed him a new Land Cruiser. Given Brooke is now officially the McTavish estate (courtesy of DNA results), I'm sure he's hoping for the newest model. And Jasper and Harriet, well, they're just a red smear on the side of the Ghan. You'll have seen that photo in the papers.

Majors's plagiarism accusations are now much more public, so she'll get the lawsuit she wanted. I can't prove this, but I have a feeling she was going to shred whatever confidentiality agreement she'd signed at the same time as Lisa. Besides, you can't defame the dead, so she could accuse McTavish of whatever she wanted now. I also suspect she knew a little more than she was letting on about everything. Why else would she invite McTavish, Royce and Lisa all together on the same trip? Perhaps she and Lisa had planned it together: a chance to expose McTavish once and for all for both of his crimes. Of the other guests, we were truly just barnacles: Wolfgang was invited, as she'd told me, for the grant funding pedigree, and me, well, now I know I wasn't invited at all. Majors had a spare slot and wanted Juliette to give her a blurb.

I know you think I'm being harsh on Simone. I don't care about the one-star review, really I don't. But if she'd told me about the ghostwriter earlier, instead of hoping I'd solve some riddle so the book would be more complex, Wyatt and Jasper would still be alive. Probably Harriet too. And maybe Harriet should have lived to face just punishment. Though it's far from the worst lie told on that train, it's opened up a strange chasm between Simone and me, so I feel it's best we end our professional relationship.

But the actual ending, therein lies the problem.

One of the fallacies of most books written in first person is the perception that everything is happening in real time. That's why readers are able to indulge suspense when, say, a character scrambles across the roof of a train—It's a tacit agreement that they won't acknowledge the author, sitting in a hotel room in a sling, bashing away at the keys. But underneath it, we always know. It's why readers anticipate that I survive this book the whole way through.

We're about as close to real time as we can get, seeing as they won't let me out of the hotel. I don't know how long it will take to verify the facts in the case, but I do know that Hatch isn't a detective worthy of writing books about. By this I mean he may well be precise, methodical and competent, but he doesn't really have a grasp on pace, does he? Plus the drugs they've given me for my shoulder (which I still can't move, by the way—should I be worried?) make my fingers fly. That's how I've been able to get the story down so quickly.

Another upside is that I've had plenty of time to google things. Did you know Mathison is Alan Turing's middle name? You know, the bloke who made the Enigma machine to do the Nazi code-cracking—he's considered the father of machine learning. Or, as we now know it, AI.
Ha. Classic Wolfgang

And as to your complaints: yes, I did say seven writers would board the train. But McTavish hadn't really been a writer for a long time, had he? Plus Juliette and Jasper, it all adds up. I said five would leave the train alive at the end of the line too. Again, without counting McTavish as a writer: Jasper dies in the fall—yes, I saw him go under the wheels (ick, that's dead body number ten for me)—and Juliette departs halfway. Leave it in as a clue for the mathematicians, I reckon?

As for Aaron and Cynthia, no dark pasts to report there. But I can't omit them from the book entirely. Someone has to work on the train, right? I can't just ignore that they were there. If a reader wishes to consider them a red herring purely based on the fact that they exist and haven't done anything to contribute to the plot, that's on them for reading too many books with unfair twists. I said at the start it wasn't a butler-dunnit.

Another thing I said was that in books like these, two cases always spin together. Andy's business is, apparently, booming with calls after his poppy thief turned out to be a multiple murderer. I let him have his narrative. I even told him he can do all the media—and the festivals—this time.

So, back to the epilogue. I know you want the big-ticket item: the re-union between me and Juliette. The embrace and the tears and the one knee down (note to self: do Pilates). Obviously Juliette and I have talked, and I've apologized. But there's only so much you can do on FaceTime. She should get here soon. It was hell getting out of the holding cell at Alice Springs, for starters, and then there were no flights because of the bushfires *and* the cops *and* the media. Now she's got a rental car, but it's like a fifteen-hour drive and it's safer with a couple of stops.

I did joke that maybe she should catch the train. That was *not* well received.

My point is that the big reunion hasn't happened yet. I know you'd love a bit of romance to cap off the book, but all I can tell you is what happened: which is, at the moment, nothing. An improvement on the last proposal, granted, but that's not saying much.

Of course, I know how I'll apologize. Writing it all out has made me think about that a lot. When I started, I thought this story was about legacies. That's why writers write things down, after all. From Royce's vanity, to Majors's truth, to Wolfgang's principles, to Lisa's rage, to my memories. It's to leave something behind. I thought that's what a legacy was: putting your name on something.

But legacy isn't a stamp left by the people with ink. It's not about leaving your fingerprints, it's about having fingerprints left on you. In the case of books, the legacy isn't created by writing it, it's created by the people who pick it up, who expand and enrich and enlighten your words with how they reinterpret, remember and relive them. It's passion, it's tears.

It's internet forums, it's MongrelWrangler22. It's Juliette secretly giving her invitation to me instead. Jasper Murdoch knew that his name was the least important thing about his work, and now I know that too. A book isn't a book until it's read.

I'm saying all of this because I've had time to understand what Juliette said to me. She asked me whose story this was.

Now I know the answer.

Best,
Ernest

P.S. Speak of the devil, someone's knocking at my door. Maybe you'll get your epilogue after all.

# CO-WRITER

# EPILOGUE

This is not the place for gloating, but I did warn Ernest his stupid rules were going to get him killed.

How many times did I tell him his real life wasn't going to play out like a mystery novel? But does he listen to his girlfriend? No. Here's the proof: first person does not equal survival. Of course you can't write about your own death, that would be impossible. But a book *can* finish before the story does. You could get hit by a bus dropping the manuscript off to the publisher. Or, as it just so happened to Ernest, attacked in your hotel room by a woman you'd seen fall off the side of a train four days ago.

I don't know how Harriet tracked him down, but I do know that's why Hatch kept him sequestered to first the train, then the hospital and then his hotel room. For protection. Fat lot of good it did. The bodies were hard to find, shredded under the train as they were, but it quickly became apparent that, due to some fluke of physics and airflow, only Jasper had gone under the wheels. Hatch told Ernest they were still finding all the pieces of the bodies. Which wasn't technically a lie, it was just that there was one big piece they were really missing: Harriet.

So, back to the hotel room. Harriet's stolen a car, made it to Adelaide and knocked on the door. She's got blood and dirt caked over her face, two teeth missing, one arm hanging so far from her shoulder it's like a wind sock on a still day. But her other arm works just fine. Fine enough to grip the knife she's brought.

Fine enough to stab Ernest right in the stomach.

Be it fate or just miraculous timing, I arrived to an open hotel room door and chaos inside. Harriet was on top of Ern, dead arm swinging like an elephant trunk, her other raised to slash down, screaming that Ern had taken Jasper from her. I've never punched anyone before, and I was surprised by how quickly I knocked her out. I also broke four of the bones in my hand. They don't tell you that in books.

Ern's not dead, by the way. I got to him in time. I just wanted to make a point. And while it feels a bit childish to rub it in while he's doped to the eyeballs with two pints of someone else's blood in him, well, he should've thought of that before he accused me of being a murderer.

So that's really the end. Ern's awake and talking, but he asked me to write this chapter for him. To sum it all up. I've gone in and fixed up his name tally too. Harriet lands on a crisp 106 (granted, five of those are mine) for those playing at home.

One last thing. Sequels aren't always a disappointment, you know. Sometimes a second go at things is exactly what you need. A chance to fix up the mistakes you made the first time around. Or to ask a certain question twice. I said yes the second time, is what I'm saying.

The reason I did is very simple. I imagine it's the same reason he asked me to write this epilogue.

Ernest finally told me whose story this was: ours.

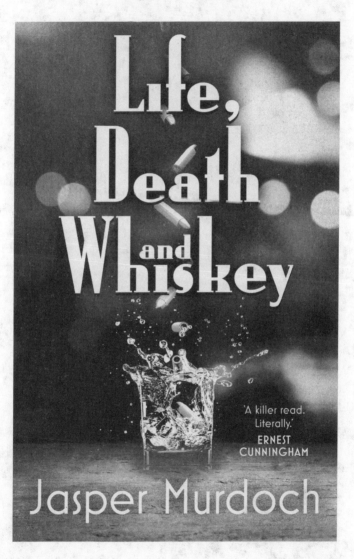

# AUTHOR'S NOTE

## OR

# AN APOLOGY TO FERROEQUINOLOGISTS

Those with a knowledge of trains will have noticed I've made some deliberate changes to the real-life Ghan to meet the needs of the plot. The most obvious of these are that the Ghan does not have a smoking deck, and I have teleported the Chairman's Carriage from a different train. Consider my inaccuracies to also extend to both the murderousness of the clientele and any deficiencies portrayed in the comfort of the journey. In particular, I am grateful to the truly exceptional staff, who didn't once call the police as I questioned them on the feasibility of various murders.

# ACKNOWLEDGMENTS

None of the characters in this book are based on real people, and, if anything, they are the complete opposite of the incredibly welcoming community of talented writers and booksellers and publishing professionals who have boosted me up in so many different ways, not only with this book but throughout my entire career.

Ernest learned something in this book that I've known all along: no book is written alone.

I am grateful to be on the receiving end of many people's talents: my amazing publishers (Beverley Cousins, Katherine Nintzel and Grace Long); my brilliant agents (Pippa Masson, assisted by Caitlan Cooper-Trent, for books, and Leslie Conliffe, assisted by Kris Karcher, for film, and my endless thanks to Jerry Kalajian); superb editors (Amanda Martin and Molly Gendell); the incredible marketing and publicity teams (Tavia Kowalchuk, Tanaya Lowden, Hannah Ludbrook, and Jennifer Harlow); those involved with international rights (Sarah McDuling, Neil Godwin and Anna Ristevski of Penguin Random House Australia, and Kate Cooper and Nadia Mokdad of Curtis Brown London); my cover designer

(Adam Laszczuk); proofreader (Sonja Heijn); and typesetters (Midland Typesetters).

Thank you to every bookseller who pressed *Everyone in My Family Has Killed Someone* into someone's hands over the last year and a half, and for again supporting this book with such passion and kindness. Thank you to every reader—what Ernest says about fingerprints and legacies is true, and thank you for leaving yours here.

Lastly, and always, thank you to my supportive, welcoming family: Peter, Judy, Emily and James Stevenson; and Gabriel, Elizabeth, Lucy and Adrian Paz.

And Aleesha Paz. Our story is my favorite story.

# ABOUT MARINER BOOKS

Mariner Books traces its beginnings to 1832 when William Ticknor cofounded the Old Corner Bookstore in Boston, from which he would run the legendary firm Ticknor and Fields, publisher of Ralph Waldo Emerson, Harriet Beecher Stowe, Nathaniel Hawthorne, and Henry David Thoreau. Following Ticknor's death, Henry Oscar Houghton acquired Ticknor and Fields and, in 1880, formed Houghton Mifflin, which later merged with venerable Harcourt Publishing to form Houghton Mifflin Harcourt. HarperCollins purchased HMH's trade publishing business in 2021 and reestablished their storied lists and editorial team under the name Mariner Books.

Uniting the legacies of Houghton Mifflin, Harcourt Brace, and Ticknor and Fields, Mariner Books continues one of the great traditions in American bookselling. Our imprints have introduced an incomparable roster of enduring classics, including Hawthorne's *The Scarlet Letter,* Thoreau's *Walden,* Willa Cather's *O Pioneers!,* Virginia Woolf's *To the Lighthouse,* W.E.B. Du Bois's *Black Reconstruction,* J.R.R. Tolkien's *The Lord of the Rings,* Carson McCullers's *The Heart Is a Lonely Hunter,* Ann Petry's *The Narrows,*

*nimal Farm* and *Nineteen Eighty-Four*, Rachel
*t Spring*, Margaret Walker's *Jubilee*, Italo Calvi-
*le Cities*, Alice Walker's *The Color Purple*, Margaret
's *The Handmaid's Tale*, Tim O'Brien's *The Things They*
*ed*, Philip Roth's *The Plot Against America*, Jhumpa Lahiri's
*nterpreter of Maladies*, and many others. Today Mariner Books
remains proudly committed to the craft of fine publishing established nearly two centuries ago at the Old Corner Bookstore.